# HEALING THE CAPTAIN'S HEART

## RESOLVED IN LOVE - BOOK 2

## PENNY FAIRBANKS

ALSO BY PENNY FAIRBANKS

*For my parents and brother for always supporting my dreams.*

# CHAPTER 1

*V*iolet tugged on the fabric, pulling it taut to encourage the buttons to meet their appropriate openings. Her face contorted in concentration, glad that her mistress faced away from her so as not to see her struggle.

"Oh, drat it all," Lady Neil moaned. "Another dress that will need altering. I had so hoped this one would still fit. I can't believe how much I grow day by day."

"Never fear, my lady. We are just about...there!" Violet exclaimed with relief as the back of the dress finally closed. She bit her lip as she noticed how the delicate buttons strained against the increased tension.

"My dear Violet, would you take this dress with you after breakfast and see what you can do to let it out?" Lady Neil sighed as she turned to face her maid, her chest heaving after the struggle to get her morning dress on. A hand rested on her belly, long elegant fingers drawing gentle swirls over the fabric.

"Of course, my lady. But are you sure this will be comfortable for you? Is it not too snug?" Violet eyed the dress that hugged her mistress's form. The fabric clung to her waist and cascaded over her round stomach. Violet had been in an endless cycle of altering Lady Neil's dresses. The little one in her belly indeed grew larger with every passing day, making it difficult for Violet's alterations to keep up.

"Yes, this will do for now. You fret overmuch, Violet." Lady Neil chuckled as she moved to her vanity, ready to begin her hair styling.

"It is my duty to fret over you, my lady." Violet smiled as she helped Lady Neil down onto the plush bench. "I'm happy to alter as many dresses as needed and assist in any way I can. I must confess that I am quite excited to welcome this new member to the family."

"Goodness!" Lady Neil jumped in her seat, a hand patting her stomach. "It seems my child is anxious to make your acquaintance as well. I think he or she just said hello."

Violet giggled as she pulled Lady Neil's long honey-blonde hair over her shoulder, threading her fingers through the soft strands to prepare it for brushing. "I hope it did not hurt you too much, but it must be a good sign that the little one is happy and healthy."

"If a tad rambunctious." Lady Neil smiled at her reflection in the mirror, her blue eyes melting into a gentle excitement.

Violet smiled as well, pondering what this tiny life would be like after entering the world, and who it would become over the years. Her eyes flicked down to her own stomach, flat beneath her dark gray dress. For a fleeting moment she wondered what a kick from within her own body would feel like.

"Not sure which of the latest fashionable styles for expectant mothers to try out?" Lady Neil asked. Violet's attention snapped back to the mirror and she met the reflection of her mistress's eyes. They were patient and understanding, just as they had always been since Violet's very first day as Lady Neil's maid—or rather Miss Richards at the time.

Violet saw a hint of pink flicker over her cheeks in the mirror and she swallowed her foolish thoughts back down. She had no business thinking about childbearing save for how it affected her mistress.

"Yes, my lady. Your hair is so lovely and there are so many ways to arrange it. Your curls catch the light perfectly, like when the sun's rays sparkle off still water." Violet hoped to distract her mistress from her sudden embarrassment with a compliment, but Violet certainly did not lie in what she said. Lady Neil carried every aspect of grace, elegance, and beauty in her physical appearance as well as her temperament.

"Good Heaven, Violet." This time Lady Neil blushed and covered her wide smile with her hand. "I swear that silver tongue of yours could turn even the sourest curmudgeon into a sweet smiling cherub."

"I only speak the truth, my lady." Violet busied herself with the hairbrush, pulling it gently through Lady Neil's thick hair and avoiding her eyes in the mirror.

"And have you been transferring that silver tongue to a pen?" Lady Neil prodded, her lilting voice threaded with curiosity.

"O-Oh.... I confess I have not. I really have no need of it. Nothing I say or think is uncommon enough to be recorded on paper. Besides, hobbies such as that are the least of my concerns when there is work to be done in the house," Violet mumbled as she narrowed her eyes to sharpen her focus on the task at hand and hopefully put this line of questioning to an end.

While Violet always appreciated Lady Neil's many praises, she couldn't help feeling that they were far too generous for a woman of her station and history. Having become a scullery maid in her childhood and eventually becoming a lady's maid to her mistress, Violet had had little time to sharpen any talents of her own.

Pretty turns of phrase came easily to her, but she'd never considered putting them on paper until Lady Neil began suggesting it some months ago. But try as Violet might, any attempts to write her poetic thoughts in her journal felt foolish and fraudulent. Lord Neil was the writer of the household and a very talented one at that from what Violet had glimpsed. Not someone like her.

Lady Neil uttered a heavy sigh, her shoulders lifting and dropping with a touch of drama. "Now, now, my dear Violet. You know I do not tolerate such self-deprecating speech in my presence."

"Forgive me, my lady." Violet nodded solemnly. She so hated to disappoint her mistress but Violet knew such compliments did not belong to her.

The baroness smiled softly into the mirror as she took in Violet's face, her brows furrowed and eyes narrowed in concentration.

"There is nothing to apologize for. But I do wish you would give the idea more consideration. The bits and pieces I've managed to convince you to show me are very promising."

"I greatly appreciate your confidence in me, but even if I did have any hope of developing a true skill for poetry I'm afraid I simply don't have the time." As if to emphasize her point, Violet began working Lady Neil's hair into a complex style.

"You try to escape it but I won't make it so easy on you," Lady Neil responded slyly. Violet glanced up in alarm at the mirror to see a mischievous twinkle in her mistress's eyes.

"Whatever can you mean, my lady?" Violet asked, trying to keep her voice carefree despite the dread seeping into her stomach.

"I know this is highly unusual, but you've proven yourself as my confidante in addition to your excellent work."

"Thank you, my lady. I'm pleased to hear that I've satisfied you." Violet felt herself soften at Lady Neil's words.

"You've done far more than that, Violet. In fact, you've been a friend to me in our time together. Which is why I care about your happiness. I know most mistresses would not go this far for a servant, but I think you are such an uncommonly wonderful young woman above all else. I think you can be spared for a few hours a week to work on your craft." Lady Neil finished with a firmness in her voice that gave Violet pause for a moment, but she knew she must insist otherwise.

"I greatly appreciate your offer, my lady, I truly do. But it is really too generous. Even just a few hours a week is time that can be spent mending or cleaning or shopping for your needs. It may be my duty but I am honored to do it. I need nothing else in life."

Violet smiled at Lady Neil's reflection, forcing the muscles in her face to emulate contentment. Of course, she was content in many ways. Finding a position with the Richards family had been a miracle in Violet's otherwise tragic childhood. And becoming Lady Neil's personal maid at the age of sixteen had been a dream come true. Violet had finally achieved the security she'd always craved.

She could not deny that she did indeed love poetry. But it was not her place to indulge her interests. Not when her mistress needed her. Violet could not risk losing this blessing.

But beyond that, Violet cared deeply for the family she served. She had been overjoyed to follow Lady Neil when she married the baron. Even better, during her time in the baron's London home as well as the country estate, Gatherford Park, Violet had grown quite fond of him as well.

Violet looked up at the mirror when Lady Neil failed to respond. Her heart thumped as she realized that she may have offended her mistress by so ardently refusing her kindness. But Lady Neil did not return her gaze through the looking glass. Her eyes were lowered, sweeping over the carefully organized items on the vanity, but without seeing them.

Violet's hands stilled. She stepped to Lady Neil's side and peered into her face. "My lady? Are you well? Have I upset you?"

A small frown overtook the baroness's troubled expression. Though Violet always stayed within boundaries—at least the boundaries unique to her relationship with Lady Neil—the desire to reach out and offer a comforting touch sometimes overtook her, as it did at this moment. But she kept her hands at her sides as was proper.

"Of course you haven't upset me. Not directly at least. I just hope you don't feel that something is missing from your life, especially something that would be in my power to give. Perhaps I have grown particularly sentimental of late." Lady Neil smiled ruefully at Violet as she rubbed her stomach.

"As you wish, my lady." Violet smiled back, forcing her apprehension down. "If you see fit to allow me time to write, I shall gladly accept. So long as you are certain I can be spared without any ill effect." She hastily added, reminding Lady Neil once again that Violet still saw her duties as a maid to be of the highest priority.

Lady Neil beamed up at Violet, her smile lighting up her pretty face. "I hope you will start tonight then. If you get my night routine started, I'm sure His Lordship will be able to help me finish getting ready for bed."

Violet nodded her agreement and resumed her place behind her mistress, taking her hair in hand once again.

Just as Violet settled into her task of perfecting Lady Neil's hair, a rapid heavy knock at the door caused both women to jump. They exchanged curious glances in the looking glass before Lady Neil called the unexpected visitor to enter.

"Darling, what are you doing here?" Lady Neil asked as she stood from the vanity and crossed the room to greet her husband, who waited uncomfortably by the door. His eyes darted about the dressing room and he smiled apologetically at his wife.

Violet turned her back to the couple to hide her smile. Lord Neil must have been one of the shyest men she'd ever met. In fact, she wondered for quite some time if he disliked her for some reason when she and Lady Neil joined his household.

His serious face with its broad features and his sweeping dark hair could certainly be intimidating to those who did not know better. But Mrs. Baird, the baron's sweet and motherly housekeeper, assured Violet that Lord Neil simply took some warming up with new people.

Now, she found Lord Neil's occasional awkwardness to be endearing. Violet turned back around and knew he must feel as though he'd interrupted the ladies in their highly important morning toilette. She had also never met a man more dedicated to his wife's happiness and comfort.

"I apologize for intruding." Lord Neil coughed.

"My dear, how many times do I have to tell you? Your presence is never an intrusion, even here." Lady Neil laughed as she waved a hand over the spacious dressing room.

The baron's eyes softened as he took in his wife's face and then her round belly. "I know, Cecilia. But I hate to disturb you during your rigorous preparations. Surely I would only get in the way."

Violet returned her eyes to the floor as her master and mistress shared a brief kiss. Her heart lurched, reminding her briefly of her longing to feel such a connection.

"But tell me, Henry, what brings you here? Are you

curious to see how your wife's head manages to hold all these curls? It is quite a process to behold."

"I am certain it is and I do promise to sit it on the master-piece in progress soon." Lord Neil chuckled.

"That masterpiece is all thanks to Violet. I have very little to do with it, truly. Aside from providing the hair." Lady Neil smiled back to Violet with pride.

Violet almost smiled back, but the way Lord Neil's face fell back to its uncomfortable expression brought the corners of her mouth back down just as rapidly. His eyes met hers for a moment before darting away.

"As a matter of fact, I've come here because there is a visitor downstairs who's just arrived..." Lord Neil's hands opened and closed quickly several times. Violet had never seen him so flustered. And the sudden shallow beating of her heart indicated that it had something to do with her. But she could not fathom in what way.

Lady Neil pressed a hand to her cheek. "My goodness. Who would call upon us at this hour? It is far too early for morning calls. We haven't even sat down to breakfast yet." Her eyes were round with surprise and Violet could see her quick mind working its way toward an explanation.

Violet's apprehension only increased as Lord Neil continued to fidget. He refused to meet his wife's eyes.

"Henry?" Lady Neil brought her hand to her husband's arm, her brows drawing closer together with concern. "Let it out now. Who's come to visit? Oh no.... Is it something to do with Juliet?" Her voice fell to a whisper and she stepped closer to her husband.

Violet saw Lady Neil tense as she mentioned her younger sister. Though Violet did not know the particulars of the situation, she was well aware that the youngest Richards daughter had fallen out of favor with their parents, causing Lady Neil much anxiety.

Lord Neil shook his head quickly. "No, no. As far as I know all is well with Juliet for now. Actually...the visitor has requested an audience with Violet."

The lord and lady both looked to Violet slowly, Lord Neil with unease and Lady Neil with confusion.

"Violet, were you expecting someone?" the baroness asked, her head titled slightly to the side, her half-finished curls dangling down her neck and around her face.

Violet barely heard the question. She could only stare back at her master and mistress with equal bewilderment. A heavy sense of dread flooded Violet's body as her mind bounced through numerous possibilities, none of which seemed more likely than the other.

The only thing she seemed to know instinctively, without a doubt, was that her past must have finally found her and sought to disturb her peace. She just did not know how yet.

"No, my lady. I'm not sure who might wish to speak with me or why," Violet answered, her voice trembling with her nerves.

"Did this visitor give their identity or state the reason for their visit?" Lady Neil turned back to her husband, her normally confident and easy manner shaken by the highly unusual circumstances.

"I'm afraid not. He only said that he needed to speak with Violet. Urgently."

The baroness walked across the room, her dress flowing gracefully despite her determined air. She stood before Violet and took the maid's small hands in her own. Normally Violet would have started at such a friendly physical touch, but her world had become far too unusual in the span of a few minutes to register the action as being too familiar even for her closeness with Lady Neil.

"If you do not wish to see this visitor, whoever they may

be, you do not have to. Say the word and we will have them shown back out the door."

The seriousness of the lady's voice brought Violet back to attention. She started at Lady Neil for a moment, reading the genuine concern in her face.

"That's quite alright, my lady. I should see who has come all this way to find me. But first, let me finish your hair. We're nearly done."

To Violet's great relief, Lady Neil did not argue. She simply nodded to the baron, who quickly left the room to relay the message, and sat back at her vanity.

Violet was grateful for a few extra minutes to gather her wits about her and steel herself to face whoever might be waiting downstairs.

She could not guess who might seek her out in the country, especially not in the middle of winter. But she could feel in her bones that her life was about to change. For better or worse, she would have to find out for herself.

# CHAPTER 2

The flickering flames in the hearth did little to soothe Owen's rattled mind. He was glad for the warmth, but every moment that passed in this unfamiliar drawing room only confirmed to Owen that he should not have come here with Davies.

"Jessup, have a seat would you? Your twiddling thumbs and tapping feet are making me even more nervous," Lieutenant Francis Davies called out to Owen from his chair. His hands covered his face, barely muffling his exasperation.

Owen turned his back to the fire to face his friend. The heat raced up his thick coat which seemed to do woefully little to shield him against the freezing English winter. But it was not the coldest winter he'd known. Not by far.

"Are you sure this was the best idea?" He did not take the empty chair next to Davies, choosing instead to pace back and forth before the fireplace.

"Yes, I am sure of it," Davies groaned, leaning forward in his seat to rest his elbows atop his knees. "There is no way she would have seen me if I wrote ahead. I doubt she would have even responded to a letter if I sent one. It feels wrong to catch her off guard like this, but I know she would refuse a meeting if she knew it was me."

"If you insist. Though it does feel rather like we're sneaking up on an unawares deer during a hunt. How do you know she won't bolt out of the room as soon as she takes a look at your unfortunate mug?"

Owen smirked at Davies as he passed before the fireplace again. His friend did not truly have an unfortunate mug, but often being compared as the two handsomest in their regiment, jokes against each other's faces were a staple of their friendship.

"I don't know that. But I can hope that she will at least grant me a few minutes to hear me out. Goodness gracious, man, will you sit down? You're driving me near insane with all your pacing. What have you to be nervous for? You are not the one trying to win back your sister." Davies's frustration at his friend's agitated behavior propelled him out of his own seat. He stood with his fists on his hips, glaring at Owen.

"You are right, but I can't help feeling like an intruder. This is quite a personal mission, is it not? I still can't see why you asked me to join you."

Owen continued to refuse the seat Davies desperately wished him to take. When Davies first asked him to journey out to the country to reconnect with his family, Owen had agreed without much resistance. Wintering in small towns around the countryside had grown tiresome, and the prospect of spending some time at a great estate was a very welcome change.

And it had been Owen's own idea, after all, that Davies should try to make amends since he saw how deeply his friend's regrets tortured him each day.

But Davies had failed to tell him that his long-lost sister did not know he was coming until they were packed into their carriage and on the road to Gatherford Park, home of the Baron of Neil.

Knowing enough of his friend's tumultuous past, Owen perfectly understood Davies's desire to apologize to his estranged sister. And holding his own family dear to his heart—his father being an earl and his mother a supremely patient woman to wrangle himself and his two equally high-spirited older brothers—Owen appreciated just how precious their time on this earth was.

He had known many, many good young men who had longed for their families every day but never returned.

Despite all that, Owen felt out of place in this unfamiliar drawing room, in this unfamiliar home, waiting for an unfamiliar woman who in truth was little more than a stranger even to Davies.

"Gentlemen." The deep voice of Lord Neil echoed into the large, quiet room and his serious face soon followed. "Miss Davies will be down shortly after she is finished attending Her Ladyship. Shall I have coffee or tea brought up?"

"Yes, my lord, tea would be much appreciated." Davies nodded enthusiastically as he walked to stand by Owen. Lord Neil gave a tight-lipped smile before leaving to inform the servants of their request.

"Do you think he is simply surprised that we've called at this unusual hour or does he already dislike us for some reason?" Owen whispered to Davies, leaning toward his shorter friend so that no one passing by in the hall might hear.

Owen continued to watch the door of the drawing room, puzzling over the somber master of the house. Davies failed to answer and Owen turned to face his friend. "Davies? Did you not hear me?"

Davies too stared at the door with round hazel eyes, a muscle in his jaw twitching. He looked nearly as ashen as when they'd set foot on the ship that carried them to the Continent.

"Davies? Is anyone home in there?" Owen stepped before his friend to block his view of the door and waved a hand before his blank eyes.

The lieutenant started and focused his gaze on Owen's face, his Adam's apple bobbing up and down with a nervous swallow. "Yes, indeed, Lord Neil is an unusual fellow," he mumbled, giving his head a slight shake as he returned to the moment.

"That is not what I asked, but I suppose you are correct. Though he does not seem unkind. Perhaps just reserved. But what ails you, friend? I haven't seen such a look on your face in over a year. This isn't a battle, you know."

Owen put a hand on Davies's shoulder and gently steered him back toward the chair near the fire. With just a slight pressure of Owen's hand, Davies sank into the chair. He ran a hand through his messy black hair.

"It may not seem like a battle to you, but the anxiety coursing through my veins feels far too similar for my liking. Perhaps in a way it is like a battle. I'm fighting for forgiveness. In truth, I hadn't expected to make it this far in my quest. What shall I do when she sees me? What will I say?"

The distress in his voice surprised Owen. He knew this was important to his friend, but he hadn't registered just how important it truly was. Perhaps Davies had sought to keep his expectations in check by speaking of it only briefly when he spoke of it at all.

Owen took the seat next to Davies and leaned forward, looking his friend earnestly in the eye. "Be yourself. The self you have become. Say what is in your heart. We can't know if she will accept your words, or if she will even stay long enough to listen. But, regardless of what happens next, you can at least be satisfied that you made the attempt."

Davies took a deep breath and smiled weakly. Owen could see him trying to fortify himself from the outside in. He clapped Davies on the knee at the same moment a footman entered the room with a tray of tea. Despite being a battle-hardened, fearless lieutenant, the man jumped in his seat at the interruption.

Owen took it upon himself to serve the tea, not trusting the steadiness of Davies's hands and securing them a few more moments of privacy. His friend's eyes continued to dart to the door and then back to the elegant surroundings in the room. The wait looked like it would kill him long before any possible confrontation with his sister would.

A pit of guilt opened in Owen's stomach. Seeing one of his dearest friends' nerves during this important moment reminded him of his own lucky family situation and that he would likely never be in such a position himself.

He knew Davies had grown into a fine man during their years of service—far from the haughty, nearly insufferable weasel he'd been when they first met as green soldiers. He had watched it happen before his very eyes. War rarely left any man the same by the end as when he started—in some fashion or another.

And Owen knew how much Davies's past mistakes haunted him. He wished for his friend's sake that today's outcome would be a step toward putting those demons to rest. Davies had gone above and beyond to assist Owen during their time on the battlefield, and they remained fast friends in the year since the war ended. The least Owen could do was offer his support.

They sipped their tea quietly for several minutes, Davies's foot tapping faster and faster as the time ticked by. Owen opened his mouth to offer a word of encouragement when the soft sound of footsteps entering the room caused them both to jump and turn toward the door.

She had only taken a few steps into the room when she halted, her dark gray skirts swishing about her feet.

Large green eyes stared at the men in shock, her small mouth falling open slightly. Her pale skin went paler still, offering a pleasing contrast to her shining dark brown hair pulled back into a modest bun.

Owen stared back, immediately struck by her pretty features, perfectly blended on her heart shaped face. But if Owen knew anything of his fellow humans, he could see that this young lady was far from pleased. Though she remained composed, a ripple of anger passed through her eyes, their striking green color almost flashing in the firelight.

"Violet!" After his own moment of surprise, Davies jumped up from his seat, nearly tripping over himself with his heavy boots in the process. "I'm so very glad you came."

He stepped forward tentatively. She stepped back.

"If I had known it was you, I'm not sure I would have come." Miss Davies's voice was quiet, but there was no mistaking the harsh resentment in it. "Why are you here?"

"Please, Violet, if you can just give me a few minutes of your time.... I can't say I'll be able to explain, because there's no way to explain away my actions. But I would like to apologize." Davies's voice faltered as he took another hesitant step closer to his sister.

This time Miss Davies did not step back. She stood firmly in her spot, her chin jutting forward. She glared at her brother, though Owen swore he saw her eyes briefly dart to him. "I see now. You did not write ahead because you knew I would likely deny you. Another clever deceit."

Even Owen shuddered at the coldness in the young woman's voice. He was suddenly very glad to be here with Davies, and not just to offer his support during this quickly deteriorating situation.

All the same, he had to admire the elegant and determined air Miss Davies maintained in the face of shock—as well as her flashing eyes.

"Please," Davies pleaded again. "I know you have every right to throw me out of this house at once. I would not blame you at all if you did. But I must beg you to hear me out, even just for five minutes. If what I say cannot change your mind, you are free to go and I will bother you no more."

Miss Davies's lips pursed together in a tight line but again she did not back down. She stared at her brother, seeming to carefully observe him and calculate whether a five-minute conversation could make it worthwhile to relive years of damage.

Despite the palpable tension in the room, Owen could not help admiring Miss Davies's resolve. Of course he agreed with his friend's statement. The lieutenant had played his own ignoble role in the tragic, sordid past of the Davies family.

But Owen knew Davies had changed for the better. He could see in Miss Davies's eyes that she was trying to read her brother to determine for herself if such a change had indeed occurred. From what Davies had told him, even he had been surprised that that vile young man had turned into the brave and honorable lieutenant he now knew.

"Consider yourself lucky. It is not within my powers to throw you out. Only my master or mistress can do that. But I will hear you. For five minutes. I must ask my mistress first for a brief respite from my duties."

Without further ado, the young lady turned abruptly and slipped through the drawing room door. Owen watched her turn down the hall, his eyes glued to her form until the last possible second when she escaped from view entirely.

"Thank God..." Davies sighed with relief and returned to his seat. His strong legs seemed unable to support him any longer.

The sound disturbed Owen's trance and he rejoined his friend in his own plush chair. "What was your sister saying about her master and mistress?"

"Did I not mention?" Davies looked curiously at Owen. "I discovered in my long search that she is a lady's maid here to Lady Neil. Though she also served Lady Neil for many years before her marriage to the baron. But thank God she has agreed to speak with me! I've often wondered what I might say if I found myself in this moment, but I must choose the best parts to suit the timeframe. I only hope I can convey my heart's deepest regrets in so short a time."

Davies's fingers tangled and untangled themselves in his anxiety and he bit down on his lip as his eyes stared into the distance, his mind no doubt working out the best way to move forward.

The corners of Owen's mouth turned down in an annoyed frown. "No, you had not mentioned that. Yet another important detail you've neglected. But I suppose it does make sense as to how she came to live in such a place. For all your acuity in battle plans and remembering the minutest detail of formations, your memory is quite terrible."

But his friend seemed not to hear him, embroiled in planning how much he could say in such a short period.

To Davies's obvious relief, they did not have to wait long. But the person who entered the room was not who they expected. Miss Davies had not returned. Instead, a tall, exceedingly graceful woman with neatly styled blonde hair— and clearly with child—strode across the thick carpet toward the seated men. The baron followed behind her.

Owen and Davies both stood quickly and bowed to the lady. She curtsied in response, eyeing them both carefully with perceptive blue eyes.

"Good morning, gentlemen. I am Lady Neil. I understand you have business with Miss Davies. My husband and I would be delighted if you could join us for breakfast. Miss Davies will join us as well. Afterwards you might have a private word with her. This will give us an excellent opportunity to get acquainted—or reacquainted in some cases."

She smiled politely and spoke with impeccable manners, but Owen sensed that her guard was up against these two strange men who so unexpectedly turned up at her doorstep so early in the morning, seeking an audience with her maid, no less. Lord Neil did not speak but simply watched the exchange, an air of uneasiness about him.

"Of course, we would be delighted as well!" Davies enthusiastically accepted the invitation.

"Excellent. Follow me to the breakfast room." Lady Neil took a few steps forward with the men in tow before pausing and turning back to her guests. "I apologize, but I don't believe we've learned your names yet. Due to the unusual circumstances."

"Lieutenant Francis Davies, my lady." Davies bowed his head as he properly introduced himself and Owen quickly followed suit.

"A pleasure to meet you, my lady. I am Captain Owen Jessup."

∾

JUST AS OWEN SUSPECTED, breakfast was an exceedingly awkward affair for numerous reasons.

The tension between Miss Davies and her brother could not be denied. Though they sat across from each other, neither seemed comfortable making prolonged eye contact with the other. Miss Davies seemed particularly engrossed in carefully cutting her ham into miniscule pieces while her brother accepted heaps of helpings and put them into his mouth too quickly to have much time for looking anywhere else but his plate. Nor did they speak directly to each other, preferring to allow Lady Neil to ask pleasant generalized questions on their behalf.

But the tension did not end with the Davies siblings. Lord and Lady Neil were both extremely attentive to their guests, with Lady Neil seeing to the majority of the verbal duties necessitated by a breakfast joined by visitors. But Owen did not miss the way Lord Neil curiously observed Davies and his sister—and occasionally Owen himself when he happened to glance up at the head of the table.

And of course there was yet another layer to the tension, though this layer likely only concerned Owen.

He simply could not remove his eyes from Miss Davies. After their long ride to Gatherford Park—passing through the nearby town without so much as a break for a refreshing drink—Owen felt that he should be ravenous. Yet his food held little interest for him. Not when a beautiful young lady sat on the other side of the table.

Owen hoped his observations were subtle enough. He kept his gaze down, viewing her from the corner of his eyes. The longer breakfast went on, the more Owen found Miss Davies's manners to be very intriguing.

The maid looked uncomfortable at such a grand table and Owen sensed that she felt very out of place dining with her master and mistress.

But still she held herself with as much grace as she could muster with so many pairs of eyes upon her. She glanced continually to her mistress and tried to match the long elegance of her neck and her delicate handling of the silverware.

No doubt Miss Davies knew that her every action, even in this unorthodox situation, would reflect upon the woman she served.

Owen admired Miss Davies's dedication to make herself

worthy of her spot at this table, no matter how singular the experience might be.

She answered all of Lady Neil's questions with the utmost politeness and an exceptional way with words. The maid was very well spoken, even for a servant of the highest degree. The remnants of her upbringing were still evident in her all her manners.

Because Owen's attentions was so fixed on Miss Davies, he certainly noticed the many cautious glances she sent his way. She surely wondered who he might be to her brother and how he came to accompany Davies. She had only looked to him once or twice in the drawing room and hadn't said a proper word to him since her first appearance.

Naturally, Owen knew that her focus must be on her brother's sudden reappearance in her life. Her brother's strange friend was simply another oddity amidst the real event. His eyes met hers only a few times through all of breakfast, when their sideways looks happened to be well timed, but she always quickly returned her gaze to her food.

Owen found himself wishing that she would look at him just for a moment longer, so he could take note of the shades of green in her eyes, so he could understand the many thoughts running behind them. For in his stolen observations, Owen felt certain that Miss Davies possessed a sharp intelligence that she employed at every second to make her own observations of her brother and Owen himself.

As if hearing his wish, Miss Davies's eyes happened to meet Owen's once again as she chanced to look up from her plate in his direction. Owen's heart jolted at the connection and he offered a small smile in the hopes of putting her more at ease. The morning sunlight turned her eyes into a shimmering emerald. Owen's smile grew wider.

But before she could look away of her own volition, a

clattering sound coming from the direction of Lady Neil, seated next to Miss Davies, distracted them both.

"Goodness, there goes another fork. Have my fingers swollen so much they can no longer grip cutlery, or have the footmen been polishing our silverware a little too thoroughly?" The lady sighed and chuckled in good humor, looking ruefully to her fellow diners.

She began to reach down for the fork, grimacing briefly with the effort, when both Lord Neil and Miss Davies jumped up to assist.

"Allow me, my lady!" Miss Davies's voice rang out clear and firm through the breakfast room. Faster than Owen thought possible, she was out of her chair and at her mistress's side, collecting the fallen fork and removing it to the cabinet with spare silverware. Even Lord Neil could not match her speed, still half out of his own chair. He sat back down and took his wife's hand in his, his deep brown eyes searching for any sign of discomfort.

The display tugged at a bittersweet chord in Owen's heart. From his brief time in their presence, he could see that the baron and baroness clearly adored each other. Though they seemed quite different in temperament, the difference seemed to balance them both out. But Owen knew he had no chance of experiencing such a bond. At least, not if he could help it.

When Miss Davies returned with a clean fork for her mistress, she lingered by the lady's side and asked her several times if she needed anything else and if she felt quite well. Before resuming her seat, she also asked Lord Neil if he was in need of anything.

Owen knew such attentiveness was a maid's duty, but, watching their interactions, he could see that Miss Davies genuinely cared for and worried after her master and mistress. He knew instantly that Miss Davies would go to any lengths for the people who mattered most to her. Such a quality was of the utmost importance to Owen, and he greatly respected anyone who possessed it with humility and sincerity.

To Owen's surprising regret, breakfast finally came to an end. Lady Neil summoned the butler, Mr. Taylor, to return Davies and his sister to the drawing room and show Owen to the morning room while the reunited siblings spoke privately.

Somehow Owen found himself wishing that he could join them. He did not want to leave Miss Davies's presence so soon. He wanted to learn more of her.

Instead he followed behind the butler. He knew his part in this quest was over. The rest was up to Davies and the two did deserve time to reacquaint themselves with each other and determine if they could start their relationship anew.

Owen could only hope that he might catch a glimpse of Miss Davies before they left Gatherford Park, possibly forever.

# CHAPTER 3

*M*r. Taylor showed Captain Jessup into the cozy morning room with a flourish of his wizened hand. Violet noticed his discerning eyes narrow just slightly as the man turned back to the rest of the group and bowed his head.

Violet also noticed the way the captain's brown eyes darted to hers as Mr. Taylor continued down the hall, calling for Violet and Frank to follow him.

The time had finally come to find out what all this business was about—why Frank would come after her all the way at Gatherford Park after all these years.

Though Violet could have easily led Frank to the drawing room herself, she was glad to have Mr. Taylor's quiet strength nearby for a few moments before truly being left alone to face her brother. But she did not enjoy feeling as though she were being treated almost like a guest as well. She was not a guest in this house. She would never be a guest in any house.

Recollections of Captain Jessup's eyes upon her, just now at the morning room and all through breakfast, kept Violet somewhat distracted as they made their way to the drawing room. He was just as foreign to her and she could not guess why he'd accompanied her brother on this mission, but she found something about the crinkles near the corners of his eyes when he smiled and their warm brown color to be comforting.

With almost no information to justify her assessment, Violet felt sure that the captain's eyes conveyed a kindness in his character.

"Here we are," Mr. Taylor announced. Violet blanched as she realized that they stood before the drawing room door.

"Thank you, sir." Frank nodded as he stepped into the room.

Violet paused at the threshold, her heart thundering and her breath faltering. She felt a gentle nudge in her side and she glanced up to see Mr. Taylor peering down at her with a raised eyebrow.

"I'll be fine." She answered his unspoken question with a weak smile. She stepped into the room and turned back to Mr. Taylor, still lingering at the door.

"Do ring if you need anything," he announced, looking between both of them but holding Violet's gaze for a touch longer before leaving the room.

Finally, Violet was alone with her older brother for the first time in over a decade. She still faced the door, hoping that Mr. Taylor would return and whisk her away from this unpleasant situation.

Instead, she felt her brother stand next to her. His presence by her side felt almost like that of a stranger. She had lost contact with her remaining family years before. Though they may have been bonded by blood, Violet did not know this man standing next to her.

She only knew her memories of him, of the terrible things he'd done.

"Violet..." Frank's voice came out nervous and tentative. Perhaps he really had changed. Violet had never heard such a tone in his voice during her childhood. Or perhaps he simply acted the part of a regretful big brother, trying to trick her into some scheme. "Why don't we have a seat? Then I promise to explain as much as I can in five minutes."

She turned to him but still could not look at his face. She did not wish to see the deceit behind his eyes. Some very small part of her, Violet had to admit, longed to understand and perhaps even forgive. But the larger part could not trust him enough. Not yet. Not after everything he'd put her through.

But she nodded and followed him to a pair of comfortable chairs near the warm fire. As Violet sat, she finally mustered her courage up to look at her brother. The proud defiance she'd felt earlier seemed to diminish with every second leading up to this moment.

He looked quite similar to what she remembered, but her childhood memories had distorted his features over the years. The Frank she remembered was a hulking giant, coming into his adult form with all the excitement of youth. His face had seemed cold and harsh, sometimes even villainous.

But today, sitting next to her and peering anxiously at her face, her brother did not seem so tall and threatening. Of course, she too had grown since the last time she'd seen him when she was just ten years old. She was taller herself, and her heart had been strengthened by the struggles she'd endured in the past twelve years.

Frank no longer looked like one of the monsters who haunted her dreams. He was just a man.

"You may speak and I will hear you. But I cannot promise anything more than that," she said, hoping that she sounded calm and collected but firm. She forced herself to hold his gaze, to read into the regret and miniscule hope she saw in his eyes and return it with cold strength.

Frank gave a small smile, his shoulders sinking slightly with relief. "Thank you, Violet. I hope what you hear will soften your opinion of me, even just a bit. But again, I understand if you hold me in the same contempt. Where to begin...

"I suppose you might like to know what I've been doing since we last saw each other, which will also help me explain my radical change of heart. You see, after the downfall of our family I spent a few aimless years barely surviving, still drinking my way deeper into debt. I'm not sure how it happened, but I eventually came to the realization that I was becoming more and more like our father and our two oldest brothers.

"Something in me revolted against that idea. Perhaps I had grown tired of living such a pathetic life. I couldn't imagine spending all the rest of my days in the same fashion —begging for a hot meal from kind innocent strangers, drinking myself into a stupor every night, being kicked out of inns and sleeping in alleyways."

Frank paused and swallowed, the discussion of his horrid past looking as though it left a bad taste in his mouth. He looked down at his hands clasped together in his lap, his brows furrowed and eyes squeezed shut against the memories. For a fraction of a second, Violet's imagination played out the scene her brother described and she almost felt sorry for that pitiful man.

"I felt I needed to change lest I end up in an early grave like Father, or doing God knows what Samuel and Charles ended up doing. As you must have guessed by the way Lord and Lady Neil referred to me, I had a lucky night at the tables and won a sizeable amount of money—enough to allow me to purchase a commission. I knew the instant I won the money that I had been blessed with an opportunity to change my life. I entered the army as the vile man you remember, and came out a lieutenant—and, I think, a much-improved man.

"In fact, that is where I met my friend Captain Jessup. With his help, and the harsh realities of life in the army, I grew out of my old awful ways which had been practically bred into me, bred into all us Davies boys, by Father. Violet, I cannot express to you how shocking are those horrors of war that I lived through for years. I saw countless families destroyed as I watched sons, brothers, husbands, and fathers fall all around me, from both sides.

"I have long known that the part I played in our family's destruction, and the horrible disregard with which I treated you, are near unforgiveable, regardless of who I am now. Nothing can change the days I spent at the club with Father and our brothers, drinking and gambling away our fortune. Nothing can change the fact that we all blamed you for our rapid decline in wealth and the loss of our mother. Nothing can change or excuse the fact that I abandoned you when our estate was lost and fled to live a life of debauchery, away from the responsibilities I should have claimed if neither Sam nor Charlie saw fit to step up."

Violet grimaced as she listened to Frank enumerate the many faults of their family, the many ways they'd harmed her though she was just an innocent child. It had taken her years to realize that she could hold no blame for their father's inability to cope with their mother's death and his insistence on dragging his sons down with him while treating his only daughter like some vermin to be disposed of.

Frank looked up from his hands, a tear glistening at the corner of his eye. "I should have protected you. I should have stood up for you when Father screamed at you for killing Mother and for driving him to drink and waste his life away on bets. I should have taken you with me and found somewhere for both of us to grow up and be happy. I have regretted my actions, the pain I've caused you, every moment of every day for the past decade.

"I know it is far too little and far too late to be saying these things now. You've done a remarkable job making a life out of the wreckage we left you in. Clearly you do not need me. You never have. I know my time must be up but if I may be so bold…. Violet, I so desperately wish that you and I can be a family again. Will you forgive me?"

Frank bit his lip, a tortured expression stretched across his face, pulling his skin taught. His hazel eyes watered, pleading with Violet.

It was Violet's turn to look down at her hands in her lap, her fingers unconsciously twisting in the fabric of her skirt. She could feel her own tears poking at the corners of her eyes, threatening to break free, but she willed them away.

She could not deny that her heart had been moved by Frank's speech, but her tears originated primarily from the sudden rush of memories from the darkest years of her life, her childhood spent in fear and anguish knowing she was hated by those who were meant to cherish her.

She had locked up these memories in a deep corner of her mind, keeping herself so busy with work that she had no time to reflect on them. But now they were dragged out of their vault as her brother laid his heart bare.

Despite her many misgivings about this situation, something deep in Violet's heart felt that Frank was indeed sincere. She could not yet rule out the possibility of a well-rehearsed act, but she also could not stop herself from longing to reach out and believe him.

"What you say is all very nice, Frank…but why did you wait until a year after the war to meet with me? Why bother finding me now after abandoning me twelve years ago?"

Violet dared to lift her gaze, to meet her brother's eyes and discover what might be hiding there.

But when she did, she saw that her words must have injured him. He frowned and shook his head, not at her but at himself.

"In truth, I did not originally plan on seeking you out. I selfishly thought that it was better if I knew nothing of you and completely buried my past. But I thought of perhaps trying to trace your whereabouts to at least know that you were doing well. I thought it extremely unlikely that you would want anything to do with me even if I tried to atone for my actions." He glanced up at her nervously, his face still contorted with shame.

"My friend Captain Jessup is the one who encouraged me not just to find you and gather news as to your health and happiness, but to reach out and attempt to make amends. You see, he reminded me of the many men both familiar and foreign to us that would never be with their families again. If the chance is there to right a wrong and offer an apology it should be taken, even if the other person does not accept. That is what he told me."

Frank's face softened slightly as he spoke of his friend. His words sparked an unexpected curiosity in Violet. Just who was this captain and how had he managed to have such a profound effect on her brother? If he could help turn Frank around from the unsavory young man he'd been, he must surely be a miracle.

Violet squeezed her eyes shut to banish these unwelcome thoughts of Captain Jessup out of her mind. This was not the time to think about him. This was between Violet and Frank and their future as a family. Perhaps later, after all this business was done and over with and Violet could resume her normal life, she could spare a moment or two to think about the handsome captain who'd stared at her with his kind, warm eyes.

"What do you say, sister? May I call you that again?" Frank shifted forward to the edge of his chair, anticipating Violet's answer with wide, almost innocent looking eyes.

"You wish to call me sister again and surely you wish that I will call you brother. And while I do sense sincerity in your words.... Frank, you left me behind to make my own way in the world when I was just a child of ten years old. That was over twelve years ago now. You've been a stranger to me longer than you've been my brother. How can we possibly hope to mend these wounds in our family history?"

Violet flushed as her voice cracked with tears that strained against her crumbling resolve.

She used to be terrified that her brothers would come looking for her and steal her away from the secure position she'd found with the Richards family.

After their father had been laid to rest in a pauper's funeral, Violet's brothers fled the estate as quickly as possible. Mr. Davies had gambled it off to the man who'd killed him in a duel when he'd tried to worm his way out of the bet he'd lost—and it would not do well for his sons to be nearby when the winner came to collect what was owed.

Young Violet had wandered about the town near their home, forgotten about in the mad rush, until some passersby travelling through on their way to London took notice of her.

Those passersby had been the young Miss Richards's family and she had begged her parents to stop the carriage and give shelter to Violet. But they'd had no interest in accepting an orphan until Violet urgently offered to earn her keep.

And so she had been with the family ever since, eventually becoming Miss Richards's maid. And when Miss Richards became Lady Neil, she had followed her then, too.

Violet had lain awake through the night in those early years, her heart pounding as painful memories flooded her young mind. Every creak of footsteps in the hall made her jump, fearing that her brothers had returned to now blame her for their father's death.

And here one of them sat, begging her to allow him back into her life.

She knew from the moment Lord Neil had said the visitor was for her that it must be someone from those old days looking for her. Her past come to haunt her present.

Could she accept Frank's words as they were? Or was she opening herself up to another chapter of pain after working so hard to put that life behind her?

She must have been silent for too long for Frank stood and walked a few paces away, turning to face Violet.

"I understand your concerns and you have every right to feel as you do. I myself do not have an answer for that question. Our history is dark, perhaps too dark to be overcome. But I thank you for taking the time to hear me out. I hope you will be happy and healthy all your days."

Frank's voice was solemn as he bowed low to Violet and made his way to the door. A surge of panic shot through Violet.

"Wait!" she found herself crying out.

Frank started from the sudden exclamation and turned back to face Violet once more. His eyes were wide again, with surprise and hope.

Violet stood from her chair, her hands trembling as she walked across the room to stand before her brother.

"Perhaps you should not go yet," she mumbled, glancing down to her feet in sudden embarrassment. Her fingers continued to worry away at the folds of her skirt.

"I cannot promise that I will ever feel a deep sisterly connection for you, or even a general fondness. But...I would like to try and work towards it. I wish to know more of you —who you are now. But you must understand that my trust in you has been nearly damaged beyond repair. I cannot say that it will be easy to mend."

Frank stood silently for several moments, leaving Violet to continue staring at his boots until she could take the silence no longer. She looked up at her brother's face and saw utter amazement in his expression. When their eyes met, a smile slowly spread across his countenance until he grinned so widely Violet thought he looked like an entirely different person. Perhaps this person was worth getting to know. Maybe even worth forgiving.

"Frank?" She asked, peering up at her brother curiously. His silence and transfixed gaze almost worried her.

"Do you truly mean it? You will give me a chance to prove myself a changed man, to make up for all those years you suffered?"

Frank beamed down at her almost like a child receiving a present. But because he was seven years older than she, Violet could not remember what he looked like as a child, nor did her memory of the family portraits in the gallery of their estate help her in producing a true likeness. Still, at this moment, she felt she could imagine it well enough.

"Yes, I truly mean it." Violet couldn't keep the small smile from tugging at her lips. "I shall ask Lord and Lady Neil if they will allow you and Captain Jessup to stay with us. Perhaps a fortnight to start. But I must remind you that I will be very busy with my regular duties."

"Thank the Lord!" Frank clapped his large hands together and then grabbed Violet's hands in his.

The sudden touch shocked Violet and she snatched her hands away, but not before she noticed a few scars on the backs of his hands. They looked far older than the rest of him.

"I-I'm terribly sorry," Frank stuttered as he brought his own hands rapidly back to his sides.

"You surprised me," Violet whispered, clasping her hands to her chest as if she'd just touched a hot tea kettle without a mitt. She felt that he meant well, but there was only so much she could handle at a time.

"I will be more restrained from now on, I swear it. I simply let my excitement get the better of me." Her brother smiled sheepishly, tugging on his coat and straightening his back to adopt a serious air.

Violet put a hesitant hand on her brother's arm. "It's alright, Frank. One step at a time."

As DINNER APPROACHED, Violet paced over the stone floor of the servants' hall. Lady Neil had been more than happy to accommodate Frank and Captain Jessup for as long as Violet wanted, so long as it was truly what Violet wanted. But she went a step further by offering to host a private dinner for the three of them.

Violet almost refused, but she had already tried to deny her mistress's kindness once today and did not wish to anger or offend her.

After all, if she truly wished to mend her relationship with her brother, she would have to start the process at some point. It might as well be over a quiet, delicious meal.

And she found she did not mind that Captain Jessup would also be there. He was a guest as well and had played a large part in bringing her brother back into her life. Besides, she looked forward to learning more of him and appreciating his very pleasant countenance.

"Dear Violet, you are going to polish this floor smoother than a river stone if you keep up your pacing." Mrs. Baird's warm voice startled Violet to a halt. She looked toward the fire, where the sweet-tempered housekeeper stood with hands clasped together at her waist, a patient expression on her wise face.

"I'm sorry, Mrs. Baird. It's just that I am a nervous wreck in regards to this dinner. Frank and I have only just met again today after over a decade. My intuition tells me that I can trust him, but I simply cannot allow myself to go that far yet. I fear it will be terribly awkward."

Violet sighed as she gave voice to her worries and she sank down onto one of the chairs at the long table where the Neil family's servants took their meals or worked on projects for the household.

Mrs. Baird sat in the chair next to Violet and took one of her hands in her own. The elderly woman's hands may have been roughened by age and decades of work but she always handled everything she touched, including Violet, with such gentle care.

Violet looked over to Mrs. Baird and gave a tired smile. The unexpected turns this day had taken—on top of Violet resuming her normal duties after her meeting with Frank—had drained her more than she realized. But holding Mrs. Baird's hand, Violet felt as though she could borrow some strength from the older woman.

Violet had never known her mother, but she had finally found someone who could fill that gap in Mrs. Baird. And Mrs. Baird seemed particularly fond of Violet from the start, treating her as Violet imagined a daughter might be treated by a loving family.

"I know you are scared. You do not want to be taken advantage of, to be hurt like you were in the past. But it sounds like your brother has gone through a great deal of trouble to find you and offer himself to you for acceptance or rejection. I sincerely hope that he is being truthful and wishes to do right by you now. The choice is ultimately up to you. Keep your wits about you, but be open to second chances. Especially when that second chance is accompanied by a very handsome friend."

Mrs. Baird smiled slyly at Violet's shocked expression, her gray bun bouncing slightly as she laughed quietly. Violet had never heard the housekeeper speak so candidly on the subject of men. They had had a few visitors to Gatherford Park since Violet had come to live there, including the exceedingly charming and attractive Earl of Overton, but Mrs. Baird had never once commented on them beyond their well-bred manners or sharp outfits.

The older woman laughed in earnest as Violet continued to stare at her. She gripped Violet's chin and gave it a squeeze. "Don't you think it's about time to head to your special dinner?"

Violet glanced to the clock on the mantle of the fireplace and saw with dismay that it was indeed the appointed time. "Send me off with luck," she whispered to Mrs. Baird, standing stiffly and smoothing out her skirts.

"I doubt you will need it, but I will send it all the same." Mrs. Baird patted Violet on the shoulder and steered her out of the servants' hall.

Nerves fluttered through Violet the whole way to the guest wing of the grand home, where Lady Neil had had rooms prepared for Frank and Captain Jessup, as well as the smaller dining room in that side of the house for their meal.

She waited at the closed door for a moment to take in a deep breath that rattled all the way down, the tension in her body refusing to dissipate. But finally she put her hand on the brightly polished knob and entered.

Both men stood immediately upon Violet's arrival.

Captain Jessup bowed his head and Frank crossed the room quickly to give his arm to Violet. After a beat of hesitation, Violet took her brother's arm and allowed him to lead her to her place at the table.

The guests sat across from her, giving Violet ample opportunity to observe them.

Frank began the conversation with simple questions, his voice a touch too lighthearted as if it required effort to seem so relaxed, encouraging Violet to share her day since he'd last seen her that morning.

Violet found that she could barely respond for the food was too delicious. As servants of a very old and wealthy family, they ate quite well. But all the best meals were of course reserved for the master and mistress—and their guests. Violet ate as much and as quickly as she could without appearing disgraceful. She couldn't remember the last time she'd tasted such wonderful food. And she could not guess when she would have the honor again.

But Violet also knew that she kept her answers short because she still did not wish to open up entirely yet despite Mrs. Baird's advice.

Just as the housekeeper's words jingled in her head again —including her comment about Frank's friend—Captain Jessup spoke up.

"I swear, this meal is almost as fantastic as the very first meal we had back on English soil. There is something so comforting about a hot, lovingly made dinner after an extended period of travel."

Violet started at the sound. She hadn't yet properly heard Captain Jessup's voice as he had been almost completely silent during breakfast, save for a few quiet answers to Lady Neil's questions.

Now he spoke with his full voice, powerful and rich but cheerful at the same time. It sounded as though it gathered from every corner of his chest and rose up to his lips on warm air.

"Oh, you remember it?" Frank shot back. "I seem to recall you sleeping through most of that first meal. You never could rest well on a swaying ship." Violet noticed the smirk her brother directed at the captain, who returned his jabs with an unbothered shrug of his shoulders.

"I think I was simply tired from running about Waterloo and seeing that our regiment was packed up and accounted for."

"Waterloo?" The question slipped out from Violet before she could check herself. Though it was only one word, it was the first question she'd asked either of them.

"Yes indeed." Captain Jessup smiled, the corners of his mouth creating creases that spoke of a lifetime of smiles and laughter. His eyes locked on Violet's and she marveled at the fact that this seemingly carefree man had fought in the war for years and had even been at Waterloo.

"Did not the lieutenant tell you?" he continued, his bright voice carrying through the room. "We were both at Waterloo, yes. Quite a frightful time, in truth. But your brother fought very valiantly many, many times over."

There was no mistaking the respect in Captain Jessup's voice as he spoke of Frank. Violet found herself wishing to hear more of her brother's accomplishments, and perhaps some of the captain's as well.

Captain Jessup continued. "Yes, indeed, I daresay I owe Frank my life. During a smaller skirmish I received a truly nasty shot to the leg and your brother is the reason I was able to keep that leg, and possibly even my very life. He carried me off to the medic as quickly as possible and they were able to operate immediately and retrieve the bullet."

He spoke with such ease that he could have been telling Violet about shrubbery sculpting. But still her eyes widened at the unexpected frankness with which he told his story. He did not shy away from discussing the reality of war in the presence of a woman, though such details were generally thought too distressing for the gentler sex.

From the corner of her eye she noticed Frank observing her with a furrowed brow, no doubt watching to see how she would react to his friend's story. When Violet looked at him head on, with a small smile and less guarded eyes, Frank visibly relaxed. Clearly his sister would not be put off by their experiences.

"That is very heroic indeed," Violet said with a hint of admiration as she looked between the two men who sat across from her. She felt as though she could suddenly see them more clearly. The veil she had kept over her eyes to protect herself slowly dissolved, allowing her to peek through and truly see her brother as he was now and of course his handsome and honorable friend.

"Oh, it sounds more dramatic than it really was. I believe the real hero to be Captain Jessup in that situation." Frank waved away Violet's compliment, a slight blush creeping over his face, but Violet could see by the smile he tried to hide that he was very glad to know his sister thought him heroic.

"Is that so?" Violet couldn't help prodding, looking over to the captain. She wanted more of their exciting tales, more opportunities to see into both of their characters. After all, few situations tested a person's true mettle like the battlefield.

"Absolutely. Captain Jessup was helping an innocent family to safety. They weren't able to escape the area quickly enough before the fighting broke out. He caught a bullet in the leg just as he saw them off to shelter, probably a villager who didn't realize he was helping the family rather than trying to harm them. It can be hard to read the intentions of an enemy uniform. Luckily I happened to be nearby patrolling when I heard the sound and carried him back to camp right away."

Violet's eyes remained fixed on Captain Jessup as Frank told the rest of the story. She tried to read his expression but he seemed suddenly closed off. His dark eyes darted to hers for a moment before returning to his plate.

"That is also incredibly heroic. I'm sure that family would thank you ardently for your help if they had the chance."

Violet's words felt hollow, unsure of how to comfort a man who has been through such an ordeal. But she wanted to say something, even something small, to bring peace to Captain Jessup. She knew he deserved it. She was overwhelmed by that same feeling she got near Lady Neil at times —the desire to reach out and touch and soothe.

Captain Jessup looked over to Violet and held her gaze for a moment. His eyes rendered Violet breathless. "Thank you for saying so, Miss Davies. I only wish I could know what became of them."

Violet's heart sank as she understood his suddenly stoic expression. He'd had no issue discussing his injury because the wound wasn't nearly as important to him as the circumstances that had caused it. He did not regret the injury, but his heart still longed to know that the family was safe.

"I'm sure whatever became of them, they would thank you all the same for bringing them a moment of safety." Violet smiled warmly and her heart lifted again when the captain returned it. She marveled at how even a small smile could completely transform his face.

Frank squirmed in his chair, sensing the heavy atmosphere. "But war is not all heroism, you know. I can't tell you the many foolish things we got up to when we weren't busy running about the battlefield. Surely you must remember the latrine, Captain Jessup?"

The lieutenant turned to his companion with a raised

eyebrow and a smirk. Captain Jessup groaned and dragged a large hand down his face in exasperation. "You never give me the chance to forget, my good man."

"Ah yes, latrines. My favorite topic of conversation for dinner," Violet giggled. A sudden lightness washed over her. Perhaps she could get used to this company.

"See!" Captain Jessup cried, waving a hand in Violet's direction. "Clearly the lady jests. No one wishes to hear of latrines at the dining table."

"On the contrary, captain," Violet quickly interjected. "I declare we must not leave this table until we have heard all about this latrine business."

She shot a sly smile to Captain Jessup, whose wide eyes stared back at her in shock. He ran a hand through his thick light brown hair and sighed dramatically. "Alright, let's have it then."

Frank beamed at Violet and immediately launched into the humorous tale, abandoning his food in favor of waving his arms about for emphasis. Violet pressed her lips together at first, trying to hide her laughter. But the first time she caught the captain's eyes and saw the corners once again creased with mirth, Violet could no longer help herself. She let out a quiet laugh, covering her mouth behind her hand but unable to still her shaking shoulders.

When Frank finished his embarrassing tale, Captain Jessup returned one of his own involving Frank's habit of talking in his sleep. The two men seemed to think it a game of who could share the least flattering story about the other.

As Violet watched the two argue over some detail Frank claimed Captain Jessup had embellished, she realized that she genuinely enjoyed herself. The Frank before her was not the Frank she remembered. He made jokes, he teased his friend, he endlessly complimented the meal and the home and the kindness of their hosts, he endeavored to learn more about his sister's life.

Violet felt herself slipping into the ease with which the two army officers spoke with each other and drew her into the conversation. None of the anecdotes they shared betrayed any of Frank's old misbehaviors. In fact, Violet would not have believed anyone who described Frank now and claimed him to be the same brother who had caused her so much grief. The change was remarkable, almost unbelievable. Yet Violet found herself wanting to believe.

"Violet, would you perhaps like to join us for coffee or tea in the guest drawing room?" Frank asked as their meal came to an end.

The question surprised Violet. She hadn't considered taking refreshments in the drawing room after dinner. Her brother suggested it as if she were a guest as well, at liberty to do as she pleased when she pleased.

Violet looked back and forth between the men, both with expectant expressions on their faces. Despite her earlier anxiety about the dinner and the many times she'd considered feigning illness or some other excuse to avoid it, Violet found that now she did not wish to part from her brother or Captain Jessup so soon.

She still had much to discover about both of them.

But a quick glance at the clock told her that she had already likely used up too much of her borrowed time— though she knew Lady Neil would be generous enough to allow her time in the drawing room if she asked. The thought of her mistress sent a pang of guilt through Violet. Besides, she could use some time away from Frank and Captain Jessup to digest their conversation and assess her changing feelings about her brother.

"I thank you for the invitation, Frank, but I really should get back to my duties. Unfortunately the mending will not take care of itself and Lady Neil is in need of much mending due to her condition." Violet quickly stood and curtsied to the guests, who also stood and bowed their heads as she left the room.

She quietly closed the door behind her and leaned her back against it for a moment. She could not have guessed that she would undergo such a transformation in one simple dinner. But as she smoothed out her skirts and listened to the soft clicking of her shoes against the floor as she made her way back downstairs, Violet reminded herself that she must not get too carried away.

Her trust could not be completely rebuilt over one meal. And regardless of her brother's presence in her life, Violet owed her first duty to the family she served. She could not be distracted and allow the quality of her work to slip lest the Neils find fault with her and banish her.

Violet would not be banished ever again.

# CHAPTER 4

$\mathcal{W}$inters always seemed so bleak and gray to Owen regardless of how brightly the sun shone. But English winters had the advantage of being comforting, only for the fact that it was home. Even still, he'd considered escaping to some exotic location with permanently temperate weather on more than one occasion. His winters at war had changed Owen's opinion of the season entirely.

Yet he found himself out on a walk about the grand Gatherford Park grounds on a winter afternoon. The sun blazed in the monotone sky but the chill temperature ensured that Owen did not feel it.

The snow had held off and Owen had been prevailed upon to join the residents of the estate on a walk. The cool air's invigorating properties had been the bait to entice him. Owen had still been tempted to refuse until he learned that another certain resident of the house would also be joining them.

He stared at her now, bundled in a simple but thick pelisse, her arm threaded through Lady Neil's. The path was large enough for the two ladies to walk ahead side by side while the men remained a few steps behind. Though Owen could not see Miss Davies's face, he could hear her soft voice conversing with her mistress about the scenery, household plans, new fashions, and other minor subjects.

"Dear, are you sure you're quite alright?" Lord Neil called out to his wife once again. They hadn't been on their walk long, but the baron certainly seemed apprehensive about having his very pregnant wife out in the elements though she was thoroughly bundled as well.

"Yes, my love, I am quite well. I so hate to be cooped up in the house and I am still very capable of taking a simple walk," Lady Neil responded over her shoulder, smiling patiently at her husband. "Besides, who knows how long this weather will last? Surely the snow will be coming soon and we'll have no choice but to be cooped up." She craned her neck to look up at the sky as if searching for the first sign of snowflakes.

"I must say I quite agree, Lady Neil," Owen blurted. "Being out of doors is always so refreshing when one can take advantage of it."

"It that so?" Davies asked, a hint of suspicion in his voice. He looked over at Owen with raised eyebrows, his chin lifting into the air. He knew he'd caught Owen in a lie. Or at least he thought he did. "I thought you hated winter, Captain Jessup? I'm surprised being out of doors during this season is at all agreeable to you."

Owen had to resist the urge to roll his eyes and thank goodness, too, for Miss Davies peeked over her shoulder curiously at him.

"Of course I find it agreeable to walk out of doors in winter if I can do it in such lovely company. In truth, I prefer to be active out of doors; my main objection to winter is that it puts an end to so many of my favorite pastimes."

Owen smiled to himself at his sound answer. Davies

would not catch him out this time, as they so often tried to do to each other. And his answer was only the truth. He did hate being trapped indoors. He was a man of action and activity, preferring horseback rides or driving the carriage or hunting to any activity that could be found within the walls of a home. But during winter, he had to be more selective about his hobbies and when he participated in them.

"My favorite season must be summer. Some will say it is too hot to enjoy, but I don't mind the heat at all. Early summer in London is always so exciting," Lady Neil offered, looking back and forth over the browning landscape of naked trees and dying grass. "What about you, Violet?"

"O-oh..." Miss Davies stuttered before falling into a thoughtful silence. She seemed surprised at being directly addressed while her master and mistress showed the guests around though she had been invited on the walk as well.

"Spring. I like waking up each day and seeing more flowers appear, seeing the grass grow greener and taller. It really is like a rebirth. Just when it seems that winter will never end, when you've almost forgotten how bright and lively the world can be, spring surprises you."

Owen smiled at her response, her voice so gentle and quiet he almost didn't hear. In fact, it sounded almost as though she spoke to herself, forgetting that she was surrounded by company.

Following suit, Davies and Lord Neil both shared their own thoughts on the seasons but Owen hardly paid them any mind. Miss Davies captured his attention, even if he could only catch glimpses of her round cheeks and soft looking lips and curved chin beneath her bonnet.

The more he thought of her response, the more he realized how thoughtful and observant the young lady was. After their dinner on the day he and Davies had arrived, he'd had very few opportunities to speak with her. It was a terrible shame that their fortnight neared its end. Her mistress had given her time off each day to spend with Davies. Sometimes Owen joined them, but even then, the siblings' conversation primarily involved each other. He knew this was perfectly normal as they had over a decade to catch up on and he was only a tagalong stranger.

And Miss Davies did seem rather engrossed in her work. He came across her at times around the house but she was always rushing this way and that or so focused on the task at hand that he did not feel it right to interrupt her. Beyond being a very intelligent and well-spoken young lady, Miss Davies was also a dedicated employee who served her family with pride.

The conversations within the party floated in and out of Owen's attention. Everything seemed to quieten as he observed Miss Davies. He felt out of sorts, a strange sickly feeling settling into his stomach. Regret, he realized. He did not want to leave so soon.

That thought sent a ripple of anxiety down Owen's spine.

"Jessup? Whatever is the matter with you?" Davies's voice sounded brash against Owen's ears, pulling him away from his troubling thoughts.

"What's that now?" Owen shook his head and refocused his attention on his friend.

"You've fallen quite behind. I wouldn't have noticed it if the baron hadn't pointed it out." Frank nodded further up the path where the rest of the party continued, their hosts and Miss Davies now walking side by side. Lord Neil now guided his wife, leaving Miss Davies's arm unoccupied. For a distressing moment Owen wished to loop his arm around hers and walk beneath the barren branches that he imagined looked lush and vibrant in the spring.

"My goodness, I had no idea you cared so little for me. I could have fallen down a ditch and you probably wouldn't have noticed my absence until dinnertime." Owen gave his friend a slap on the shoulder and picked up his pace to regroup with the rest of their party.

Lord Neil heard the crunch of their boots on the dry gravel and turned back toward his male companions. He said something to his wife before extracting his arm from hers and falling back to meet Owen and Davies, resuming their previous formation.

A wild desire overtook Owen and he nearly lurched forward as he saw Lady Neil hold out her arm for Miss Davies to take again, hoping that he could substitute his own instead. Though he realized that it might seem strange offering his arm to the maid rather than to the lady of the house.

Luckily, Lord Neil interrupted this foolish notion with a whispered question to Davies. "Lieutenant, how goes your progress with your sister? Lady Neil and I are more than happy to host both of you for the rest of the winter if that is agreeable to everyone. My wife is right, as she is about most things. It should begin snowing in earnest soon."

Davies glanced up nervously to the ladies walking before them, but they were far enough ahead and engrossed in their own conversation that they did not hear. His head drooped between his shoulders and he gazed at his boots, not bothering to hide the sadness in his eyes.

Owen felt the melancholy air about his friend and couldn't help being affected by it as well. He looked at Miss Davies again but this time with a frown. He knew his friend still struggled to make headway with that stubborn young lady.

"Unfortunately, my lord, I do not think that will be necessary. But I thank you both for the kind offer. No, I imagine

Captain Jessup and I will be departing at the appointed time. We are on better terms and we converse more easily. But I do not believe she will ever truly be warm to me. I think the best I can hope for at this point is the occasional correspondence. I do not wish to force her into accepting me as her brother again, so it is best we leave as planned."

Davies kicked at a rock in the path and sighed as he confessed his dashed hopes. He looked ahead to his sister with such a heart-wrenching sadness that Owen wrapped an arm about the lieutenant's shoulders for a moment. He so hated to see his friend in such a state, knowing that he was so close to accomplishing his mission but unable to bridge the gap.

"I'm terribly sorry to hear that." Lord Neil nodded solemnly. "Perhaps she will still come around in time. These matters are very delicate and the human heart is a complex creature."

The human heart was a complex creature indeed—an annoying, frustrating, foolish creature. Though he felt bad for his friend's struggle, Owen wondered if perhaps it was best to leave now. His mind took him to strange, uncomfortable places where Miss Davies was concerned and he did not wish to give them any more time to strengthen.

"Is there anything I can do to help bring you comfort?" The baron asked Davies. "Might I suggest a hunt? I confess I do not often hunt. My father was much more of a sportsman than I so I know my property is excellent for hunting."

"A wonderful idea!" Frank exclaimed immediately. "Hunting is a favorite pastime of mine and Captain Jessup's. Jessup in fact is a very skilled marksman. It's been so very long since I've enjoyed a hunt on a grand estate such as this. Perhaps a little thrill will take my mind off my struggles for a bit."

Owen quickly offered his own hearty agreement. He did

indeed love the hunt, but he also needed his mind taken off his own struggles.

"Then we shall set out early tomorrow." Lord Neil smiled, pleased that he could offer some farewell entertainment to his guests.

All Owen had to do was find other ways to distract himself until tomorrow morning.

*BLAST IT ALL*, Owen cursed silently to himself. He had missed yet another shot and startled all the animals in the vicinity away once more.

"Tough luck, Jessup," Davies muttered as he clapped Owen on the shoulder. The lieutenant shrugged at Owen with a puzzled expression.

The situation was so unusual that even Davies could not find joy in teasing his friend for being a poor shot. One poor shot might have emboldened Davies to offer some snide remarks to his friend. But dozens of poor shots in a row was nearly unthinkable for a man with Owen's marksmenship.

Davies looked positively embarrassed for Owen. Owen gritted his teeth and trudged forward behind the baron who led them to another spot in the distance where they could try again.

Even Lord Neil fared better than Owen.

This hunt had been far from the distraction Owen had longed for. Since their walk yesterday, it had taken all of Owen's willpower to suppress any thoughts of Miss Davies, always returning his mind to the hunt.

But he could not escape her even out here. Her some-times sweet and sometimes stubborn face floated into his mind's eye when he should have been preparing his shot. Her voice swam through his thoughts, replaying the few phrases he'd had the opportunity to hear her speak.

Owen was no fool. He knew by now what this meant. What had started as a simple admiration for the young woman in the face of such a jarring situation accompanied by many painful memories transformed into something else.

Not just admiration, but interest. And Owen could not tolerate interest.

His mind felt stretched thin as he both longed to stay and learn more about the intriguing maid and longed to run away and put an end to this nonsense.

But soon it would not matter and Owen could return to his usual activities and thoughts. He and Davies were scheduled to leave the day after next.

Their hunting excursion did not last much longer and for once Owen was glad to see it come to an end. His growing frustration only made it more difficult for him to focus. The three men returned to the house in near silence. Perhaps they sensed that Owen was in no mood for conversation. The sooner he could get himself back to his guest room with a fire lit, a warm change of clothes, and a packed suitcase the better.

Lord Neil left his guests to their own devices in the foyer, going off in search of his wife to check on her health. Owen wandered with Davies about the house, listening to his friend lament about their poor luck. Every word grated on Owen's nerves. He knew Davies spoke primarily of Owen's performance.

He was so distracted by trying to keep himself from blurting out the real reason for his sudden lack of skill that he did not realize they'd wandered all the way to the servants' hall. Owen stopped in his tracks once he noticed his boots clacking on hard stone instead of polished wood.

"Davies, what are we doing down here in the servants' area? If you need something just ring for it."

"Oh, I thought we could tell Violet about our hunting excursion," Davies answered with a nonchalant shrug of his shoulders.

"Or do you mean to say you wish to tell her that you shot better than the famously talented captain?" Owen mumbled, hardly able to keep his annoyance at bay.

Davies scoffed. "Come now, even I would not expose you so harshly. Perhaps in a few years after the event becomes humorous. You would nearly punch any man who mentioned the latrine, remember? Now you laugh about it in good nature."

In truth, that was not the only reason Owen wished to avoid the kitchens but he dare not confess that out loud. Let Davies believe it was only a matter of wounded pride.

"Don't you think it rather unusual that the guests are showing themselves into the servants' hall?"

"Perhaps, but these past two weeks have already fallen well outside the boundaries of what is normal. What harm could there be in visiting my sister down here?"

*There could be plenty of harm in it for me.* Owen grimaced as they rounded a corner and came into the main servants' area.

There sat Miss Davies by the large fire, a notebook in her hands. She scribbled something across the page, so focused that she did not hear the two men enter. The orange and gold flames lit up her face and Owen could see that she seemed to greatly enjoy whatever she wrote. A small peaceful smile graced her lips and her eyes glowed in the firelight.

A jolt shot through Owen from head to toe and his mind ripped away from his present surroundings, transported to another fireside on a vastly different winter night.

He saw one of the many camps he'd spent countless freezing days and nights in. He saw his fellow soldiers going about their duties or trying to entertain themselves. He saw their wives, the ones who had followed their husbands to the battlefield, huddling around the campfires for warmth. He thought of the many thousands of other wives and sweethearts who had remained at home, sitting by their own fires and no doubt thinking of and praying for their husbands and beaus.

Owen squeezed his eyes shut to banish the memories and he returned to the servants' hall of Gatherford Park.

Miss Davies still sat by the fire, unaware of anyone watching her, content to write in her notebook without any worries or fears.

"Let us not disturb her now," he whispered to his friend. "She looks quite engrossed in whatever it is she's doing. I'm sure she has little enough time to herself as it is."

Frank nodded his agreement and turned back down the hall while Owen followed behind.

But just before they went around the corner, Owen looked over his shoulder. He took in the peace and warmth that emanated from Miss Davies as she looked lovingly down at her notebook, her pen gliding across the page with ease.

The image felt bittersweet to Owen as he tore his eyes away and marched down the hall. Though his interaction with her had been minimal, Owen knew that Miss Davies was an uncommon young lady in all the best ways—save perhaps for her stubborn streak, but he could not blame her for her guarded attitude.

He admitted to himself that he was sad to leave her forever without having a chance to sufficiently know her. But he knew this was the right way. If he really knew her, it would make it that much harder to part eventually.

And if she already held this power over Owen, he knew he could not remain near her for long.

Here at Gatherford Park she was safe. She was warm. She was happy. As she should be.

Owen's duty necessitated forgoing all those luxuries at times. But he loved and served his country first and foremost. He would not force someone he cared about to endure the possible heartache that such a life entailed.

# CHAPTER 5

*V*iolet could barely see out the window of the foyer as the heavy snowfall swirled against the panes. The wind howled like a crazed animal, seeping into the house and chilling every room despite the many lit fires fighting to keep the residents and guests of Gatherford Park warm.

"What awful timing..." She lamented to herself as she paced at the window.

Frank and Captain Jessup were scheduled to leave tomorrow but that would obviously be impossible if this weather continued. The storm had started in the morning and continued to rage all day.

A pinch of guilt made her stomach turn. Of course she did not want to risk harm to the two guests if they did venture out in such unfavorable conditions. But nor did she want them to remain here any longer than they'd agreed.

Violet decided to take her nervous energy to the servants' hall and find something to occupy her hands and mind. But instead she found Mrs. Baird carefully stoking the fire as two footmen and one of the kitchen maids huddled around it.

"Ah, Violet. Why don't you come by the fire, dear? Warm yourself up a bit before you go back upstairs."

"Thank you but I'll be fine here. I'd just like to work on my sewing for a while." Violet gave a tight smile and made her way to the cupboards to retrieve her work.

"Have a seat first. You do not look well," Mrs. Baird insisted as she approached Violet, taking Violet's hand and leading her to the table before she could open her cupboard. "Tell me."

For a moment Violet contemplated lying and insisting she was well. But if she'd learned anything about Mrs. Baird since she'd joined the Neil family servants, it was that the woman had a far too keen eye and she would uncover any truth if she deemed it necessary to uncover.

Violet sighed, her shoulders sinking slightly. Now that she sat with Mrs. Baird, she found she wanted to give voice to her distress.

"You may think me awful for saying so, but I so hope this nasty storm will clear up before the morrow. My brother and the captain are supposed to leave and I do not wish for them to be delayed."

Mrs. Baird narrowed her eyes at Violet. Violet had not gone into detail with anyone about her meetings with her brother or how she now felt about him.

"And why is that, may I ask?"

"I just want to return to my normal life. I do believe my brother has changed. He seems like a very good man now. But I just cannot let go of my past. Our past. I would like to communicate with him but I do not know that I am ready to begin acting like a real family again.

"This here is my life now and I cherish it. I'm too confused with this new layer to my life. I liked how things were, before Frank came back. Is that horribly selfish?" Violet's voice trailed off as she hesitantly peered up into the housekeeper's face, fearing the judgement she might see there.

But all Violet saw was patience and understanding as Mrs. Baird looked back at her.

"Of course not, dear. You've worked hard to become the woman you are today. Nothing and no one will change that. I'm glad you have opened yourself up to your brother, but that does not mean you need to act as though nothing happened. The scars left behind from your past are great and they will not disappear immediately. You've made the life you want and it is natural for you to wish to hold on to it. Take your time coming to terms with all this."

A tear pricked at the corner of Violet's eye at Mrs. Baird's kind words. Violet smiled appreciatively, feeling a calm wash over her as she stared into the housekeeper's warm brown eyes.

"Thank you, Mrs. Baird. I will do my best."

"I know you will, Violet. You always do." Mrs. Baird wrapped an arm around Violet's shoulders. Violet allowed herself to sink into the sweet motherly touch for a moment before squeezing Mrs. Baird's hand and standing up from her chair.

"I'm feeling much better now. At least well enough to tackle the mending." Violet smiled again as she made her way to the cupboard. But upon opening the door she found that her mending was missing. She realized she must have left it in her chamber upstairs, where she often worked by candle-light before going to sleep.

After assuring Mrs. Baird that she would be back shortly with her materials, Violet quickly made her way upstairs. While she did feel better after Mrs. Baird's inspiring words, she did not want to give herself any more time to slip back into her anxious thoughts.

As she walked past the drawing room to reach the next

flight of stairs, a rapid movement caught Violet's eye beyond the door. She stopped a few steps down the hall, her curiosity surpassing her need for distraction. She only wanted to confirm if what she saw from the corner of her eye was correct.

With quiet careful steps, Violet returned to the drawing room door and peered inside, careful to keep herself hidden. She was indeed correct. Captain Jessup, the sole occupant of the room, paced up and down the far wall, glancing many times to the large window. His brow was furrowed, the corners of his mouth turned down in a deep frown, and his broad shoulders hunched forward slightly. He looked to be in deep concentration. Or deep worry.

Now that she had her answer, Violet turned back to the hallway to continue her mission. But a squeeze in her chest told her that she could not go just yet. Biting her lip, Violet returned to the doorway and stepped inside.

Entirely engrossed in his thoughts, Captain Jessup failed to notice Violet enter the room. "Captain, is there any way I can assist you?" Violet kept her voice quiet and gentle so as not to startle the man, but he jumped anyway at the sound of her voice, stopping so quickly in his tracks that he nearly lost his balance.

"Miss Davies. Good afternoon," he mumbled, taking a moment to gather his bearings and pull his coat straighter.

Violet struggled to keep her face neutral and professional. But the captain made it difficult when he appeared so endearingly flustered, such an unusual look compared to his typical confidence. Violet reminded herself that he must be surprised at having his private moment interrupted by a servant and the smile she fought quickly slipped away.

"Is there any way I can assist you, Captain Jessup?" Violet repeated her question, her voice hitching just slightly. She ardently hoped that the man hadn't noticed it.

"If you could put an end to this cursed storm that would be a good place to start." He chuckled nervously, his hand brushing a fallen lock of light brown hair away from his forehead.

Violet's feet moved of their own volition, carrying her further into the room, closer to the captain.

"Unfortunately, I believe influence over the weather falls outside the abilities of a lady's maid. But I am quite capable of fetching tea," Violet offered with a quiet chuckle. A sudden shyness stole over her as the captain's expression brightened.

"Perhaps some company for a moment or two will suffice —if you have a moment or two to spare?" He lifted an eyebrow curiously and Violet hated the way her heart jumped at the look, and the way her heart sank the very next moment as she remembered that the captain was supposed to leave tomorrow with her brother.

Violet nodded and joined him by the window, looking out at the vast white expanse she could barely see between the angry flurries of snow falling hard and fast.

"You must be anxious to be on your way. I know your time here can't have been terribly interesting since the primary quest has more to do with Frank than yourself." She kept her voice light and conversational but a tingle ran down her spine as she felt the captain's body tense next to her.

"My time has been quite enjoyable, as a matter of fact. Everyone I've had the pleasure of meeting in this house has been very kind." He gave a half smile as he looked down at Violet from the corner of his eye. "It is just as I said the other day. I hate winter."

"Is it because of the winters you spent out of doors and exposed to the elements during the war?"

The question slipped out before Violet could stop herself. A fierce blush spread over Violet's cheek at the imprudent question and she was immensely glad that they both faced the window so that the captain might not see.

Yet beneath the initial embarrassment at being so forward, Violet realized that she did not wholly regret the question. Her opportunities for learning more about Captain Jessup rapidly dwindled and she did wish to learn more before he left her life, most likely forever.

But the guilt and embarrassment quickly returned in full force when the captain coughed, turning the uncomfortable sound into an awkward laugh. "As I said previously, I am simply an energetic man. I enjoy the outside world—riding my horse, driving a carriage, walking, hunting, landing myself in precarious situations. I feel trapped if I cannot be out and about."

Violet swallowed the lump in her throat as Captain Jessup made his answer. She knew immediately from his hesitation, from the stilted casual tone in his voice, that she had hit upon the real reason for his intense dislike of the season.

Now Violet did regret the question. She must have brought up distressing and painful memories for him. The man made every effort to live his life with cheer and positivity despite his hardships—at least on the outside. And Violet had prodded too deeply, too closely to a subject that was meant only to be shared on his own terms.

"I fear I must be going now," Violet muttered weakly, feeling every bit the coward as she quickly left Captain Jessup to return to his fretting and his unhappy memories.

"THANK GOODNESS," Violet whispered to herself as she looked out the small window of her bedchamber. She was still not used to having her chambers situated in the house proper rather than in the attic with the other female servants, but her mistress wished for her to be as nearby as possible. Every view outside her window, the window that belonged only to her, was a miracle. But this view was a particular miracle.

The wide sky swirled with light pink and orange wisps as the sun climbed higher, the snow beneath glistening as it spread over the entire landscape.

A wave of relief washed over Violet and she felt as though a weight had been lifted off her. Snow still covered the ground but the sun shone strong and bright. The roads would likely be cleared up for normal travel to resume. Surely Frank and Captain Jessup would leave as planned.

And especially after her embarrassing encounter with the captain yesterday, Violet could hardly wait for the appointed hour.

In the meantime, Violet readied herself for the day and went to Lady Neil's room to ready her mistress. Her duties would keep her occupied until the men announced they were ready to leave.

Unfortunately, it seemed Lady Neil was not so willing to allow the subject to slip into the background.

After Lord Neil left his wife's side with a loving kiss on the cheek and a pat on her belly, Lady Neil fixed Violet with a pointed stare. She still sat on the bed in her nightgown, leaning back on one hand while the other cradled the bottom of her stomach as if to hold it up.

Violet sensed her look and hurried over to help the baroness up and make their way to the dressing room. She gripped Lady Neil's arm and slowly pulled her to her feet until she had her balance.

"Let's get you dressed, my lady. I just finished more alterations yesterday so this morning dress should fit you just right," said Violet cheerily, doing her best to ignore the way her mistress stared at her.

But Lady Neil did not move. She remained in her spot,

continuing to watch her maid.

"Are you well, my lady? Shall we sit you back down?" Violet did not like Lady Neil's unusual behavior. The staring, the silence, the stillness—it unsettled her. And with the lady being so near her time, Violet scrutinized every action and expression for signs of distress or illness or some other affliction that could harm her mistress and the baby.

"Are you sure?" Was all Lady Neil said in response, a surprising firmness in the question. Her eyes searched Violet's face but for what Violet had not a clue.

"I'm afraid I don't understand your meaning, my lady."

"Are you sure you're alright with this? Your brother leaving, I mean," she clarified, a soft concern in her voice.

Violet clenched her jaw and looked down at her hands. Why must Lady Neil ask her this when she was so close to finally putting this strange chapter behind her?

"Yes, my lady. Quite sure. Positive, in fact." Violet met her mistress's eyes again and hoped the baroness did not see any of Violet's misgivings there. She felt as though her smile wavered upon her face as she tried to look as certain as she claimed.

In truth, Violet had second guessed her decision many times over the course of Frank's stay at Gatherford Park. One moment she was certain she wanted him gone somewhere far where she only had to think of him on the occasion of writing a letter. But the very next moment she felt it cruel to send him away after all his effort to improve himself and make amends to her.

And of course there was his dashing companion to toil over as well. The longer Frank stayed, the longer Captain Jessup would likely also stay. The two men clearly shared a deep bond, deep enough to convince the captain to come along on a mission that did not concern him in the least if only to support his friend.

But Violet had said so many times now, to herself at least, that she needed Frank to go so she could return to business as usual, so she could live the life she'd fought so hard for without distraction and constant reminders of her traumatic childhood. So she could be safe.

"I understand your decision." Lady Neil offered her arm to Violet and they walked through to the spacious dressing room, where Violet had already laid out her morning dress and prepared the vanity. "I just want you to be sure you are making the decision that is truly right for you."

Violet sat Lady Neil in a nearby chair and rushed over to the dress, assessing its drapes and seams, especially in the areas she'd let out. She wished to be rid of this topic of conversation as quickly as possible, but if Lady Neil wished to discuss it then discuss it she must.

"I think it is right for now, my lady. I plan to correspond with him and perhaps visit from time to time. But I think it's best if I resume my normal habits."

As Violet turned around to begin readying her mistress for the dress, Lady Neil gave her a cautious look. Violet smiled again, hoping to assure her that all was well.

"Very well. The storm let up last night and everything is calm now so they are preparing to leave in the early afternoon. They'll be in the next county by nightfall. You must join us for lunch before we send them off. Did you have a pleasant time with Lieutenant Davies and Captain Jessup?"

"I must admit I was not terribly optimistic at the start. In fact, I rather dreaded the idea of having one of my brothers back in my life. I feared he might try to abuse me again or try to get something from me. But...Frank has changed. I do not believe him to be disingenuous in his words and actions since he's been here. But it is not so easy to let go of my memories. I just wish to live my quiet, simple life here with you and Lord Neil," Violet explained as she began buttoning Lady Neil's dress.

"He does seem to be a kind man, if a little boisterous at times. But I think his amiable nature can excuse it," Lady Neil chuckled. "Did the lieutenant have any news to relate of your other brothers?"

"It seems he's lost all contact with Sam and Charlie as well since our family fell into destitution. They likely went their separate ways but I would not be surprised if they ended up the same as our father. Frank was always the lesser of those three evils. My brothers, I mean. My father was an evil all his own."

Violet frowned as she recalled her two eldest brothers. Frank had emphasized that he often followed in the footsteps of Sam and Charlie, though he did not claim this as an excuse for his mistreatment and neglect.

And looking back on her memories, Violet seemed able to confirm this for herself. She had seen Frank more often than the other two and he did not constantly berate and belittle her or lock her away in dark rooms on the occasions they did see each other as Sam and Charlie had done.

"But what of the captain?"

Violet started at the unexpected question, her hand slipping the loop for the last button. "What of him, my lady?"

"He is rather dashing, don't you think?" She prodded, looking over her should to glance slyly at Violet. "It is a shame to see such a well-bred, heroic man go."

"Indeed," Violet mumbled through tight lips. "But I am sure they both have better things to attend to."

"If you have any interest in seeing your brother again do let me know. We would be happy to adjust your schedule and accommodate him. And anyone else he might wish to bring."

Lady Neil smiled warmly as they moved to the vanity but Violet sensed that her meaning carried more weight than she let on.

Violet took a deep breath to steady herself. She had made her decision. In a few hours' time her life would be as if nothing had changed. She only needed to hang on until then.

LUNCH WAS a quiet affair and Violet was very glad when it was over—not just because it meant that Frank would be leaving soon but because the whole ordeal carried such a heavy air that she nearly felt breathless.

Conversation was scarce, even for Lady Neil. She still seemed pensive about the departure of her guests and Violet's true feelings about the situation but she did not push Violet to change her mind for which Violet was very grateful.

The men shared their travel plans, stating that they would be spending some time with Captain Jessup's oldest brother, Baron of Campston. They shared their many thanks to the baron and baroness for their hospitality and assured their hosts of a very enjoyable stay. Frank also professed his happiness to Violet, thanking her for allowing him the opportunity to reconnect with her and expressed his wholehearted desire that they remain in contact.

Violet accepted her brother's words to the best of her ability, hoping that her anxiety did not make her seem insincere.

Captain Jessup, much like at their very first meal, was all but silent unless spoken to by Lord or Lady Neil. He had nothing to say to or about Violet, it seemed.

Thankfully lunch did not last long as her master and mistress seemed to sense everyone's unease and hurried along to the goodbyes. They walked together from the dining room down to the foyer, where the carriage Frank and Captain Jessup had arrived in waited to carry them away.

"Lieutenant, Captain, it has been such a pleasure to meet and spend time with you both. And we are certainly glad that you had an equally enjoyable time with us."

Lady Neil smiled graciously to her guests and Violet could see from the warmth in her eyes that she meant every word she said.

"I cannot thank you enough for allowing these two ruffians into your lives in such an unusual way." Frank took Lady Neil's hand in his and bowed low over it, his voice thick with sincerity.

Lord Neil chuckled as he shook both men's hands. "Unusual indeed, but life needs a little unusualness from time to time to keep it interesting."

"Please do write if you are ever in the area again or if you wish to visit. We would love to have your charms brighten our home again," Lady Neil insisted, an edge of strictness in her voice that made all of them laugh. All except Violet.

"Do not fret, my lady. You will be the first to know if our charms are nearby." Captain Jessup took his turn to bow over Lady Neil's hand, his bright smile conveying nothing but gratitude. But Violet noticed that the smile did not touch his eyes, did not make those lovely crinkles appear at the corners.

With those formalities taken care of, Lord and Lady Neil quietly retreated to allow the others some privacy.

Though their parting moments were not as awkward as the lunch had been, Violet still felt a stiffness in the atmosphere.

In a moment of panic, as she watched Frank shift his weight from one foot to the other, Violet nearly blurted out for them to stay.

But she managed to snatch her composure by reminding herself that having another person in her life to care for would only distract her from her mistress, the person she'd sworn to serve and care for above all others.

"May I?" Frank stepped forward, his arms outstretched slightly. His eyes searched Violet's, hopeful that she would accept.

Violet nodded and stepped into her brother's arms, allowing him to wrap her in a brief hug. He hadn't tried to be so physically close to her as he had on their first day. She appreciated his willingness to keep his distance and allow her time to come around to him. Violet couldn't help smiling sadly against Frank's shoulder and as he pulled away, she finally found the words she wanted to speak.

"Frank, I hope you know that I am glad we can resume contact. I apologize for taking so long to warm to the idea. I promise to write as often as I am able and I hope you will do the same. This is a good start for us. Perhaps given more time we can find a path that will carry us toward new memories," she said with a weak smile.

Frank returned her smile, his hazel eyes softening into a sad but understanding expression. "I quite agree. I would be more than happy to write as often and as quickly as I receive your replies. I hope you will be well. Please do not hesitate to contact me if you are ever in need—of anything someone who might be a brother could assist with."

His last sentence caused guilt to squeeze Violet's chest. He took a few steps backwards but didn't let his smile fall.

Captain Jessup took Frank's place before Violet. Her breath caught in her throat as she suddenly found herself staring at his wide chest. Her eyes slowly traveled up to his face.

The captain looked down at her with such intensity that

Violet felt a jolt of electricity shoot down her back. He took her small hand in his, the soft glove unable to mask the strength of his fingers. Captain Jessup leaned over her hand for a parting kiss, his lips whispering against her skin. Her heart leapt at the contact, barely there but impossible to ignore.

"It was a pleasure to meet you, Captain," Violet mumbled, barely able to keep her eyes on his. They continued to pierce her with an expression she could not quite read.

"The pleasure was all mine, to be sure. I look forward to furthering our acquaintance someday soon." The captain smiled his wide, charming smile and returned Violet's hand to her side before stepping back next to Frank.

She offered well wishes and safe travels as a footman held the door open for them and then closed it just as quickly, removing them from Violet's sight.

Violet turned her back to the door and resolved herself to return to the servants' hall and continue mixing cosmetic solutions for her mistress. But her foot barely left the ground before the guilt in her heart froze her limbs.

Despite her insistence that she would be glad once her brother and Captain Jessup left, Violet rushed to one of the foyer's grand windows to catch one last glimpse of them.

The drapes served as her camouflage as she watched the two men climb onto the seat of their carriage, Captain Jessup taking the reins and giving the horses a tap to spur them forward. Violet's heart sank.

But she remained at the window, watching the carriage rumble down the driveway toward the tunnel of trees that separated the main estate to the rest of the vast grounds. She wondered what Frank and the captain spoke about, what they would do once they arrived at the village, if they would enjoy their stay with Captain Jessup's brother.

Violet had never felt such a strong wave of regret twist

through her stomach. She should have given more effort to mending her relationship with Frank. He had tried his best, yet Violet had forced herself to remain guarded and distant.

Even in the moments when she could envision a happy family bond with her brother, Violet's memories interrupted the feeling and reminded her of all she'd suffered at the hands of her brothers and her father. When Frank laughed at something Captain Jessup said, her mind transposed the image of him jeering at her as their father and other brothers railed against her or shoved her in a cupboard for days at a time to keep her out of their sight, forcing the sympathetic servants to sneak her bits of food.

But as she watched the carriage roll away with her brother inside, Violet knew that he was not that man anymore. In truth, he had still been a boy then. Nearly a man, but still easily influenced by the father and brothers he looked up to and learned from. He'd had to go to war to understand how precious life was but he carried the lesson with him in everything he did.

And then there was the matter of the captain. Violet had to admit that part of her regret also stemmed from his departure. She had no right to feel as she did. Captain Jessup was merely her brother's companion, along for the journey only because his friend asked for his support and encouragement.

They'd had little contact, giving her almost no reason to feel even the slight attachment she did now. But she'd sent him away, too, ending her opportunities to know him better.

But even if she did, Violet reminded herself, a captain would have nothing to do with a maid, and a maid had only to do with the family she served. It was just as well that the captain should leave with Frank. They could only be distractions from her true purpose. They could only threaten the security she'd finally found.

As if reading her thoughts, a footman called out to Violet.

She turned away from the window, pushing her distress away and resuming her professional demeanor.

"Yes, Andrew?"

"Lady Neil requests your assistance in the library."

Violet nodded and hurried away. Lady Neil needed her, and Violet would work every day of her life to pay back the great opportunity and kindness she'd found in her mistress.

A SLIVER of moonlight filtered through Violet's small window, adding a cool glow against the candlelight surrounding her. Violet hunched forward to better see her stitching in the low lighting. Lady Neil had assured Violet that she need not do any such work in her chambers, especially at night when the lighting was so poor. And Mrs. Baird had scolded her for doing the same, exclaiming that her eyesight would be ruined before she reached middle age.

But Violet did not mind, especially in these last several months when her mistress's dresses needed more frequent altering to accommodate her growing stomach. Besides, whatever work Violet could get done after hours left her with more time to attend to other duties during the day.

And on a night like tonight, when confusing and distressing thoughts swirled through her mind like yesterday's blizzard, Violet needed something to keep herself busy.

"Ow!" Violet cried as the needle slipped and poked her finger. She stuck her finger in her mouth to soothe the tiny wound. "Perhaps it is time I put this away and got some rest," she mumbled, sitting up straight in her chair and stretching her arms high above her.

A sudden clatter in the hallway caused Violet to jump as she folded up her mending. Her heartrate spiked at the sound of rushing feet and hurried voices, highly unusual for this late hour. A pit opened in her stomach as her thoughts flew to Lady Neil. Though the baby was not expected for some time yet, Violet knew that babies often insisted upon coming early—but the earlier the baby came the greater the risk of complications for both mother and child. Violet had been an early baby, too, and it had killed her mother.

As Violet took a step forward, poised for action, the door flung open. On the other side stood Mr. Taylor, his normally smooth gray hair sticking up every which way. His chest heaved as if he'd run all the way here, beads of sweat forming at his hairline.

"Mr. Taylor!" Violet cried in shock. She knew something serious must be happening elsewhere in the house, but she had never seen the dignified and decorous butler in such a disheveled state. The image surprised Violet and she knew that the situation must really be dire.

"Whatever is the matter? Is it Lady Neil?" Violet asked as the older man leaned against the doorframe to catch his breath.

"No, no. Lady Neil is fine." Mr. Taylor waved a hand at Violet's concerns before wiping at his forehead with a hand-kerchief. "You must come downstairs with me at once."

Violet nodded hastily and asked Mr. Taylor to close the door. She slipped out of her nightgown and into a dress as quickly as she could manage and rejoined the butler.

They wasted no time, rushing down the two flights of stairs. Despite Violet's fears, she couldn't help being impressed at the speed with which Mr. Taylor moved. She had not expected it, especially since Mr. Taylor typically did everything with such composure. But the emergency spurred them both on.

They finally made it to the foyer. Violet came to an

abrupt halt when she saw who waited there with Lord and Lady Neil.

Captain Jessup.

His eyes flew to hers as soon as she entered the room. Her blood froze as she took in his expression. She knew instantly that something terrible must have happened if the captain had returned nearly in the middle of the night with such a look of misery on his face.

But if Captain Jessup had come back...where was Frank?

"What's happened?" Violet's voice cracked as hundreds of dreadful scenarios flooded her mind in an instant. Her stomach churned and she felt she might be sick with worry.

Captain Jessup closed the distance between them, standing just a few feet away. He bent his head down and spoke in a low voice.

"Your brother has just been brought to the fireside in the servants' hall. The roads were still icy from the storm, too icy for us to feel safe continuing to the village. We had actually turned back to see if we could stay one more night here and were quite nearby. Unfortunately, our carriage went over a slick patch while you brother was driving and the horse lost its footing. I managed to throw myself off in time but the lieutenant was pinned under the carriage.... I'm afraid he's suffered a terrible break in his leg."

Violet covered her mouth with her hand as a gasp escaped her. "Good heaven..."

A whirlwind of feelings swept through her as the captain's words sank in. She was relieved beyond belief that Frank was alive. But the fear did not let go. A broken leg could be a fatal injury depending on the severity of the break and how quickly a doctor could get here. And the situation could have been so, so much worse.

Captain Jessup stepped even closer and took Violet's

hands in his, giving them a gentle squeeze. Normally Violet would have been shocked at the touch, but her mind still swirled with too many horrible images of the accident and the gut-wrenching fear that Frank could still be lost.

She looked up long enough to see the concern in his eyes —concern for both herself and Frank—before he let go of her hands and dashed off to the servants' area.

Lord and Lady Neil approached Violet next. The baroness wrapped her arms around Violet and whispered soothing words in her ear. Violet returned the hug and felt a hand settle on her shoulder. She peered over her shoulder to see Mr. Taylor behind her. Lord Neil stood slightly apart from them but his gaze on Violet was soft and kind.

Their comfort brought Violet a sliver of peace and she allowed herself to absorb it for a few moments. But when she pulled back from her mistress, the lady knew exactly what Violet would ask next.

"We sent for the doctor immediately upon their arrival. I hope it will not take him long to get here, but we did tell the messenger to be careful on the roads and inform the doctor as such as well. We will ensure that your brother is cared for as best as we can in the meantime."

"Both Captain Jessup and myself have some medical experience, so we will be tending to him until Dr. Slaterly arrives," Mr. Taylor offered.

He straightened out his weary shoulders and nodded sharply, giving Violet his most determined expression. The butler had always prided himself on running the household impeccably and providing his assistance in any and every situation to the best of his ability. But Violet could see the concern and even fear in his eyes.

Violet nodded, anxiety rattling her bones. It would not do to have the doctor thrown from his carriage either, but

Violet prayed that some miracle would speed his travels. Surely Frank must be in agony, and he risked infection with every passing moment. Tears gathered in her eyes as she imagined her brother in the servants' area, writhing in pain, and as she imagined how close he had been to a much worse outcome.

This was Violet's fault for sending them away. If only she hadn't been so stubborn and had allowed herself to accept her brother. No one would have been hurt and she and Frank could be well on their way to forming a new bond. Instead, she had held on to her pain and pushed him away and now he suffered for it.

Her knees went weak and Lord and Lady Neil had to catch her elbows to keep her from falling to the ground.

"Oh dear, let's bring her to the sitting room." Violet heard Lady Neil whisper to her husband and the butler.

Violet allowed herself to be steered deeper into the house and onto a chair in the sitting room. She was in a daze, her mind working over the details she'd just heard and the part she had played in it.

"I did this.... This is because of me..." She mumbled to no one in particular, staring down at the intricately designed rug before her, unable to will her eyes to focus.

"Leave us. Check on Lieutenant Davies and see if there is anything that can be done for him now," Lady Neil commanded Lord Neil and Mr. Taylor, the authority in her voice unmistakable.

Violet heard them exit the room and felt her mistress sit in the chair next to her, a groan escaping as she struggled to lower herself carefully.

Violet snapped back to attention, jumping out of her chair. "Forgive me, my lady. Are you alright?"

She gripped Lady Neil's forearms to steady her as she slid

the rest of the way down. Lady Neil waved Violet back to her chair.

"I am quite well, Violet, thank you. You need not worry about me under the present circumstances. Sit and explain what you mean, about this being because of you."

Violet sank back down into her chair, her voice trembling as she confessed her fears.

"This is my fault. I've been too stubborn and guarded. I thought I was doing the right thing by protecting myself and forcing Frank away. And now look what's happened. He's been terribly injured, and if Dr. Slaterly is delayed then Frank could lose his leg, or worse." Violet buried her face in her hands, hot tears breaking free.

Lady Neil leaned forward and took Violet's hands away from her face. Violet looked miserably into the baroness's face, too distraught to care how she looked or what her mistress might think of her working herself up into such a state.

"Shh now, dear Violet. Blizzards and icy roads are no one's fault. I know it is easier said than done, but try not to fret about the worst-case scenarios just yet. The doctor will be here soon, I am sure of it. And Dr. Slaterly is the best in the area. He will see that Frank is properly mended. Until then, Taylor and the captain will do what they know.

"You can't have guessed that this would happen. But perhaps...you can view this as a blessing in disguise. A second chance to give your brother a second chance. I knew you battled with the decision to send him away. Now he will likely have to remain here for some time until his leg heals enough for long distance travel. Though of course we all deeply regret his getting hurt, maybe there is a silver lining in all this. Perhaps an unspoken prayer has been answered."

Lady Neil brushed a thumb over the back of Violet's hand

as she spoke and occasionally dabbed at her maid's face with a handkerchief. Violet could only stare in disbelief at the lady's incredible compassion. She knew very few lady's maids could cry before their mistresses and receive such tender comfort.

"Thank you, my lady. You are too kind to me. I fear I have disgraced myself before you and yet you care for me when I should be caring for you," Violet sniffled. "I think you must be right. Though the circumstances are grim, I have been given another chance to heal my past and welcome my brother back into my life. I must take advantage of it." She sat up straighter and lifted her chin, nodding sharply with her newfound resolve.

"I am very happy to hear it. And I am very happy to assist you when I can. No one can expect another human being to remain composed during such an unhappy event." Lady Neil smiled warmly, her blue eyes full of understanding and empathy.

"My lady, how did Frank and Captain Jessup make it back to the house?" Violet asked, a sudden curiosity overtaking her.

"As the captain said, they were thankfully quite close to the house when the accident happened, perhaps half a mile by the sound of it. Captain Jessup used his quick thinking and practical skills to fashion a sort of brace to keep the lieutenant's leg as stable as possible. Then he carried him the rest of the way."

"Thank God for the captain," Violet whispered in awe, imagining Captain Jessup carrying her brother half a mile in the near freezing cold.

"He is quite an amazing man," Lady Neil agreed with a chuckle.

"Please may I see my brother?" Violet asked.

"Violet, I am sure such a sight will be terribly unpleasant to witness," Lady Neil cautioned.

"Please, my lady. I wish to be by his side for as long as I can. I've already wasted this past fortnight pushing him away. I do not fear what I might see," Violet pleaded. "He is my brother. He needs me."

# CHAPTER 6

*urse this cold and snow and all things winter,* Owen grumbled silently as he found himself once again walking around the Neils's estate. He glared at the pair walking ahead of him as he trailed behind.

In truth, he did not need to follow along. But Owen had found himself volunteering to join his friend and Miss Davies on the lieutenant's first outing since his injury two and a half weeks ago.

Owen pulled his heavy coat tighter about him as a breeze whistled by. He noticed the way the wind rustled Miss Davies's bonnet and her hand shot up to steady it.

Though Owen was thrilled that his friend felt recovered enough to enjoy some time outdoors in a wheelchair, he knew the real reason he'd come along was Miss Davies. Perhaps it was some sick twist of fate that had stranded him at Gatherford Park just when he'd thought he could safely escape the maid's captivating green eyes and sweet smile and eloquent words and return to his usual life of wandering the country with his friends, engaging in all manner of revels without a worry for anyone but himself and his companions.

Instead, Owen found himself trapped and he would need to fend off his unwanted interest for who knew how long. For all he knew, they could be stuck here all winter.

But watching Miss Davies carefully push her brother over the gravel path around the barren estate, chatting amiably and pointing to this spot that had the prettiest blooms in spring and that spot where a flock of chickens had run loose last summer, provided a certain warmth.

Her attitude was quite changed from just two weeks ago when they'd prepared to set off. He'd been sure that she could not wait to be rid of them. Perhaps Miss Davies saw this as an opportunity to bridge the gap between herself and her brother.

Owen was pleased for his friend. Despite his broken leg and the pain that accompanied it, Davies's spirits seemed almost as high as when the war finally ended. Maybe he felt the war to win his sister back had in fact ended in victory.

For that reason, Owen forced himself to be content with staying until the doctor cleared the lieutenant for travel. Owen would simply have to exercise caution until that day came, keeping himself as neutral toward Miss Davies as possible despite the longing in him to get closer and learn more. So far, as this walk proved, he could not claim success.

As they walked, Davies shared more stories of their time in the army, both the humorous and lighthearted tales of everyday life among soldiers as well as the harrowing and disturbing stories of treacherous terrain and living conditions, hard fought battles, and lives lost.

Miss Davies listened intently, hanging on her brother's every word. Sometimes she chimed in to offer her opinion or ask a question about some detail or other. But never did she shrink away from the harsh details of war. Even many men who hadn't experienced it for themselves would blanche at some of the things the lieutenant now spoke of. But not Miss Davies.

Owen should not have been surprised that she was made of sterner stuff. After all, she had waited in the servants' hall with himself and the butler, holding Davies's hand and wiping the sweat off his forehead and offering conversation to distract him as much as possible from the pain.

Her eyes had widened and she'd gone pale when she saw the state her brother was in. Owen and Mr. Taylor both tried to dissuade her from coming nearer, but the fierce determination that had flashed through her green eyes told them that she would not be shooed away.

Regardless of any of his other feelings for Miss Davies, Owen had to admire her bravery.

"Jessup, you've fallen behind again. Are you telling me you can't even keep up with a man in a wheelchair?" Davies called out over his shoulder. Miss Davies also turned to peer at Owen, her eyes turning into half-moons as she giggled. Owen scrunched his nose at the insult and increased his pace to draw up next to the pair.

"My goodness, I must still be recovering from the physical feat I accomplished in carrying you back to the house." He smirked down at his friend playfully.

"Too right you are, my man. I cannot say enough how dearly I appreciate it." The lieutenant's voice grew grave and he stared down at his gloved hands resting atop a thick blanket over his lap.

Owen squirmed at the sudden seriousness of the conversation. He infinitely preferred lighthearted banter to any kind of thanks for doing his basic duty.

"Just don't make me do it again, Davies. I don't think I could survive it," Owen chuckled, hoping to lighten up the mood again. He'd had more than a lifetime's worth of dour circumstances and gloomy conversations. He turned the talk to a person, and subject, he found far more enjoyable. "Miss Davies, do you have any particular hobbies you indulge in during your spare time?"

Miss Davies laughed a little and Owen's eyebrow raised in curiosity. He didn't think it a particularly funny question.

"I hardly have any spare time for hobbies, captain. But when I do, I like to read poetry. I've even begun to write some myself. Her Ladyship has graciously set aside some time from my duties each week for me to work on it though I fear I'm taking advantage of her kindness. I do not wish to slack off on my work, or make it appear as such."

Her voice was light but Owen did not miss the sad smile that overtook her face for a moment. This news came as a revelation to Owen. He did not read much himself and never had. Whenever his governess approached with a book Owen had escaped and scampered up a tree or jumped into the pond instead. It did not often cross his mind that anyone willingly read poetry let alone wrote it.

"Is it very difficult? Writing poetry, I mean. I must confess I've always found the stuff to be a bit dull," Owen admitted. He watched her from the corner of his eye, hoping that he hadn't offended her with his honesty.

"I too find some of it dull. It's simply a matter of finding the right words, the words that interest you and inspires you. I follow the same policy when I write so I don't find it terribly difficult. It can be challenging, yes, but very rewarding."

Miss Davies looked up at him, this time with a genuine smile. His heart gave an uncharacteristic flutter at the expression. She seemed pleased to be able to speak of her interests with someone. She must not have had many opportunities to do so.

"Won't you let me read your writing sometime, Violet?" Davies pleaded, glaring up at his sister from his chair.

"Absolutely not. I won't say my poetry is awful, but it is certainly not worth showing around." The resoluteness in Miss Davies's voice was almost comical and Owen could see her good-natured smile as she denied her brother.

The two bickered back and forth for a while and Owen gladly observed that they seemed more and more like real siblings every day. Perhaps Davies's injury had been some sort of strange blessing in disguise.

Owen also gave himself over to observing Miss Davies in particular, his curiosity overwhelming his caution. With the knowledge that the maid was also a poet, her behaviors made more sense to Owen. He saw the way her eyes floated over the landscape, lingering here and there over crooked tree trunks and bushes buried under melting snow—all things that anyone else would completely disregard, including Owen himself if he hadn't thought to look through Miss Davies's eyes.

And of course he saw the way she saw him. Her gaze, though often brief, seemed to seek a deeper understanding of him. On the one hand it made him feel exposed yet on the other, he wished to open himself to her understanding. But Owen knew this must be avoided at all costs.

It would not, however, keep him from admiring her keen sight and sharp mind that surely turned even the most mundane events and objects and sensations into beautiful lines of poetry. Perhaps if Owen could read some of her work he would enjoy the artform.

Miss Davies pulled the wheelchair to a stop and came around to the front. She adjusted her brother's blanket which had slipped slightly over the course of their walk, mindful of his injured leg made bulky and awkward by his wooden cast.

"Are you sure you're quite alright? Are you warm enough? Comfortable? I can remove my shawl and bundle it up against your back if you need to be propped up further," Miss

Davies inquired as she fussed over the lieutenant. Her eyes scanned him up and down for anything amiss.

Owen also admired how attentive she was to those in her care. She stopped often to check on Davies and ensure all was well and she handled his chair with caution, carefully pushing it over the shoveled path to avoid any bumps. He could tell she was sincere in her concern for both Lady Neil and her brother, not simply driven by obligation.

"As a matter of fact, I am feeling a bit cold and tired now. Let's head back if that's agreeable to you all." Davies did indeed sound winded and weary and his sister agreed immediately. She slowly turned his chair around and they began the walk back, the grand house looming large ahead of them.

Owen allowed himself to slip behind the Davies siblings again. The lieutenant's mention of being cold had caused Owen to realize that he had been so caught up in watching Miss Davies that he hardly felt any chill at all. The realization troubled him. He could not even hate winter as much when the maid was nearby.

He caught back up before Davies could scold him again and joined into their conversation. They spoke more of army life as Miss Davies seemed very curious about it. She asked about everything from meals to sleeping quarters to uniforms to daily duties. She asked them to explain the differences in ranks and what responsibilities each entailed.

For the first time in a long while Owen felt as though he were a normal man. Once most people found out he'd been in the army and fought in Belgium, their demeanor toward him changed. Some gave him pitying looks and lamented over the struggles he must have endured. Others changed the subject, not willing to confront such a grim subject. Others seemed afraid of him as they wondered what terrible things he must have done.

But not Miss Davies.

Talking with her of his life in the army felt relaxed and natural. He did not feel the need to mask his experience to protect her sensibilities as he so often did. He could speak of it as he could speak of anything and he knew she would listen with real interest and understanding.

It felt relaxed and natural, but Owen constantly reminded himself as they walked and talked that it was far from right. At least for a man like him.

He sighed with relief when they reentered the house and Miss Davies went off to the servants' hall while Owen pushed the lieutenant to the saloon turned bedroom. Dr. Slaterly had determined that it would be a while yet before Davies could begin using a crutch to make his way around the house so the Neils had the ground floor saloon transformed with almost all the same comforts of a real bedroom.

Owen started the fire and situated them both nearby to thaw themselves. Davies requested his book brought over and Owen complied, rolling his eyes at his friend's smug expression. Surely the lieutenant saw the advantages of his condition, including commanding Owen around for once.

Davies lost himself in his book while Owen lost himself in the fire. He pulled his chair even closer and stared at the flames, relishing in the heat that nearly drowned him—and his recollections of their walk.

Owen did not know how long he sat there, leaning toward the fire, gazing into its red and orange and yellow tendrils as it consumed the wood underneath. The fire turned green sometimes, in his imagination—the color of Miss Davies's eyes in the sunlight. The crackling of the flames on the logs turned into her gentle laugh. He knew he should not indulge these imaginings but surely a few minutes could not cause too much harm.

He must have been lost in thought long enough for

Davies to look up from his book and call attention to it. "You must be watching a captivating play in those flames, Jessup."

Owen jumped at the sound and hoped that the shadows cast by the firelight concealed his reddened face.

"Just thinking," he mumbled.

"I did not realize you were capable of thinking for so long a period," Davies laughed. "What could be holding our attention so firmly?"

"Just this and that."

Davies let out a raucous laugh. "You do not fool me, friend. You never could. You've always been a terrible liar."

Owen nodded in agreement. It was true that he could not tell a convincing lie, but he did not often have anything to lie about therefore he'd never developed the skill. But this was one topic Owen did not wish to broach with Miss Davies's older brother of all people.

The lieutenant did not push Owen to reveal his thoughts directly. Instead he sought a subtler route.

"Do you not think my sister is a lovely young lady?"

"To be sure," Owen acquiesced, keeping his voice as neutral as possible.

"I really do feel so awful for all the things I said and did to her. She was just a child, she did not deserve to be treated in such a horrid fashion. It's a wonder she turned into such a kind woman with all that in her past. Coming from a family like ours could turn anyone bitter and cruel." Davies sighed and he closed his book, now taking his turn to stare thoughtfully into the fire.

Owen frowned at his own miniscule worries and instead turned his attention to comforting his friend. "You can't change the past, Davies, but you can change the future. And you're well on your way to doing just that. Miss Davies seems to warm up to you more each day. She's a cautious young lady and rightfully so. She just needed more time to come around."

Davies gave a hesitant smile. "I hope you are right. It does seem as though she's beginning to regard me as a brother again. I also notice that she seems to regard you with some interest as well. You know, if you developed an attachment to her I would not be opposed to such a thing."

The lieutenant shot a sly look to Owen, who wanted to kick himself. He'd been trapped in Davies's underhanded plan to discover his thoughts. It only went to show that their years serving side by side had forged a mental connection that awarded them both with easier access to the other's mind.

Owen should not have been surprised that Davies had guessed the situation exactly for what it was. He sighed and shook his head in resignation. His eyes returned to the flames but instead of the fireplace in the saloon in Gatherford Park, Owen saw a miserable campfire with soldiers and their wives or widows huddling together and towns ablaze, homes and livelihoods destroyed.

"You know as well as I do that another war could come along at any moment. And if it does, I will take up arms again. That is the oath I swore to myself—to protect my country and my countrymen. What point is there in developing affections for anyone, let alone marrying and starting a family? I could be called away for months or years or forever. My duty is to protect, not cause pain and suffering."

Owen did not mention Miss Davies by name, but she was the only woman to come to mind as he spoke his fears. He'd never allowed himself to come this close to harboring a real interest and thus far it had been easy to keep any female acquaintances at arm's length as far as the romantic realm was concerned. He did not understand why it should be such a struggle now, but it was and he would have to deal with it until they could leave.

Davies sat in silence for a moment, pondering Owen's words and formulating his own. Owen fidgeted as he observed the solemn look on his friend's face.

"I do not say this simply to recommend my sister. A hundred more wars may come, but they may just as easily not. But do you not think that is all the more reason to enjoy life and find happiness while you can? For God's sake, I lived through a war and was nearly killed by an overturned carriage."

He laughed ruefully at the realization and Owen knew he was right, at least on one count. Life was fickle indeed. He should know that better than anyone else.

But when Owen imagined Miss Davies sitting by the fire, writing mournful poetry over a lost beau, he did not think he could bring himself to agree with the rest.

Could happiness now possibly be worth heartbreak later?

# CHAPTER 7

The clacking of the knitting needles soothed Violet into a content trance. Her eyes focused on the tips of the needles threading through the soft white yarn. She did not mind stitching, but if she could she would knit everything. It wouldn't be very practical or comfortable, but knitting had a way of calming her and easing her mind into a blissfully blank state.

She did most of her knitting in the summer and early fall before the chill settled in so that Lady Neil would have new scarves and shawls by winter. She made some for herself and the other servants if she had time and extra material.

But a baby was an excellent excuse to put her beloved knitting needles to use. Violet had gotten a later start on her project than she would have liked with her brother and her poetry writing taking up a fair amount of her allotted free time, but the tiny garment and blanket set were coming along well.

Violet was so given over to her task that she failed to hear Mrs. Baird approach the long table in the servants' hall where she liked to work. She did not even notice when the housekeeper stood before her in silence, watching her work.

"That is a lovely little set you're working on," Mrs. Baird said, causing Violet to start.

"Thank you. I think I shall be happy with the outcome and I think Lady Neil will appreciate the gift." Violet smiled down at her handiwork, envisioning the baby that would soon wear it.

"I am sure she will be thrilled. I have never had a kinder mistress, save for the late Lady Neil. I think the two would get along swimmingly if she'd lived to meet her daughter-in-law." Mrs. Baird lowered herself into the neighboring chair.

Her words sparked Violet's curiosity. She'd learned much of Lord Neil's family since she'd come to serve under his roof, primarily from Mrs. Baird's anecdotes. She'd come to the house when the late Baron of Neil was but a teenager, she'd seen him wed and become a father, and she'd attended his funeral. Now she would soon see his son become a father.

It made Violet wonder how many generations of Neils she would come to know in her time with the family, if she was lucky enough to stay on for decades like Mrs. Baird.

For a flash of a moment she saw into her future. She still mended and tidied and attended to her mistress's toilette. The only difference was the hurried clicking of tiny feet on the hardwood floor and high-pitched laughter floating into the air. Violet blinked and shoved the vision away, returning her attention to her project.

"How have things been with your brother? He's been here over a fortnight since his accident, a month in total. Are you glad he's stayed longer?"

Violet spoke as she worked, an easy enough division of concentration for her.

"I am glad. My reservations still have not completely dissipated but I am more open to him with each passing day.

Whenever my thoughts turn to that ugly period in my life and remind me of his cruelty toward me, I simply remind myself that the Frank I see now is the real Frank. This is who he was always meant to be. This is who he would have been if not for our wretched father."

Violet saw Mrs. Baird's smile from the corner of her eye. "I'm very glad to hear that, dear. Continue keeping your heart and mind open. You don't need to forget your past, you just need to learn how to grow from it. It sounds like Lieutenant Davies's presence is helping with that."

"Yes, I think you're quite right," Violet agreed. She hadn't considered that welcoming one of her antagonists back into her life could actually help her heal. But that did very well seem to be the case, slowly but surely.

"Though I am far too old to indulge in such fancies myself, I must admit that I am quite happy Captain Jessup has stayed as well. I may be old, but I can still appreciate a handsome fellow," the housekeeper chuckled.

A stitch slipped from Violet's needle at the mention of the captain. Violet gulped, suddenly overwhelmed by nerves. She couldn't remember the last time she'd dropped a stitch.

Of course Mrs. Baird noticed this as well. "It seems the captain's name causes you to fumble. Is it possible that you admire him?" she asked teasingly.

Violet could feel a fierce blush burning across her cheeks. She swallowed again before answering. "I certainly admire him. But not in *that* way as you seem to be implying." She picked up her dropped stitch and quickly fixed her mistake before continuing. "I do not admire anyone in *that* way. I don't believe I ever will."

"And why ever not?" Mrs. Baird frowned, the creases between her gray brows deepening.

"You know as well as I that servants are rarely allowed or

able to marry. A family would take up too much of our time and energy for us to do a proper job."

Mrs. Baird remained silent for a moment too long. Violet's head whipped around and she stared at the woman by her side. Guilt thundered through her as she realized that she very well may have offended the housekeeper.

She knew Mrs. Baird was only called Mrs. Baird because of her position in the house. She had always been a Baird. As Violet had unthinkingly pointed out, she was one of the many who had never had time to marry and have a family of her own.

"I'm sorry, Mrs. Baird, I didn't mean—"

"Hush now, Violet. You are right, of course." The older woman smiled ruefully, the lines at the corners of her eyes more prominent than ever.

"I do not regret my choice to dedicate my life to service. But you do not have to make the same choice. I am proud of my life and my work. I should think you'll have more opportunities than I ever did in any case. I never had much besides my work ethic and good character to recommend me to any man. Surely you must know that at least a couple footmen here think you rather pretty. But I seem to notice another man in this household of late who thinks you not just pretty but very fascinating as well."

It was Violet's turn to furrow her brow. She'd never given any thought to the footmen she served with. They ranged in age from their late teens to late thirties if she had to guess. And they ranged in looks from plain to attractive and in manners from simple to noble. Most importantly they all did their duties very well.

She couldn't fathom any of them taking a liking to her since she rarely had any interaction with them besides those necessitated by work and the bits and pieces of conversation exchanged during the servants' mealtimes.

But she knew instantly who Mrs. Baird alluded to when she mentioned a man who thought her both pretty and fascinating. She must speak of Captain Jessup based on their conversation thus far though Violet was not sure she agreed with that assessment.

"Even if someone did have any affection for me, I don't think I could return it. And not just because I'm a lady's maid." Violet's voice trailed off into melancholy. She had never come this close to revealing her deepest fears surrounding the topic of love.

"And why might that be?" Mrs. Baird prodded gently.

"Coming from a family like mine—if it can even be called much of a family—and being treated the way I was.... I fear history will repeat itself. I will find myself in the same situation. How can I be sure that the man I marry will not turn into a man like my father?

"He was a good man when he married my mother. I know it broke him when she died and he coped with it by drinking and gambling away our fortune and estate and by abusing me for killing her and throwing the family into debt by my unwanted birth.

"Life can be full of unexpected tragedies and difficult circumstances. Will my husband handle them with strength and honor or will he implode like my father? Will my children be safe and happy? Will they turn into cruel monsters who make little girls cry for fun? Will our family crumble and become destitute?

"I cannot risk it. I cannot risk suffering such circumstances again, or allowing another generation to suffer them."

Violet felt as though she'd been deflated after she finally confessed just how deeply her scars ran. They affected every aspect of her life, including her unwillingness to shackle herself to someone and bring more lives into the world who might end up hurt or hurting someone else.

"Goodness me..." Mrs. Baird muttered after a moment of heavy silence. "That is quite the burden you bear, my dear. I can appreciate your hesitation, certainly. You've never known what a loving family is like. I suppose you have no reason to believe they exist at all."

"Except for Lord and Lady Neil," Violet quickly offered. "Lady Neil's family was not always a happy one either. But I truly believe she and His Lordship will create their own wonderful family. They're the closest I've come to knowing a loving family. And you as well, Mrs. Baird, if I may be so bold."

Violet blushed at her frank words and looked down at the partially completed garment in her hands. She might have come to view Mrs. Baird as a mother figure, but that did not guarantee she felt the same.

"I am honored that you think of me with such fondness." Violet could hear the smile in the housekeeper's voice and she looked up at her with relief. "But that does not mean you can never experience a happy family of your own creation."

Mrs. Baird patted Violet's hand gently. Violet gave a small nod, considering her words. But before she could thank Mrs. Baird for her advice, one of the bells on the opposite wall chimed, signaling that someone upstairs needed assistance.

The bell danced over the placard that read "Lady Neil." Violet stared at it quizzically for a moment. It was still early in the morning. Her mistress should have still been sleeping.

Panic surged through her as she dropped her knitting and apologized to Mrs. Baird for leaving so abruptly. Violet knew that the baroness could go into labor at any moment, or suffer some complication, or have fallen on her way to the water closet. Violet needed to be at her side at once.

She rushed through the house, gathering her skirts up to

allow her feet easier movement up the stairs. She did not notice the footmen or maids she flew past, her eyes locked on the next landing.

Only the sight of Captain Jessup coming down the stairs from the guest wing slowed Violet, but only by a fraction of a second.

"Miss Davies, how do you do?" The captain called out to her with a bow of his head.

Violet ignored him and continued quickly up the steps. He'd paused at the top of the stairs presumably to converse with her, but Violet hurried straight toward the next flight of stairs.

She slipped past Captain Jessup on the landing, feeling a whisper of air pass between them created by her haste.

Suddenly Violet found herself jerking back slightly, her feet forced to come to a halt. She felt a strong hand grip her elbow. She looked to her side to see the captain's gloved hand wrapped around her arm and his face staring down at her intently, that same troublesome lock of hair sweeping over his forehead. His brown eyes, normally so jovial and light-hearted, burned with something new.

*Longing.*

Violet's heart jumped at the thought. But she had never seen what longing looked like in a man's eyes, not when they gazed into hers. She could not be sure that she saw correctly.

"Miss Davies, if I could have a moment of your time. I'm very glad we've crossed paths as I hoped to ask you if you would like to accompany me on a carriage ride about the grounds later today. I've already been out on horseback and the day is quite fine. I think it will only improve from here."

Violet sensed something forced in Captain Jessup's voice. A forced ease, perhaps. Beneath it she swore she heard what she'd just seen in his eyes. Longing.

She felt her breath leave her body as she stared back at

him, too shocked by what she heard to make a response. The captain wished to go on a carriage ride with her. Just her, by the sounds of it. He hadn't mentioned Frank or Lord and Lady Neil.

*Lady Neil!* Violet's mind cried out to her, reminding her of her urgent mission. How much precious time had she lost standing here with Captain Jessup? Her mistress could be in distress or agony at this very moment.

Violet pulled her elbow out of the captain's grip a bit too harshly. But she had no time for manners or regard to the captain's feelings when Lady Neil needed her.

"My mistress has called for me and I fear it may be urgent. I must go. I do not have time for carriage rides and it is not my place to decide when I shall go on carriage rides." She gathered her skirts again and trotted toward the next flight of stairs. "If you really must ask, please direct your question to my master or mistress," she called over her shoulder, her eyes grazing over his hurt expression for just a moment before she returned all her focus to her mission.

Her heart raced as she finally came upon Lady Neil's bedchamber. She paused at the door, straightening her dress and drawing in a deep breath to appear calm and capable. She tapped her knuckles on the door to alert Lady Neil to her presence and then turned the knob.

Violet found her mistress in bed, grunting and squirming against her several layers of blankets. She ran across the room and bent over the baroness.

"What's happened, my lady? Should I send for Dr. Slaterly?" Violet took a handkerchief from the bedside table and dabbed at Lady Neil's face which had developed a fine sheen of sweat.

"No, no. It's not quite time for that yet. I've just been trying to get out of this cursed bed. I can't seem to get enough leverage to right myself. And His Lordship has gone early to his study." Lady Neil grimaced as she tried to maneuver herself into a seated position.

Violet gripped her arm and pulled her the rest of the way up. Once seated, Lady Neil was able to swing her legs over the edge of the bed. She breathed heavily from the effort and likely from her belly pressing against her chest. The baroness groaned and put a hand over her stomach.

"You are up quite early. Does something trouble or pain you?" Violet prodded nervously, watching Lady Neil's every fleeting expression. She knew there must be something amiss.

"I am alright now. The feeling has passed. My stomach has grown tight in these past couple days but it always subsides quickly. I've heard that this is a sign that the baby is preparing to enter the world. But the pain is not very great. It is more uncomfortable than painful. It will get far, far worse when it is really time. That is what I have heard, at least." She gave a hesitant smile as she pondered her very near future.

Violet glanced down at the baroness's swollen belly. She found it hard to believe that a child lived there and harder still to believe that it could find its way out. One moment the little one was in her mistress's stomach and the next moment it would be in her arms, alive and breathing and wailing.

"Are you afraid, my lady?" Violet asked quietly. She wasn't sure why the question came over her. Lady Neil looked off into the distance as she considered her answer.

"Yes and no. I am terrified of the experience. Even in our modern age anything could happen during childbirth. But my excitement to be a mother and my love for this child eclipse my fear. It has always been my dream to make a family and I am thrilled that I can make a family with such a wonderful man whom I love and cherish with all my heart."

Lady Neil gazed softly at her stomach and slid her hands over her protruding nightgown. Violet could see the love she spoke of. It lit her face from within with such a sweet peaceful glow.

As she observed her mistress and gave her a moment to gather her breath, Violet's thoughts suddenly turned back to Captain Jessup and his offer of a carriage ride. She shook her head just slightly enough that it wouldn't be noticed, but enough to shove the thought out of her mind.

This was no time to think of carriage rides with handsome men. It should not have even crossed her mind.

"Accompany me on a walk about the house, Violet. I think some movement will put me more at ease." Lady Neil held out a hand and Violet pulled her to her feet.

"Of course, my lady." Violet nodded and smiled, willing herself to focus on the baroness and nothing else.

As she readied Lady Neil for her day, Violet forced a mantra through her mind countless times.

*This is your place. This is your place. This is your place.*

# CHAPTER 8

$O$ wen paced across the rug in the breakfast room, anxiously awaiting the arrival of Lord and Lady Neil.

Miss Davies's words circled through his mind like a mantra.

*I do not have time.... It is not my place....*

The words had stung Owen then and they still stung now. It had been such a cold brush off that Owen wondered if he might be attempting to get closer to someone who did not wish to get closer to him.

He shook his head. That could not be. He knew he'd seen a hopeful surprise in her eyes when he asked her to join him in his carriage. He could not have imagined it. At least, he sincerely hoped he hadn't.

Owen played her words in his mind again. He could only assume that the baroness was well despite the urgency with which Miss Davies left him behind. Surely if she had gone into labor or some other illness or injury befell her the whole house would know by now.

Once again, just as he'd done numerous times in the past

month he and Davies had stayed at Gatherford Park, Owen felt the stirrings of a kindred connection in Miss Davies.

But now that sameness in their spirits caused an unexpected issue.

Owen had sworn himself to serve and protect his country without regard to possible loss of life or limb.

Miss Davies had sworn herself to serve and protect Lady Neil without regard to her own personal interests or desires.

He understood her concerns. She felt she needed to be available to her mistress at all times. He knew she continued to work for Lady Neil's benefit even when she should have been sleeping or enjoying her mealtimes. Her mistress's well-being was never far from Miss Davies's mind. At times she could not even spare a moment to look Owen's way or provide more than a one- or two-word answer.

He also understood that he had no claim to her attention. She had a job to do and she took it very seriously. Serving the baroness was her calling. Serving England was Owen's.

Yet he could not stop himself from wishing to spend more time with her. Even if he knew their time together would not and could not last. He enjoyed being in her presence and he hoped to enjoy it as much as he could while he and Davies were still here. Owen toed a dangerous line but he would prove to himself that he could spend time with Miss Davies and then shut away his interest when it came time to leave.

Thus he found himself pacing in the breakfast room. Normally he supped with Davies as he often took his meals in his temporary bedroom when he was too tired or pained to journey down the long hall to the dining room. But today Owen had a query for his hosts.

Surely this could not be a good idea. It would be far safer to keep his distance for the remainder of their time at the Neils's estate. But Owen had never been a safe man.

The click of the doorknob turning snapped Owen out of his troubled thoughts. He stood at attention, his arms stiff against his sides and his shoulders pulled back as if he were a green soldier again waiting for his commanding officer to inspect him.

"Captain Jessup!" Lady Neil chirped with surprise when she spied Owen by the fireplace. "Will we have the honor of your presence at breakfast today?" She smiled warmly as she and her husband made their way toward Owen.

"Is Lieutenant Davies well?" Lord Neil asked.

"Yes is he. I told him I would like to dine with our gracious hosts today and he sent his assurances that he should soon feel well enough to join everyone for meals once more. He gains strength and stamina every day."

Owen's words came out quick and sharp much like a report he might give to his commander. His anxiety had turned him into a nervous young cornet eager to impress.

"Excellent. We're very glad to hear it." Lord Neil gave a satisfied smile and wandered toward the sideboard. Lady Neil started to follow.

"Lady Neil, a moment please?" Owen called her attention as quietly as possible.

The baroness turned back to face Owen, an expectant smile on her face. "Of course, captain. What can I assist you with?"

Under Lady Neil's patient gaze, Owen felt even worse than a bumbling brand-new soldier. He felt like a shy little boy, working up the courage to ask his governess for a bonbon. He looked down at the tips of his boots, her curious expression increasing his anxiety. Rarely did he buckle under anyone's eyes. Not his superiors nor his enemies. Such a sensation was almost entirely foreign to him.

Owen knew that Lady Neil was exceedingly kind and generous, especially when it came to Miss Davies. But he also knew that asking this question would likely give her a certain impression of his intentions toward her lady's maid. Besides, he had developed a great respect for the lady. He found he did not wish to make a fool of himself before her.

She waited patiently for Owen to gather himself and he finally found the strength to push his pride away and say the words burning in his heart.

"Lady Neil, I know this is a rather unorthodox request, but I wondered if I could perhaps steal Miss Davies away from you for just a couple hours this afternoon or next or whenever you think best. I thought I might take her for a carriage ride."

The words rushed out in one breath. He swallowed as he watched her blue eyes read his face and absorb his words. Her face was blank for a moment and Owen feared he had indeed made a fool of himself or offended his hostess.

But a surprising smile flashed across her face as she answered, "Yes, Captain Jessup, I think that will be splendid. I shall clear Violet of her afternoon duties. It is too lovely a day not to take advantage."

Now Owen felt like a pleased little boy whose governess had indulged him and given over the dearly desired treat. His body hummed with excitement as he walked Lady Neil to the table. He could barely keep his grin at bay throughout breakfast.

The sheer volume and intensity of his excitement surprised Owen. Perhaps he had not realized how badly he wished for his request to be granted until it had been. What had started as a simple idea for a carriage ride around the grounds had transformed into an event of grand anticipation.

Owen did not know how he would wait until the afternoon for their ride. He should have asked Lady Neil if he could take her this very moment. But he knew it best not to interrupt her busy morning. Owen had gotten what he wanted and he would have to be happy with it for now.

His reservations about his entire situation with Miss Davies melted to the back of his mind. For now, he would relish this feeling of eagerness. But those persistent reservations did not disappear entirely. They continued to prod at him from time to time out of the corner he'd temporarily banished them to.

Beneath his happiness, Owen knew that this was only one small victory in a war he was bound to lose.

OWEN KNOCKED on the door of the saloon. It was nearly the appointed hour.

A muffled "Yes?" signaled Owen to enter. Just as he'd expected, he found the lieutenant seated in his wheelchair. By his side sat Miss Davies.

"Ah, Miss Davies. What might you be doing here at this hour?" Owen asked, feigning curiosity. He knew very well why she was there.

The maid bristled at the question and Owen bit his lip for being insensitive. He hadn't meant to imply that she had abandoned her duties. He hoped this would not cast a shadow over the rest of their day together.

"Lady Neil has kindly given me the afternoon off, though she did not say why. I thought I could still put myself to good use and attend to my brother."

Miss Davies floated around the lieutenant, eyeing every inch of his chair and even brushing off some imperceptible dust from his shoulders.

"As it so happens, I took the advice you gave me this morning, Miss Davies. I had breakfast with Lord and Lady Neil and asked your mistress if you might have some time off this afternoon for that carriage ride I suggested." Owen could hear the smile in his own voice but he tried to steady himself and mask his eagerness.

Miss Davies's head snapped around to stare at Owen. Her green eyes were wide and her mouth slightly ajar. He knew in an instant that she had not thought he would actually trouble the baroness with his request.

"T-That is very generous of you, captain, but I really think I should remain nearby. Lady Neil needs—" Miss Davies began to protest, her eyes darting about the room for an escape.

"Hush now, Violet." The lieutenant interrupted his sister with a chuckle. "If Lady Neil did not think it prudent to allow you out for a short while today surely she would have said so. Besides, this house is packed to the gills with staff. They can help Her Ladyship if needed and of course she has His Lordship to rely on as well."

Miss Davies flushed at her brother's insistence. She looked down at her hands, wringing the fabric of her skirt, in time for Davies to flash a knowing look and wink at Owen.

Owen scowled in response. Perhaps he should have pulled Miss Davies aside for a quiet word instead of announcing their outing in front of her brother—who had clearly already expressed interest in a possible match between the two. No doubt this would only fuel his fire and Owen knew he would be bombarded with questions later.

"Very well..." Miss Davies finally agreed after a moment of uncertainty. "But I shall instruct one of the footmen to come for me should anything happen to Lady Neil. There may be many servants in this house, but none of them know Her Ladyship like I do..." The firmness in her voice when she spoke of commanding the footmen trailed away into an almost self-conscious admittance.

Owen quickly stepped forward and reached out a hand as

if to touch her but he stopped himself short. Instead he said, "And no one would suggest otherwise. You are clearly invaluable to your mistress. But I am sure she will be fine as we will not be gone long. And if it would put you at ease, we will make our exact route known to the footmen."

Miss Davies nodded, fixing Owen with a serious stare. He knew how much Lady Neil's health and safety meant to her and he would not fall short of his promise to ensure everyone in the household remained on high alert while they were away and knew where to find them.

"Let us wrap ourselves snugly and meet in the foyer in a few minutes," Owen declared.

A strange fluttering sensation overcame Owen's heart when he saw Miss Davies's shy smile and the hint of excitement in her eyes. It may have been hard to tear her away from her work, but that look alone was worth the struggle to Owen.

Owen left the room and took the steps up to the guest wing two at a time. He quickly pulled on his winter coat and gloves and rushed back downstairs but slowed to a stop when he saw his companions.

"Will you be joining us, Davies?" Owen asked his friend. He clearly looked dressed for an outdoor trek.

"Yes, Violet asked that I come along. But this charming gentleman will push me behind the carriage. It's been some days since I've properly been outside and a little fresh air will do me good." Davies waved to the footman at his side and slipped on his gloves.

"Excellent." Owen nodded stiffly. He hadn't expected his friend to tag along. He'd only planned on himself and Miss Davies with a footman. But no matter. He had gotten this far in his plan to share a simple conversation with Miss Davies. Her brother would not spoil that because there was nothing to spoil, Owen reminded himself.

He turned his attention to Miss Davies. She looked very smart in her winter outfit. He held out his arm to her and she took it with a small smile.

The carriage already waited for them and Owen gripped Miss Davies's fingers as he helped her up onto the seat. Even with both their gloves between them, that same flutter of the heart afflicted Owen once again. He swallowed his nerves down and went around to his side of the carriage, taking the reins from the stable hand.

As Owen had predicted that morning, the day had become even finer. It was cold, but with their layers of clothing and the sunshine beaming down on them, Owen found he did not mind it.

Of course, having Miss Davies seated next to him certainly helped. She radiated warmth, whether physical or emotional. And his heart pumped fast enough to keep his body heated.

He watched her out of the corner of his eye. She seemed to relax now that they were on their path. She looked out at the scenery, her observant eyes absorbing and appreciating everything.

Owen too cast his gaze over the grounds. He had to admit that the patches of melted snow and the way the sun glinted off the soft white, creating sparkling diamonds in his vision, had a certain charm to it. Even the trees with their shivering and naked branches looked stately and imposing.

In truth, the grounds were beautiful, even in the winter when the landscape drowsed beneath blankets of snow. He couldn't help noticing it when he saw the world as he imagined Miss Davies saw it.

"How was Lady Neil this morning? It seemed quite an urgent summons," Owen inquired, keeping his gaze forward over the horse's head. He asked out of genuine curiosity, not to bring back that unpleasant moment. He hoped Miss Davies wouldn't interpret the question as jab at her.

"It wasn't as urgent as I thought," the maid admitted. "She needed help getting out of bed and wanted to go on a walk. Her condition makes every day more challenging. I just fear that every ring of the bell could mean something more serious than a need for tea or a curl that's come loose."

Now Owen glanced down at her and he saw the worry in her expression, brows drawn together and a slight frown pulling her plump lips down at the corners. He felt guilty for a moment for pulling Miss Davies away from her sacred duty. Surely she worried about it even now.

But when an unexpected trill of birdsong caused her to look up into the sky with wonder and curiosity, searching for the creature who dared brave the cold to sing for them, Owen felt justified in his decision. Lady Neil needed her, no doubt, but Miss Davies also deserved some time for herself, especially out of doors. He guessed that before her brother's arrival, Miss Davies only had an opportunity to go outside when her work made it necessary.

The sun bathed her face in a soft glow as she continued to search the skies and Owen thought it a terrible shame that the sun was deprived of her.

"What a pretty little song. I wonder where that bird could have come from. I hope it gets home to its warm nest soon." Miss Davies smiled as she gave one last curious look to the sky.

Owen kept the conversation to nature, asking Miss Davies about her favorite creatures and favorite flowers, if she ever walked by the pond in warmer weather, what sorts of fruits and vegetables they were able to grow here.

Miss Davies had an answer for each of Owen's queries, given with confidence and little hesitation. She loved many animals, but small soft rabbits were her particular favorite.

She thought it might be nice to keep one as a pet. Every flower was beautiful but she preferred tulips above all else. She insisted that the pond was excellent for walking as a variety of fish and birds and other wildlife could be seen from its banks. The gardeners grew all manner of fruits and vegetables. The baron had long been a favorite of his country neighbors due to his luxurious gifts of various fruits.

Owen marveled at her wealth of knowledge about the estate though she was only a recent resident and he enjoyed hearing her opinion on every topic they happened upon.

A swift breeze blew past them, bringing along with it a biting chill. Owen shuddered as the wind hit his exposed face but the red in his cheeks produced by the cold was quickly replaced by a different kind of blush.

Miss Davies huddled a little closer to Owen's side, her shoulders tucked up by her ears to shield herself from the breeze. Whether she did this consciously or unconsciously Owen could not guess. Either way he found himself warmed to his core. He glanced down to see just the top of her bonnet as she continued to press her arm to his, keeping her head lowered.

The corner of Owen's mouth pulled up as he took in the sight and the sensations running through him, from the firmness of her presence next to him, to the heat he received from her proximity, to the gentle humming that radiated through his chest. In short, he felt utterly content.

Miss Davies sat up, creating distance between them again. Owen quickly looked forward, training his gaze on the path ahead.

"Which poets are you fond of these days, Miss Davies? I must admit I do not spend much time on poetry but I have read some works by that popular yet scandalous Lord Byron fellow and I enjoyed those."

Owen was nervous to approach the subject of poetry with an

actual poet. In truth, he'd taken advantage of Lord Neil's library since their unexpected return to Gatherford Park. Taking Lord Neil's recommendations into account, Owen began reading poetry in earnest. At first he thought he was simply curious about the artform knowing Miss Davies's strong attachment to it. He wanted to see if he could understand what she saw in it.

But over time, Owen found himself enjoying it. Not every poem or poet he read, but he found a select few that did not bore him to death. At times, when he sat in the library by the fire with a particularly interesting volume in his hands, he imagined conversations between himself and Miss Davies about the poem he'd just read.

Even deeper than that, Owen realized as he sat nervously beside the maid awaiting her response, he hoped to impress her. He did not deny that he had always been more brawn than brain but something about Miss Davies encouraged him to improve his intellectual faculties. He did not wish to embarrass himself in front of such an intelligent and insightful woman.

"I am very fond of Lord Byron's writing," Miss Davies agreed happily.

Her whole countenance transformed into joy as she listed off her favorite poems by the famous writer and her favorite aspects of each. Owen found it difficult to keep up. He hadn't read all of the man's works yet and many of Miss Davies's observations were a bit out of his reach.

She seemed to understand meaning that did not exist explicitly on the page. In fact, some of her words mystified Owen, even when she spoke of poems he did know. He resolved to head straight to the library after their ride to reread them and try to see what Miss Davies saw.

But for now Owen was more than happy to listen as the maid shared her thoughts with him. How could he not be happy to listen when she was clearly so thrilled to speak of her passion with someone who knew a little about it—even if it was very little—and who was willing to listen.

The realization came like a bolt of lightning to Owen. Until now, Owen had been under the impression that Miss Davies's interest in poetry was just that. Interest. But Owen now saw that this was false. It wasn't merely interest. It was passion.

He watched her as she spoke and saw the gleam in her eyes, their cool emerald green shifting into a fresh spring lawn swaying in the breeze, vibrant and alive. He saw the animated and eager smile that never left her lips as she spoke.

When she paused to take a breath, Owen seized the moment to interject.

"Have you given any thought to publishing your own poetry? I know Lord Neil has connections at a publishing house in London. I'm sure he could be of great help if you were interested in sharing your work with an audience."

A rosy tint spread across Miss Davies's cheeks as she stared up at Owen with wide eyes. He felt a powerful urge to slide his gloved finger down her round cheek.

"I'm afraid, Captain, that you have no way of knowing whether my poetry is worthy of being published. I can assure you it is likely best left for my eyes alone. Besides..." Her voice faded away, carried off by another stiff breeze. She looked down at her hands in her lap, her fingers pinching the edge of her coat.

"Besides?" Owen encouraged gently. He wanted to know all her thoughts and he wanted her to feel comfortable sharing them.

She looked at him again with a sad smile. "A maid shouldn't be anything more than a maid. Can you imagine? A maid who publishes poetry? Even a maid writing poetry sounds ridiculous."

"Yes, I can imagine." Owen's voice was firm but gentle as his eyes locked onto hers. "Everyone has a right to their passions. Even a maid."

Miss Davies frowned slightly, but it was not a displeased frown. It was a thoughtful frown. Perhaps she had never considered that such a thing could be possible. But Owen knew it was possible, because he'd fought for it.

It pained him to know that Miss Davies felt she could not partake in her right because of her station in life. It pained him to know that the same situation afflicted thousands of people all over England and even the world. It pained him to know that he could not change these facts of life for most people.

But if he could change it for Miss Davies, he would.

"I would love to read your poetry someday if you will allow me. I promise I do not expect perfection. Whether it be good or bad, I admire you greatly for trying at all. If the words come from your heart and mind then they will be good enough for me."

Owen smiled at the young woman, hoping to ease her self-consciousness. He truly did not care if her poems were on par with Shakespeare or if they read like a child's musings. He was not a well-read man by any means so his standards could be assumed to be low. But if her eloquent speech was any indication, Owen felt certain that Miss Davies's works must be beautiful.

Miss Davies only gave a small nod, the becoming blush returning to her face. Owen sensed her discomfort and he knew it would be best not to push the matter. He glanced over his shoulder to see that his friend had maintained a respectful distance. He seemed not to notice the pair in the carriage at all, happily chatting away with the longsuffering footman who pushed him along.

Owen could not suppress his sly smirk. He turned his attention back to Miss Davies and leaned down to whisper in her ear.

"Hold on tight."

He gripped the reins, the sound of leather against leather sending a thrill down his spine.

"I beg your par—" Miss Davies started, a quizzical look on her face. But they were off before she could finish her question.

She squealed as Owen brought the reins down on the horse's haunches and the carriage jolted forward.

The wheels rattled over the gravel path as the horse sped forward. One of Miss Davies's arms threaded through Owen's and gripped his sleeve while her other arm shot up to keep her bonnet in place.

Those first few moments of speed were glorious. Owen had dearly missed flying over the road on his horse or on the carriage box. The air was bitingly cold now as it raced past them in the opposite direction. Owen's hat flew off and he heard the lieutenant shout after them.

Just when Owen thought his exhilaration had achieved its maximum, a sudden peal of uninhibited laughter at his side sent a shock through his entire body.

He took his eyes off the path just long enough to glance down at Miss Davies and see her shoulders shaking, her eyes squeezed shut, and her lips parted in a wide smile as laughter flowed out of her.

Owen had never seen her so carefree. The image and sound immediately burned themselves into his memory. He wished he could race forever if it would keep her spirits so high.

He tugged on the reins and the horse slowed. Miss Davies

still laughed but now the sound was quiet, hidden behind her hand.

"I don't think I've ever been that fast in a carriage," she said breathlessly. "I do hope you'll forgive my noisy outburst. How unladylike of me."

She unlooped her arm from Owen's, adjusted her bonnet, and smoothed out her coat and skirts. The red was back in her face. Owen could not tell if it was from the cold or the excitement.

"You should know I don't give a toss about that. You can laugh all you like in my presence. I don't know why you ladies must pretend as if the function is foreign to you."

Owen huffed, pondering some of the stranger aspects of his society. Miss Davies, being a maid, need not hold herself to as high standards of behavior as well-born and well-married women. But her actions reflected upon her mistress and Owen knew she would never purposely do anything to bring censure upon the beloved lady.

Still, Owen did not regret getting her to laugh so freely even if just for a moment. The sound still tinkled in his ears.

"Are you surprised to see that a soldier can have fun? We're not all doom and danger and 'yes, sir,' 'no, sir,' at least not all the time."

Owen smirked at the sad image. Yet many people seemed to think that soldiers must be very serious and stoic men, all business and no pleasure. And they were when they needed to be. But at least in Owen's regiment, they usually found time for jokes and games and pranks. And now that the war was over, Owen dreaded any business that approached the semblance of seriousness.

Miss Davies smiled up at him, her teeth gleaming against the red of her cheeks. "In truth, captain, since I've come to know you I can hardly imagine you being so dour. I think if anyone knows how to have fun it would be you."

Owen smiled back with a surprised chuckle. It seemed she knew him better than he thought.

"But in any case," she continued, her expression growing contemplative. "I should hope that you and your fellow men-at-arms can have some fun. Fun and joy should be held onto even in the darkest times. How else can anyone be expected to survive?"

Owen couldn't help staring at her as he contemplated her wise words but before he could respond they heard an annoyed shout coming from behind them.

They turned around to see Davies waving at them and yelling for them to slow down. The poor footman behind them struggled to push the wheelchair faster over the gravel walkway.

Owen and Miss Davies turned to face each other at the same time and as soon as they locked eyes, they both filled the air with their laughter and giggles.

"I suppose we should go back and collect him," Owen said through his chuckle. He gave the horse another tug and they were soon turned around and walking back toward the lieutenant.

But Owen took his time, allowing the horse to pull them along at a very relaxed walk. He didn't want his time with Miss Davies to end though he knew it must at some point.

He certainly hadn't expected to have such a grand time when he asked her on this ride. He would have been happy with some light conversation and personal anecdotes. But he'd gotten so much more.

Miss Davies now sat silently by his side, shaking her head slightly as she saw the exaggerated annoyance on her brother's face. She smiled fondly as she gave him a small wave.

Owen smiled, too, as his chest swelled with such an unexpected happiness. He'd learned so much more about Miss Davies in this one ride than he had in the past month.

He had always noticed her intelligence and perception, but he greatly enjoyed seeing them in action for an extended period of time. Though she often deferred to her humble position as a maid, she had so many opinions on every subject when given the chance to express them.

He appreciated Lady Neil for not crushing the young woman's free thinking, but he knew that Miss Davies still felt it necessary to hold herself back in her mistress's presence. There could be no doubt that they were close, much closer than a lady and her maid usually were, but there still existed the barrier of class and circumstance between them.

And despite her insistence that she was nothing more than a maid, Owen saw her to be so much more. Miss Davies could clearly enjoy life if only she allowed herself to let go. Owen had seen that spark in her today. He wished he could find some way to keep that spark going and perhaps even help it grow.

At the same time, she had ignited a spark in him, too. As they made their way back to the lieutenant and Owen watched Miss Davies send teasing expressions and gestures to her brother, he wondered what life might be like if he took her words to heart.

What could be so wrong with Owen accepting joy in his life? Why couldn't he spend his days with a thoughtful, clever, caring, pretty woman? If life was short, should he not take advantage of the fun and joy and companionship he could find while it lasted?

When he looked down at Miss Davies and she met his gaze with a smile, Owen couldn't help wondering if that wouldn't be so bad after all.

# CHAPTER 9

*V*iolet's eyes snapped open, instantly alert as the bell in her room jangled. She could sense the urgency from the sound. Her room was still bathed in darkness. If Lady Neil called for her in the dead of night, Violet knew she must need her desperately. Violet knew in the pounding of her heart that the baby was on its way.

She wasted no time, not even bothering to light a candle. She dressed by the thin stream of faltering moonlight from her small window, not overly concerned if her appearance was perfect. Emergencies superseded perfection.

Violet reached Lady Neil's bedchamber in the blink of an eye, thankful that her room was so close to her mistress's. She did not even offer a courtesy knock but pushed the door open immediately and ran into the room.

Lady Neil writhed in her bed, low moans and high screeches following on each other's heels. Sweat already gathered on her forehead, turning her golden blonde hair almost as dark brown as Violet's.

Lord Neil sat on the edge of her bed, dabbing at her face with a handkerchief and whispering soothing words to his wife. They both seemed oblivious to Violet's presence, so immersed were they in their own missions—hers to bring the baby forth and his to comfort and encourage.

After taking stock of the situation quickly, Violet rushed to the bed. Lord Neil heard her footsteps approach and he turned to look at her, such a helpless expression on her face that Violet feared the man might faint from stress at any moment.

The look so surprised Violet that she nearly stumbled over her own feet. She had seen the baron in many moods and situations. Mostly content, many times in deep love with his wife, sometimes nervous and awkward, occasionally frustrated or annoyed. But never scared.

"Please," he begged. "What must I do?"

Violet swallowed the fear that threatened to constrict her throat. She of course had never been in such a situation before. Her knowledge of pregnancy and childbirth seemed all the scarcer at a time like this. She had only been taught the absolute necessities that any woman must know.

But if she knew next to nothing, Lord Neil knew less than nothing.

"You, my lord, must step aside so I can assess Her Ladyship and sort out what needs to be done next." She stepped forward, her voice firm. She needed to take control. Her mistress's life and her child's life were at stake.

Lord Neil nodded weakly and stood up, casting one last panic-stricken look at his wife before letting go of her hand.

Violet took his place on the edge of the bed. Lady Neil immediately grasped her hand, squeezing so tightly that Violet bit her lip. But her pain did not matter now.

She picked up the handkerchief the baron had left on the bedside table and continued to wipe away at the sweat that dripped down her face.

"My lady, can you speak?"

Lady Neil groaned through her teeth as another wave of labor passed through her. "Y-Yes. Barely."

"How long has this been happening?" Violet forced herself to keep her voice as calm as possible despite the fear that surged through her.

"A few hours.... They woke me...but they weren't as painful then.... Suddenly, they became awful. I fear...the baby is coming too fast," she mumbled between moans and shallow breaths.

Violet nodded to herself. "I'll fetch Mrs. Baird and she'll put you right. Hang on, my lady."

Violet extracted Lady Neil's hand from her own and instructed Lord Neil to resume his place.

"I'll bring Mrs. Baird here. She'll know better than anyone what to do. It may be difficult to see this but remain by her side whatever happens, my lord."

"Of course." A solemn determination replaced the quivering panic in Lord Neil's voice.

They exchanged firm nods as Violet flew from the room and made a mad dash for Mrs. Baird's quarters.

As housekeeper, Mrs. Baird had her own private room on the highest floor where the other female staff slept in shared rooms. Every stair felt like a wasted moment to Violet. Anxiety tore through her as she wondered what might be happening to Lady Neil at this very second.

But she ran with all the speed she could muster to Mrs. Baird's room and threw the door open with such a clatter that the older woman sat bolt upright in her bed, eyes wide but instantly alert.

Violet stood in the doorway breathing heavily but Mrs. Baird needed to take only one look at her to understand the urgency in her eyes.

"It's time," Mrs. Baird announced with a calm matter-of-fact voice. Violet only nodded, still dragging air into her lungs.

The two women rushed back downstairs to the family wing. Mrs. Baird instructed Violet to go straight back to Lady Neil's room and fetch fresh water in her bowl while she stopped at a linen closet to fetch fresh towels.

Violet did as she was bid without hesitation. She burst back into the room to find Lord Neil still in his spot, his ministrations of soothing words sounding less soothing and more dismayed by the second. Lady Neil gritted her teeth as another wave of pain carried her away. The baron remained oblivious as Violet readied what she could in the room and Mrs. Baird arrived with a bundle of towels in her arms.

"Take His Lordship away from here," Mrs. Baird whispered urgently to Violet. "This is no sight for a man. If he faints I can only attend to one of them at a time and Her Ladyship takes priority now."

"I'll see to it that he has distraction."

Violet hurried out of the room and straight to the guest wing on the opposite side of the house.

"Curse these massive homes," she muttered under her breath as she dashed down corridors and hallways. She wished Frank had stayed downstairs in the sitting room for a few more nights as it would have been faster for her to get to him there, but Dr. Slaterly had given him approval to move back to his guest room with the help of a crutch just a couple days before.

Finally she made it to Frank's door. She curled her hand into a fist and pounded on the door as loudly as she could. All her courtesy fled her when she did not receive an instantaneous answer and she allowed herself into her brother's room.

"Frank!" She cried out as she ran to her brother's bedside and tapped his shoulder.

"Good heaven, what's all this about?!" He snorted and rubbed at his eyes. "Violet, what the devil are you doing here?"

"The baby is coming. You and Captain Jessup must keep Lord Neil away from that room and distract him as best you can," Violet explained breathlessly as she pulled Frank out of bed.

"Is everything alright? Can I help?"

A tired but concerned voice came from the doorway and Violet turned to see the captain in his robe, blinking the sleep away.

Violet blushed fiercely at seeing him in such a vulnerable state and blushed even deeper when, despite the severity of the current situation, she found herself longing to see his drowsy expression again.

"Yes, Captain," she responded as soon as she forced those thoughts away. "Please help Frank dress and ready yourself as well. The baby will be here soon and Lord Neil needs to be distracted. He's in a terrible state."

"Goodness! Poor man. I can't say I blame him in the least. Birth must be a nasty business. Miraculous, but terrifying. I can imagine it must be so anxiety inducing to be in the room while my precious wife suffered so greatly and I could do nothing but watch. Leave the baron to us. We'll wait in the drawing room." Captain Jessup immediately straightened up, ready to take the lead.

His words swirled around Violet's head for a dizzying moment. *My precious wife...*

Violet chided herself to keep her wits about her. Surely she must be overwhelmed from the situation and not thinking clearly.

"No, the library," Violet insisted. "It's his favorite room in the house save for his study but I do not think he will like guests there. It may bring him some calm. Wait for us there and I will bring His Lordship to you."

Violet did not wait for an answer and quickly quit the room. She could not wait for an answer. She could not stand to be there for another moment. She needed to get the captain's words and his sweet sleepy face out of her mind. She needed to focus. Lady Neil needed her now more than ever.

She flew through the house to her mistress's room. She could hear the baroness's moans and cries of anguish from the hall now.

"My lord!" Violet called as soon as she opened the door, spying the baron in the far corner of the room. "Let us go to the library for now. Captain Jessup and Lieutenant Davies are waiting for you there."

His head snapped up when Violet issued her command. She could see beads of sweat forming at his temples and his chest heaving with shallow breaths. But he did not move from his spot.

Violet crossed the room, skirting the large bed where Lady Neil writhed and Mrs. Baird consoled and coached.

"Come now, my lord," Violet demanded. She could not believe that she was ordering her master around, but the man was clearly in no state to remain in this room.

"But Cecilia.... The baby...." He mumbled, his eyes pleading with Violet.

Violet softened at his concern. She knew he only wanted to ensure his wife's and child's safety. For a man usually so in control of his life—never having been required to yield to anyone or anything in his adult life unless it suited his fancy —bending to nature's will must not have been an easy task. Especially when it concerned his loved ones.

"Lady Neil and the baby will receive the best care possible. The best way you can help them now is by distracting yourself with prayers in the library while Mrs. Baird and the doctor do what needs to be done."

Violet stepped forward and placed a tentative hand on Lord Neil's forearm. It felt exceedingly unusual and impertinent, but the baron was clearly at his wit's end and needed a little comfort himself.

"Yes." Lord Neil nodded numbly. "You must be right. I should hate to get in the way."

With an encouraging smile, Violet turned and led the baron toward the door. He stopped at the bed first and Mrs. Baird stepped aside, joining Violet by the door to give the husband and wife a moment alone.

Violet immediately noticed the worry wafting off of the housekeeper. Of course, the situation was worrisome, but Violet sensed something else in Mrs. Baird's expression.

Before she could ask, Mrs. Baird leaned down slightly to whisper as closely as possible into Violet's ear.

Violet's heart stopped and her veins flooded with ice.

"This cannot be..." she whispered, her voice barely audible above Lady Neil's groans and pants for breath.

Mrs. Baird looked as sick as Violet felt. "Hurry now," she commanded with a tremble in her voice.

"Let us go now, my lord," Violet called out to the baron once more. He gripped his wife's hands in his and planted a soft kiss on her forehead. Lady Neil smiled with surprising strength as she patted her husband's cheek.

The baron rejoined Violet and they began the long journey to the library. They did not speak as they walked down the cold halls and empty stairways. Violet had no idea what she could say at such a time that wouldn't feel utterly trivial. Lord Neil did not seem eager to soothe his worries by speech either. Violet had learned early on that the baron was an introspective, quiet type especially when it came to troubling matters. Even Lady Neil often struggled to encourage him to share his burdens with her.

At long last they arrived at the library. Violet opened the door and followed Lord Neil inside. Thankfully Frank and Captain Jessup had already started the fire. They both turned when Violet and Lord Neil entered. Violet steered her master toward the warmth of the fireplace and sat him down in a nearby chair.

She took a step back and prepared to tell her brother and the captain the news. But before she could go far Lord Neil's hand shot out and grabbed her own. Violet's eyes widened at the unexpected gesture.

"Violet." Lord Neil looked up into Violet's face, his expression earnest. "Thank you for your help. For everything you do."

"Of course, my lord," Violet mumbled.

She knew that as a servant, her master was under no obligation to thank her for anything she did. And she did not personally interact with Lord Neil very often. His thanks, said with such fondness and sincerity, bolstered Violet and gave her a little helping of courage to face what would come next.

"The Neil family means very much to me. It is my honor to do everything I can for Your Lordship and Her Ladyship and the little one." She smiled down at her master and said a silent prayer that he would not regret trusting her with his wife's care, nor suffer any pain or heartache. He was a very good man, Violet knew. She would hate to see him heartbroken.

Lord Neil gave Violet's hand a squeeze before releasing it to her. She turned away and fixed Frank and Captain Jessup with a pointed gaze, glancing back toward the door to indicate that they should follow her.

When they were far enough away that she was sure Lord

Neil would not hear, she turned to face them. Captain Jessup stood tall and regal and certainly did not look as though he'd been asleep less than an hour ago. Frank did his best to appear alert as he leaned heavily against the crutch propped up under his arm.

"There has been some unfortunate news," Violet started, hoping the courage she'd sourced from Lord Neil's kind words overtook the nerves she still felt. The captain's brow furrowed and her brother instantly perked up.

"In addition to keeping Lord Neil distracted, you must not tell him that we cannot send for the doctor. Mrs. Baird informed me that it is snowing too heavily and I can tell by the chill in the house that it must be so. Dance around the subject as much as you need to. He is already in a fragile state and he will surely go to pieces if he finds this out. We will not worry him unless it is absolutely necessary."

"But how is the baby to be delivered then?" Frank asked.

Violet swallowed as she gave voice to her imminent future. "Mrs. Baird and I will deliver the child ourselves."

"Are you sure that is a wise idea?" Captain Jessup interjected.

Violet was indeed not sure at all, at least of her own capabilities, but she did not let this show. "It is the wisest idea we have right now. We can't very well ask Her Ladyship to wait until the snow lets up. Mrs. Baird has assisted in a few deliveries before."

She failed to mention, however, that Mrs. Baird had only acted as an assistant to a doctor and the last baby she'd helped deliver had been Lord Neil.

"You should hurry back," Frank said as he put an encouraging hand on Violet's shoulder. "We can handle things in here."

Violet took a deep breath and took one last look at Lord

Neil sitting by the fire, leaning forward with his elbows on his knees and his face in his hands.

She said her goodbyes to her brother and the captain and resumed her frantic pace through the house.

But just as Violet reached the next landing, a clatter of hurried footsteps caught her attention. She turned toward the sound to see Captain Jessup rushing up the staircase on the opposite side of the house toward the guest wing.

A surge of annoyance flooded through Violet, stinging all the more due to her already nearly snapped nerves.

What could possibly call Captain Jessup away from the library at this critical hour? She had specifically asked both he and Frank to assist Lord Neil during what surely must be one of the most frightening nights of his life.

But Violet did not have time to ponder any further why the captain would abandon his post. She raced to Lady Neil's room and rejoined Mrs. Baird, any other thoughts slipping her mind as she heeded Mrs. Baird's commands and found herself working to deliver a baby.

A FEW HOURS into labor and Violet found herself wiping away at her own sweat with the sleeve of her dress. Her other hand wiped away the sweat dripping into Lady Neil's eyes with a handkerchief.

Despite the freezing temperatures outside, the flames in the fireplace and the sheer tension in the room kept Violet from feeling even remotely cold.

Mrs. Baird's voice rang continually through the room, encouraging Lady Neil through each contraction and telling Violet what to do next. Her voice was steady, a welcome calm amongst the anxiety in the room. But Violet could see past the sharp focus in her eyes to the worry within.

The baroness's labor had gone well so far, but all three women knew that the tides could change at any moment.

Numerous nightmare scenarios whirled through Violet's head constantly and she could see the same happening to Mrs. Baird.

Sharp footsteps against wood and the heavy front door opening and closing and urgent voices coming from downstairs caused Mrs. Baird and Violet to look up at each other in surprise. Lady Neil rested in between contractions elsewise they likely would not have heard the commotion.

Even the baroness was curious about the sounds. She propped herself up on her elbows and said through shallow breaths, "What could possibly be going on at this hour downstairs?"

Violet quickly hid her small smile. That was her mistress. Always worrying about the goings on in her household, even when it was the last thing she should be worrying about.

"Violet, go on and see what all the fuss is about. If you need to, alert Mr. Taylor and have him see to whatever it is," Mrs. Baird instructed.

She nodded quickly and set aside the handkerchief next to the bowl of water on the bedside table. This time Violet did not hide her smile when she heard Lardy Neil offer a quiet "thank you, Violet" as she left the room.

But as soon as Violet closed the door behind her, her sense of urgency and curiosity returned. She rushed downstairs as quickly as she could without tripping and nearly skidded to a halt when she entered the foyer.

Captain Jessup stood just inside the door, brushing a layer of snow off his shoulders.

Next to him was Dr. Slaterly.

Mr. Taylor, still in his robe and nightcap, commanded two groggy footmen to take their coats.

"Good Heaven!" Violet cried out. "What on Earth possessed you to go out in the freezing cold and snow?"

She marched up to the captain, half wild with relief and half cross at the risk he had taken.

Captain Jessup only laughed at Violet's harshly spoken question. "If I see someone in need, I do everything in my power to help. Besides, it wasn't terribly dangerous. I'm an excellent carriage driver and I took extra care on the roads. The trip took longer but we travelled as safely as can be expected."

Violet was stunned into silence. All she could do was stare into the captain's warm, sweet eyes. He took a step closer and she noticed the tiny snowflakes caught in his eyelashes and melting on his lips. She desperately wished she could reach up and brush them away.

Violet's hand twitched as if to carry out her wishes when the doctor interrupted.

"Please, someone, bring me to Lady Neil!"

Captain Jessup coughed and the spell was broken. He nodded gently and whispered, "Go to your mistress."

"This way, Dr. Slaterly." Violet went off with the doctor behind her. She updated him on the lady's progress and answered his questions about her general health and her labor thus far.

Halfway up the stairs, Violet cast a glance over her shoulder. She had just enough view of the foyer to see Captain Jessup take off his coat, shivering slightly.

Violet vowed to thank the captain as ardently as she could at the first opportunity. He had braved the cold he hated for a woman he did not particularly know nor had any meaningful connection to.

But Violet knew what Captain Jessup had said was true. This was his nature. He helped those in need regardless of his own safety or what they meant to him. If the risk held a chance of making all the difference, Captain Jessup would take that risk.

Violet's heart swelled with deep admiration. She was immensely lucky to have the captain in her life, however briefly.

Anyone would be immensely lucky to have such a man in their life. Violet found herself hoping that her luck would hold on for a while longer.

# CHAPTER 10

*T*he heat from the fireplace did not thaw Owen quickly enough. In fact, he felt like he could step into the very flames. But he would settle for sitting as near as possible without catching himself on fire.

The sound of the crackling wood was accompanied by the baron's rapid footfalls on the thick rug and Davies's many unsuccessful attempts to calm the man down. Every suggestion to sit or read was ignored or waved away. Every question about books or the estate or the baron's life were answered as briefly as possible.

Owen laughed quietly as he listened to the lieutenant behind him ask Lord Neil how many books were in his library and he simply responded with "many." He shook his head and wondered how he'd ended up in this situation— riding out into a snowstorm to get a doctor for a woman he barely knew.

But despite the stiffness in his fingers from clutching the reins and the chill that had settled into his bones on the long ride to and from the village, Owen knew he would do it again in an instant.

He may not be an active soldier anymore, but protecting and helping others would always be his highest calling. Uniform or not.

He'd known immediately that he needed to bring the doctor to Gatherford Park as soon as Miss Davies had announced the troubling news that she and the housekeeper would attempt to deliver the little one on their own. He'd barely given it a moment of thought as he'd told Davies his plan and rushed up to his room to change for the journey. He'd barely noticed the cold as he readied the carriage and hopped onto the box, spurring the horses into the darkness.

Now that the urgency was over and the mission safely completed, Owen noticed the cold in abundance.

The door creaked open and Owen turned around in his chair to see Miss Davies enter the room with a tray of tea and biscuits. The lieutenant greeted his sister from his own chair but Lord Neil kept up his incessant pacing, eyes locked onto some unseen objective.

The cold in Owen's body melted away when he caught the maid's eye and she smiled at him.

It seemed that she too had not been blind to the intoxicating current that had passed between them upon his arrival with the doctor. He had replayed the way her eyes had darted over his face, from his eyes to his lips, since she'd walked away with Dr. Slaterly in tow.

In fact, Owen could have sworn that Miss Davies had been about to reach up and touch his face when they were reminded of the only situation that should matter to either of them.

Miss Davies placed the tray on the small table near Owen and her brother and poured each of them a cup of steaming hot tea. She handed the lieutenant his cup first before turning her attention to Owen.

Suddenly the heat from the fireplace felt far too close as

Owen's fingers brushed over Miss Davies's when she passed the cup to him. Their eyes locked for a moment though that moment felt almost infinite to Owen. He could see the way the firelight flickered against her green eyes and the way she gazed at him with something that looked perhaps like longing.

But Miss Davies pulled away and carried the last cup to Lord Neil. He held his hand up when she offered it to him but she persisted, trying a few times to put the cup within his reach but the baron continued to sidestep her.

"My lord, please sit and drink," she commanded, her light voice turning firm.

Lord Neil, surprised by the determination in the maid's voice, and perhaps at being spoken to so frankly, stopped in his tracks and stared at the young woman.

"Everything is going well. Your wife is in excellent hands. Between Dr. Slaterly and Mrs. Baird, the baby will be delivered in the best conditions. I am sure they will still do their best even if you sit for a few minutes to have some tea."

Without a word, Lord Neil sank down into the nearest chair and accepted the cup from Miss Davies. He sipped and the warm liquid seemed to instantly soothe his tense shoulders.

Owen chuckled quietly to himself as he watched the exchange. He found it amazing that such a petite young lady could put a grown man in his place, especially a grown man who was many times her social superior.

But considering the circumstances and knowing Lord Neil's kind and generous nature, Owen doubted that he would even remember this incident tomorrow and if he did surely he would not mind that Miss Davies had taken the initiative to see to his care.

After watching Lord Neil closely for a moment as if to

ensure that he would not flee his chair, Miss Davies disappeared behind one of the large bookcases.

Owen craned his neck to see where she had gone but he suspected she must need to go back to Lady Neil's room and continue assisting with the delivery. He deflated slightly and sank into his chair, the high wings of the chair back acting as blinders to the rest of the room.

After a few minutes of staring glumly into the fire, Owen heard light footsteps nearby. He looked up just in time to see Miss Davies approach with a bundle of thick fabric in her arms. The maid gave her shy smile again as she unfolded the plush blanket slightly before pausing. She looked like she had wanted to spread the blanket over his lap but thought better of taking such a familiar action.

"I thought you might need a little extra warming up." She laid the blanket on the arm of Owen's chair.

"Indeed, thank you. Will you have a seat? Or do you need to return to Her Ladyship right away?" Owen asked as calmly as he could, trying not to reveal his sudden desire to keep Miss Davies nearby. He set his cup down and unfolded the blanket over his lap.

Miss Davies sat in the chair next to Owen and poured herself some tea. "Dr. Slaterly and Mrs. Baird have everything well under control so I have been relieved of my duties for now."

"And Lady Neil? Is she well? Do they expect a safe and healthy delivery?" Owen asked as Miss Davies took a sip. Though he might not know her well, Owen would certainly never wish any harm to befall such a kind and admirable woman.

Miss Davies smiled with relief. "The doctor says she is doing very well. Her pains are great but she will not allow them to defeat her. But labor came uncommonly hard and fast on Her Ladyship and Dr. Slaterly expects that the baby could be here in just a few more hours or even less."

Owen was relieved, too. "I am so very glad to hear that. Your mistress is a strong woman."

Miss Davies's eyes locked onto Owen's and he saw a sudden urgency in her gaze. He started to ask if she was alright but her words began flowing too quickly for his query to materialize.

"Captain Jessup, I can never explain how thankful I am that you risked yourself to fetch the doctor in this storm. And I am so thrilled that you did not suffer any harm because of it. You have saved us a great deal of worry and you brought Lady Neil the expert care she requires. Perhaps Mrs. Baird and I could have managed on our own, but these things are just so mysterious.

"I so wish there was some way I could properly thank and repay you, Captain. As you know, my mistress means so very much to me, as does her family. I know you did not do this for me but your actions have affected me, too, very deeply. Lady Neil and the child will surely fare much better thanks to—"

"Hold on now," Owen chuckled as he held up a hand to pause Miss Davies's rapidly expressed thoughts. "You need not thank me. Truly. It is my honor to offer assistance whenever I can and I would happily do it a million times over." He smiled reassuringly at the maid who still stared at him so urgently and earnestly.

"I know you do not like to accept thanks, but I will give them anyway, as sincerely as I can. You very well may have just spared us all a terrible fate. But would you really do it a million times?" Miss Davies asked, a hint of tease in her voice and her narrowed eyes. "Even in this weather that you hate so much? Surely even you must have your limits."

Owen laughed, the sound vibrating through his chest and down his back.

"Careful!" Miss Davies warned as Owen threatened to spill tea on himself.

"I certainly like to think that I would. But let's not find my limit tonight, shall we?"

Miss Davies smiled, her face lighting up in the warm glow of the flames. "I think you would, Captain."

"Perhaps you have more faith in me than you ought to." Owen sipped his tea to hide the blush that threatened to travel up his neck and into his cheeks.

"I don't think so, Captain." Miss Davies smiled before giving a heavy sigh. "I must admit I was quite terrified. I've never attended a birth before and I know little of the experience. And seeing Her Ladyship in such pain and distress.... It was very upsetting, especially knowing there was nothing I could do to ease her suffering.

"But I am so thankful that she has proper medical care now. She, and now Lord Neil, are like family to me. As close to family as a servant can be. If I may be so bold, Captain, you are my hero and angel for what you did tonight."

She cast her eyes down to the cup in her hand and Owen did the same. He could hardly bear such glowing praise, especially not from Miss Davies. To be thought of as a hero and angel.... Owen had been called a hero on a few occasions, and his mother often called him an angel, but coming from Miss Davies, the sentiment carried a different weight.

"Oh dear, your cup has run low. Let me refill it for you," Miss Davies quickly insisted, setting her tea down so she could attend to Owen's and the other men.

She did not linger long enough for Owen to thank her but instead immediately carried the pot over to Davies and Lord Neil who both sat on the other side of the large fireplace.

"Violet, wait," Lord Neil called as Miss Davies finished filling his cup and went to resume her seat. Miss Davies turned back to her master with a slight tilt of her head, concern in her eyes.

"Yes, my lord?"

"Cecilia.... Are you sure she's quite alright? How long do babies take to...come out? When do you think we will hear from the doctor?"

He rattled off his questions in a low, nervous voice and kept his hand around the maid's wrist. He looked up at her imploringly, as if Miss Davies held the answer to every mystery in the world.

Perhaps, Owen thought to himself, the baron wasn't far off in that assessment. The more time he spent in her company, the more Owen realized that Miss Davies might be the answer to one particular mystery buried deep in his own heart.

A comforting warmth spread through Owen as he watched Miss Davies smile down at Lord Neil with patience and kindness. She put her other hand over the baron's which was still attached to her wrist and patted it a few times.

"I assure you, my lord, Her Ladyship was doing a wonderful job when I left. As are Dr. Slaterly and Mrs. Baird. Unfortunately, babies heed no one's schedule but their own. They can take quite some time to make their appearance. But the doctor is confident that your little one will be here in a few hours and maybe even sooner. And remember, no news is good news. For now, let us continue about our evening as normally as we can and pray for a lovely healthy baby and mother."

Miss Davies spoke with a sweet calm so deep that it could only be her nature. There was nothing of affectation or practice in her gentle words to the baron.

Owen wondered what it might be like to be on the receiving end of such caring ministrations.

His mind yanked him back to the many dreary, miserable, often freezing nights he'd spent in his camp on foreign lands. He saw the several war wives who had followed their husbands to the front, moving about the camp and assisting all the soldiers—not just their own husbands—in any way they could.

They had made tea, fed soup, mended clothes, knitted scarves, bundled up cold and weary men in homespun blankets. But most importantly of all, they constantly whispered words of encouragement, kindness, comfort.

The women who followed their men to the field seemed to know or learned quickly enough that beneath the uniforms and tough exteriors and blood on their hands that soldiers were really just homesick men—many of them just boys barely starting in life, as Owen had been when he'd first joined.

Owen squeezed his eyes shut and returned to the library. Time seemed to have stopped while he was in his memories. But he saw the purpose of their recollection now.

The way Miss Davies looked at and spoke to Lord Neil was just the same as he had seen in those wives at the camps. He knew she would make an excellent, helpful companion if she were ever in such a situation.

Miss Davies had the fortitude and tenacity to meet challenges head on without losing the kindness of spirit that enabled her to go above and beyond for the people she loved.

Owen knew he would be a fool not to admit that such qualities made Miss Davies very admirable in his eyes.

But he quickly wiped the silly grin off his face that he only realized was there when Miss Davies turned around to rejoin him on their side of the fireplace.

"Lord Neil is in quite a state. He seems dazed half the

time and painfully aware the other half," Owen said lightly as Miss Davies settled back down and refilled her own cup of tea.

"Indeed," she laughed quietly. "But he is hanging on. I am sure this experience is not easy for a husband—being shut out of the room not knowing whether his wife and child are alright, feeling helpless to take away her pain."

She glanced back to the baron sympathetically. He had returned to his mostly one-sided conversation with Davies, preferring to listen to the lieutenant rattle on about his rudimentary opinions on crops and farming practices.

"Actually, if you don't mind, Captain..." Miss Davies said quietly, a sudden nervous air overtaking her whole body. She set her cup down and toyed with the edge of her apron, avoiding Owen's eyes.

"I could never mind anything you say," Owen responded hurriedly.

Miss Davies looked up in surprise at his words.

Even just a few days ago Owen would have scolded himself for saying something so thoughtlessly forward. But he knew his ability to hide the thumping sensation that grew in his heart anytime he was near Miss Davies would not last much longer. Besides, what he said was true. Whatever was on Miss Davies's mind, Owen would gladly hear it out. He wanted, needed to hear her.

"I hope you will still feel the same in a few moments," she muttered with a blush. "You see, I've brought some of my poetry up with me. I thought I might read some to you to pass the time. If that sounds agreeable to you, of course."

Miss Davies pulled a small book out of the front pocket of her apron, her fingertips running over the back cover. She could only peek up at him nervously, seeking his approval.

Owen could see that she was clearly very apprehensive about sharing her work but his heart soared to heights he had not thought possible. The silly grin returned to his face and this time he did not suppress it.

"I would absolutely love to hear whatever you feel comfortable sharing with me."

Miss Davies smiled and let out the breath she'd been holding in anticipation. She opened the book, the same one Owen had seen her writing in when he and Davies had returned from their hunt that now seemed like a lifetime ago. Her fingers flipped through the pages at the corners, their soft rustling sounding like music to Owen.

He felt honored that she would share her intimate creative thoughts with him. Perhaps she too sensed that the distance between them shrank with each passing day. Though the act may have seemed small to anyone else, Owen knew that for Miss Davies, it was an admission of trust.

And Owen would do everything he could to honor that trust—starting with listening to her poetry.

As Miss Davies read one poem and then another and another, her voice rising and falling gently to produce a soothing melody, her words surprised Owen. He had had his suspicions that the maid undervalued her own skill and he had been proven right in these past few minutes.

But he had not been prepared for how truly beautiful her words were. They were wise and smart and eloquent. She crafted fresh and elegant phrases. But most importantly, her kind heart showed in each and every line.

Owen watched Miss Davies as she read without any fear of discovery. She was so engrossed in her words that she did not notice his stare. In truth, Owen did not think that being discovered would be such a terrible thing.

How could he look away when her face was bathed in soft firelight and glowed from within with her passion for her craft? How could he look away when her lovely eyes traced the page and changed subtly to reflect the mood of the verse, when the corners of her mouth twitched up in a small smile?

He did not even care that his host and Miss Davies's brother sat just a few feet away. No doubt the lieutenant eyed Owen like a hawk and would jab him about the enamored expression on his face when he had the first opportunity.

None of that mattered to Owen right now. All that mattered was being here in this moment with Miss Davies, enjoying her poetry, and warming up to the possibilities he heard in her voice and her words. Possibilities that could change his future.

# CHAPTER 11

$\mathcal{T}$he low heel on Violet's shoes clicked harshly against the rough stone floor in the servants' hall. She had been pacing for hours already. Though Mrs. Baird had told Violet that Lady Neil granted her a free morning for all her help during the night and the wee hours of the morning, Violet found that she would much rather be working.

Anything would be better than walking back and forth along the dining table in her anxiety to see for herself that her mistress and the baby were well.

"Goodness me, child, will you sit down?" Mrs. Baird chided from her own seat at the dining table. "The baby is perfectly healthy and beautiful and Her Ladyship is recovering splendidly. I am sure they will introduce you soon."

The housekeeper sighed, her head drooping wearily. She had been up with Lady Neil and Dr. Slaterly all night and had only snatched a few hours of sleep before the servants began their normal duties. Mrs. Baird had been given the whole day off but she, like Violet, did not do well with idle time. Violet simply clicked her tongue at the minor hypocrisy and continued her repetitive journey through the servants' hall.

The air in the house buzzed with excitement. For many of the staff at Gatherford Park, this was their first experience welcoming a baby into the family. And for those who had been around when Lord Neil had been born, the child was a welcome guarantee that the Neil family would have an heir and carry on for another generation. After all, the older staff had long since resigned themselves to the possibility that Lord Neil would never marry or father any children and the fate of their home and livelihoods would be left in the air.

But then Miss Cecilia Richards had come along and became Lady Neil. The house had been filled with a fresh joy ever since and it positively burst at the seams today with news of Gatherford Park's newest resident.

Only Violet felt that she could not share in the excitement until she had seen her mistress and the littlest Neil. And she felt out of sorts not attending to Lady Neil at this hour. To give herself something to do, and to revitalize Mrs. Baird's energy a tad, Violet set about to brewing a pot of tea.

"Violet, there's no need to do that. I am perfectly well. I just cannot sleep when I hear the noise of the house and know that I should be ensuring everything is right." Mrs. Baird had of course read Violet's mind and knew the tea was meant for her.

"Please let me do something, Mrs. Baird. If my mind cannot rest, then my body cannot rest."

"But your mind *should* rest, my dear. As I keep telling you, everyone is happy and healthy and there is nothing for your mind to fret over."

"That is far easier said than done. You should know that for yourself. If you've been given the day off, then there must be nothing for you to attend to down here and you should sleep easily. Am I not correct?" Violet shot a teasing smirk over to Mrs. Baird as the pot began to whistle and she readied the housekeeper's cup with a smidge of sugar and milk, just as she knew she liked it.

Mrs. Baird shook her head with a defeated smile. "You and I are far too alike to get either of us anywhere, it seems."

Violet set the cup down before Mrs. Baird and sat next to her. If Violet could not satisfy Mrs. Baird's request in mind, she could at least satisfy it in body.

Violet had not been in her chair for more than a few seconds when Andrew, one of the younger footmen, entered the servants' area and planted himself before Violet and Mrs. Baird.

"Mrs. Baird, Miss Davies, Her Ladyship has requested your presence in the sitting room in the family wing," he stated with much solemnity.

Violet could not stop herself from jumping up immediately and rushing out of the servants' hall, throwing a "thank you" to Andrew over her shoulder. She heard Mrs. Baird follow behind, laughing at the scene.

Finally at the door to the family's private sitting room, just a few doors down the hall from Lady Neil's chambers, Violet paused and composed herself. She took a few deep breaths as Mrs. Baird caught up to her. The housekeeper quietly opened the door and they stepped through together.

Domestic bliss. That was the picture that greeted Violet when they entered the sitting room. Lady Neil sat in a chair by the fire with a bundle of blankets in her arms and Lord Neil stood just behind her, leaning over her shoulder to peer at their baby. They both cooed and smiled and Lady Neil traced her finger down the little one's cheek.

They both looked very tired but very happy. They were already so in love with their child. A bittersweet feeling pinched at Violet's stomach as she watched the happy family, lost in their own world.

Of course she was incredibly happy for her master and

mistress. She knew they had been eager to start a family since the moment they said their vows. And now their dream had come true.

But Violet knew that such a dream was out of reach for her. She would never be part of such a loving family moment except as a bystander. She hadn't even been part of a loving family moment at her own birth. Her father and brothers had been too busy planning her mother's funeral and too full of resentment to spare much time for coos and smiles at baby Violet.

Mrs. Baird coughed by Violet's side, breaking everyone of their reveries. The new parents finally looked up and noticed their visitors. Lady Neil gave a weary but joyful smile and waved them over with her free hand.

Suddenly nervous, Violet approached with Mrs. Baird. Just as she had been terribly ignorant of pregnancy and labor and childbirth, Violet realized that she had almost no knowledge of babies. The closer she got the better she saw how small and fragile this brand-new life was.

"Isn't he beautiful?" Lady Neil asked as the two women gathered around her, but her tone conveyed a statement rather than a question. She smiled down into her son's peaceful face, her eyes glittering with the immensity of her love.

"He certainly is, my lady. Congratulations." Violet's voice caught in her throat slightly and she realized a surge of emotion threatened to carry her away.

She hadn't had an opportunity to see a baby this close before. It amazed her that he looked so real yet so doll-like at the same time. His features were still as he slept contentedly in his mother's arms, as if he would never want for a better cradle. He looked like a perfect mixture of his parents.

In an instant Violet felt that she could see just how her little master would look as he grew up, all wide blue eyes and dark windswept hair and smiles. The power of her feelings over someone else's child surprised her. She could only wonder how she might feel if the child were her own.

But Violet did not have time to chastise herself for such a useless thought. Lady Neil's voice interrupted her, asking if she wished to hold the baby. Violet also did not have time to come to her senses long enough to refuse. Before she knew it, the babe had been placed in her arms.

"M-My lady, I'm not sur—" Violet stammered as she felt the tiny body squirm.

"You're doing just fine, Violet," Lady Neil assured her. "Just be sure to support his head. You can give him a little bounce, too, if you'd like."

Violet swallowed her nerves and looked upon the little face. He seemed to settle into her arms after a moment and she breathed a sigh of relief and then a sigh of wonderment as he opened his mouth in a big yawn. Violet chuckled. She supposed he'd had a long night as well.

She tried Lady Neil's suggestion and bent her knees a few times to create a slight bouncing motion. The baby seemed to enjoy this as he burrowed himself deeper into his blanket and gripped the fabric in his impossibly small hand.

As Violet found a rhythm in the motion, the door opened once more. She looked up to see Frank limp in with his crutch, the captain right behind him.

Violet's eyes instantly found Captain Jessup's and she realized she must look very out of place holding this baby. But the captain did not seem to think so. He watched her with warmth in his eyes and a lovely smile on his lips.

"Captain Jessup, Lieutenant Davies," Lord Neil called as the two men walked toward their small gathering. "It is my pleasure to introduce to you my son, The Honorable Joseph Neil."

The pride in Lord Neil's voice hummed in every word he

said. Violet glanced over her shoulder at the baron to see the brightest smile she had ever seen grace his normally stoic face. He looked nearly giddy with love and joy.

"A charming little chap!" Frank announced as he peered down at the bundle still in Violet's arms.

"Gentlemen, I would so very much like to thank you both for everything you did to help myself and His Lordship last night—or should I say this morning. Lieutenant, thank you for keeping my poor husband company and giving him strength to get through the ordeal. Captain, thank you for rushing out in the storm to bring Dr. Slaterly. I hate to think what would have happened to you if you'd been hurt on my behalf. But you played a large part in helping our little boy come into the world safely and soundly."

Lady Neil's voice trembled and her eyes watered as she looked up at the two men from her seat, too weary and pained to stand and make a proper curtsey but no one in the room could fault her for it.

"I was happy to do it, my lady," Frank announced cheerfully as he bowed his head to his hostess.

"There is no need to thank me." Captain Jessup coughed slightly. "It was the right thing to do, and I make it a habit to do what is right."

Lady Neil frowned at this slightly. "You are too humble for your own good at times, Captain."

Frank scoffed. "Not when you have to share a tent with him, my lady."

Lord Neil threw his head back and let out a deep laugh, shocking them all. Everyone except for tiny Master Neil who slept through the ripple of laughter that engulfed the group for a few moments.

"My, my, Violet," Mrs. Baird said as she caught her breath. "You do look so very natural with that wee one in your arms." She gave a small smile to Violet and Violet suspected that she was the only one who could read Mrs. Baird's intended meaning in it.

Nevertheless, she blushed fiercely at the unusual comment and its equally uncomfortable timing. Surely Mrs. Baird could have paid this compliment before the men entered the room, or when she and Violet were alone in the servants' hall later.

"It is only because I feel so attached to Master Neil already," Violet mumbled, keeping her eyes trained on the baby's sweet face.

"Violet, why don't you give Joseph to Captain Jessup for a moment," Lady Neil suggested. Violet noticed the slightly smug expression on her mistress's face.

She blushed again but complied with the command. The captain's eyebrows shot up in surprise but he moved closer to Violet to make the exchange. He also seemed caught off guard at having a baby thrust into his arms.

Captain Jessup made a circle with his arms and Violet angled herself as best she could to shift Master Neil over to the captain. Their arms brushed against each other, the fabric of his coat and her black dress rustling as they struggled to transfer the baby safely.

She hoped desperately that Captain Jessup could not feel the heat radiating from her as her heart raced from the contact, from the wide smile stretched across his face as he took the baby, from the quiet laugh he gave at their awkward attempts to maneuver the tiny creature.

Violet took a step back and took in the captain with the child in his arms. She had heard of women swooning before but had never experienced it for herself. Violet realized that this feeling in her chest that made her lightheaded must be something similar.

The captain looked up from the baby to Violet, the inner corner of his brows tilting up with a silent question. Violet laughed behind her hand and gave an encouraging nod. Captain Jessup let out the breath he'd been holding once Violet had silently assured him that he did well.

Master Neil began to wiggle and whimper after a moment in Captain Jessup's arms but the man would not be deterred now that he'd secured this precious parcel.

"Shh now, my little friend. All is well, I promise. Though I imagine I am not as soft and comforting as your mother. And Miss Davies," he whispered to the baby. He began to bounce as he had seen Violet do earlier, continuing to offer gentle words. His eyes glowed with patience and fondness.

The scene was too much for Violet. She could not stay in the room a moment longer. Not while Captain Jessup held and soothed this darling little baby. Her heart swelled to such an extreme size that she felt sure it would break through her ribs.

"I shall fetch some tea for us all!" She quickly announced and turned her back to the rest of the party, making her way straight to the door without another glance back.

But as Violet carefully closed the heavy door she did dare to look through the crack. Captain Jessup stood perfectly framed in the small opening with the baby still in his arms. He listened intently to Mrs. Baird as she explained some of the challenges that come with newborns. The captain turned his eyes back to Master Neil every few seconds, ensuring that the baby still slept comfortably.

For a moment, Violet's heart longed to rejoin them—to rejoin Captain Jessup in this familial painting. But she quickly closed the door the rest of the way when she saw the captain's face turn toward the door and their eyes nearly met.

Unfortunately, removing herself from the room did little to calm Violet. The scene followed her downstairs and into the kitchen. It replayed itself constantly as she waited for the tea to heat and as she carried the tray back upstairs. In fact, the images began to transform themselves the harder she tried to slow her breathing and steady her heart.

Violet saw the captain holding a different baby—one that looked like him. She saw love in his eyes as he looked at this imaginary child.

To her great relief, Captain Jessup had relinquished the baby to Frank's arms by the time she returned. He sat in a chair by one of the large windows, his crutch leaned up against the wall. The captain stood with the baron and baroness and Mrs. Baird by the nearby fireplace. She could see him shyly waving away what she assumed to be Lady Neil's persistent offerings of thanks.

Violet set the tea tray down and poured for everyone but her brother. She worked quickly, not allowing her fingers to brush against anyone else's strong hands, not allowing her eyes to meet anyone else's kind, merry gaze.

She took her own cup of tea and made her way to Frank and Master Neil.

"Are you enjoying yourself, Frank?" Violet asked with a chuckle as she sipped her tea. "I'm sorry I could not pour you a cup. I fear that babies and hot tea do not mix."

"I think I shall be alright as long as he doesn't...relieve himself upon me." Frank grimaced at the idea. "But as soon as he goes back to Lady Neil I will happily take a cup if you don't mind."

Violet couldn't help smirking slightly at her brother's clear discomfort. He probably had not had many occasions to hold a baby and naturally did not know what to expect.

"He seems so quiet for a newborn. I always hear stories of babies wailing at the tops of their lungs at all hours of the night and day. Perhaps he takes after His Lordship." Violet stared down at the baby curiously. "Frank, was I a quiet baby?"

The thought hadn't occurred to Violet until she'd arrived at Gatherford Park and heard Mrs. Baird proudly share stories of Lord Neil at all ages—from the day he was born, to the day the household panicked in search of the little boy only to find him in the corner of the library asleep with a book almost half his size in his lap, to the day he was packed off to his boarding school.

After hearing numerous colorful tales from the baron's childhood, Violet had realized that she had never heard any tales from her own infancy or childhood. Had she been a quiet baby? Had she walked early or did she resist the challenge? What strange things had she said as young children are so often wont to share at unexpected moments? She had long since assumed that she would never know.

But now that Frank had reappeared in her life, perhaps she could piece together a picture of who she had been and how she'd grown up—a picture that didn't revolve around her father's and brothers' emotional abuse and mistreatment.

Frank sat silently for a moment, staring off into the distance of memory. "Hmm. I was still a boy when you were born, not yet sent off to school, so I may not remember very clearly. But I do remember you screeching bloody murder, especially in the middle of the night. How you turned into such a quiet and respectful young lady I have no idea."

He scrunched his nose at Violet teasingly and Violet laughed at the image. "I do apologize. I don't think I've done too much screeching since."

"In truth..." Frank's voice grew quiet and his gaze fell upon the sleeping babe in his arms. "I used to think that you cried so loud and so long because you missed Mother like me."

Violet's cup stopped halfway to her lips. She stared at her brother in shock. His hazel eyes had grown dark with the painful memories of their mother's passing. Violet had never known her so she could only miss the idea of her. But Frank had been just seven years old when she died. Long enough to know and love his mother dearly but not nearly enough time with her.

Frank shook his head slightly and put on a strained smile. "Of course, that was before I knew that crying was a normal function of babies. I will also have you know that as soon as you developed the ability, you loved to grab my hair and yank on it when I held you, no matter how many times I yelled for you to stop or pulled your hand away."

Violet looked at her brother quizzically. "You held me?"

"I did. I tried to, at least. Babies are not very easy for little boys to carry but I tried. It is a miracle I did not drop you dozens of times now that I think about it."

A comforting warmth filled Violet's heart as she imagined little Frank trying to carry her around the house. Perhaps Frank had been the only one in their broken family who had ever really cared for her despite his eventual participation in her torment.

A father's influence could turn any sweet, loving boy into a villain. But beneath all that, Frank had always been that sweet, loving boy who carried his sister and worried that she missed their mother. That was the Frank who had returned to her.

"Unfortunately, I feel I am not and never have been a natural at holding babies. Not like you and Jessup," Frank continued.

"Pardon?" Violet had been so lost in thought that she felt sure she'd misheard her brother's words.

"You and the captain. I daresay you would both be natural parents one day."

Frank's eyes darted over Violet's shoulder to the rest of the group. Violet turned slightly just in time to see the man in question quickly pull his eyes away from her and Frank. Or rather, just her if her own eyes could be trusted.

Violet turned back to Frank and blushed at his teasing smile. She pouted and refused to take the baby from him when he tried to hand him over. But she could not resist long and soon took Master Neil back in her arms. Violet carried the baby back to his mother, keeping her eyes on his face.

As she approached and drew parallel to Captain Jessup, the baby threw his arm out from his blanket and his tiny fingers grasped toward the captain. Everyone laughed at the endearing gesture and Violet quickly passed Master Neil to the baroness.

Was everyone in this house trying to insinuate that there was something between her and the captain, or that there should be something between them?

VIOLET PULLED her weary body up the stairs, her feet aching with each step. It had been several days since young Master Neil came into the world and Violet had been busier than ever.

Lady Neil still had a long journey of recovery ahead of her in both body and mind. Based just on the small portion of the labor Violet had seen, she could only imagine how her mistress's body continued to ache.

And of course she worried about her son at every moment. He slept in the nursery with the new nurse who had luckily arrived just the day after his birth, but Violet knew Lady Neil still got little sleep, wondering if her child was well.

The baroness could not wander far in the house yet as her body still healed but she enjoyed walking where she could on the main floors of the house despite the usual advise to remain in bed as much as possible. Lady Neil insisted that undertaking some physical activity invigorated her and helped her heal.

Though Violet's physical sphere of duties had been greatly reduced according to Lady Neil's abilities, she wagered that she had walked more in these past few days than she had in the past two weeks altogether.

Violet's sense of duty to Lady Neil had increased exponentially as she watched her mistress slowly recover. She ran from floor to floor fetching tea, warm blankets, toys for entertaining, the nurse, a towel to clean up after the baby, and sometimes they made multiple trips to and from the dressing room to change Lady Neil completely if her son's delicate stomach seemed particularly displeased.

Each day—each hour, even—brought new challenges for the new parents and Violet as they worked together alongside the nurse to understand the little being in their midst.

And Violet had to admit that on some level she appreciated the busyness. It kept her mind from replaying the scene of Captain Jessup in the family sitting room with the baby in his arms. At least, Violet thought her busyness reduced the number of times her memory pushed the image of the rowdy military man gently cradling a child to the forefront of her thoughts. Surely Violet would never be relieved of it if she hadn't been so occupied.

Her increased tasks also kept her from interacting too closely with the captain. Violet could not decide if this was a good thing or a bad thing. Perhaps in some strange way it was both. Her heart felt fit to burst when he was in the same room, even if she did not have time to stop and converse with him. But her heart longed to be near him again as soon as she quit his presence.

Despite the exhaustion of the past several days, Violet looked forward to spending time with Master Neil. He was a delightful baby. He certainly cried, but once his needs were met he went back to sleep or simply stared at the foreign world around him.

The anticipation of seeing the baby spurred Violet the rest of the way up the stairs with the heavy tea tray. She balanced it on one arm as she pushed the drawing room door open and stepped in.

And she nearly dropped it when she saw Captain Jessup holding little Master Neil once more.

He looked up and smiled to Violet, as did Lord and Lady Neil and Frank. They sat near one of the grand windows, basking in the natural afternoon light.

Violet gripped the tray handles until her knuckles turned white and took in a deep breath through her nose. She approached the gathering and prepared the tea, wishing fruitlessly that her heart would stop bouncing throughout her chest.

She served tea for everyone but Captain Jessup whose hands were full with the baby and she quickly curtseyed to excuse herself. She felt as though she might have a heart attack at any moment if she remained in this room as Captain Jessup walked in a small circle with Master Neil cradled perfectly in his strong arms, talking quietly with the baby as if they were dear confidants.

But before Violet could take a step toward the door, he began to whimper and then wail in earnest.

"Come now, Master Neil. I thought we were friends," Captain Jessup chuckled, unperturbed by the high-pitched squeals sounding just inches from his face. He bounced his arms with a little more enthusiasm in an attempt to soothe his tiny companion.

This must be Violet's demise. The ease and gentleness with which the captain handled the crying baby was nothing short of beautiful.

But a movement at the corner of Violet's eye tore her attention away from Captain Jessup. Lady Neil's neck craned up to say something in her husband's ear and they exchanged a conspiratorial glance. The way Violet's stomach turned told her that she would be involved somehow.

Lord Neil stepped forward and offered to take the baby from Captain Jessup. "It looks like someone is in need of lunch. Why don't we all move to the dining room and have some refreshments ourselves?" he announced, walking past Violet with his son in his arms. Lady Neil followed, throwing a suspiciously demure smile to Violet.

"I am indeed starving. Getting used to this crutch works up quite an appetite." Frank hoisted himself out of his chair and made his way slowly to the door. He gave Violet's arm a squeeze with his free hand as he went by.

The captain followed behind Frank. He nodded to Violet when he came up next to her. His eyes locked onto hers for a breathless moment and they remained on her face as he walked away until he was forced to break contact.

Violet took in a shuddering breath. She supposed she could have looked away first, but her eyes seemed unable to obey her. Then again, she found that she did not want to look away.

"Shame.... They barely had any tea," Violet mumbled as she set about collecting their cups back onto the tray.

A shiver shot down Violet's spine as she sensed someone watching her. She turned herself slightly to look over her shoulder as she continued to clean up. Indeed, Captain Jessup hovered by the door, his eyes on her once again.

She swallowed and wished both that he would leave and that he would come back. Her latter wish was granted. Violet's ears burned as she listened to his confident footfalls approach her.

Her heart nearly stopped when she felt his presence

behind her. She need not look to know that he was very close.

"May I offer my assistance?" His voice was low and thick with some emotion. Violet swore she felt a whisper of his breath against her ear.

She gathered herself as best she could but could only respond while keeping her hands busy wiping at the end table that did not need any more wiping. "Thank you, Captain, but I can assure you I can manage on my own. I carry tea trays many times a day."

"Of course you do." The captain seemed to realize the silliness of his offer and gave an embarrassed smile.

Violet's heart sank as she wondered if her words had come off harsher than she'd intended and she immediately sought to correct her mistake.

"As I watch you with Master Neil, I can't help feeling that you will make a great family man one day."

Violet realized what she'd said the instant the words left her mouth and her hands froze over the tray handles. Her eyes went so wide she thought they might pop out of her head. She had only intended to soothe any injury she'd accidentally caused. She had not at all mean to admit that she paid particular attention to the captain or that she had imagined him with a family of his own.

Her heart froze and then hammered and then froze and then hammered again as she awaited Captain Jessup's response. But none came for several long moments. Violet's feelings must have been shockingly obvious now, or she had offended the captain by her unintentional admission.

Holding her breath, Violet dared to look up at Captain Jessup, her hands still poised over the tray, ready to grab it and dash out of the room.

But she did not see shock or offense or embarrassment or pity on his face.

He stared at her with an intensity that stopped her heart again. She had seen this look in his eyes before.

*Longing.*

The captain's fingertips came to rest against the back of Violet's hand. The touch sent a thrill all the way up Violet's arm and into her chest, restarting her heart.

He bent his head closer and whispered, "In truth, I never saw a family in my future for many reasons. Perhaps I only needed to meet the right one, find the right reason."

Captain Jessup's mouth came down to meet Violet's, his soft lips pressing against hers for a thrilling, breathtaking, perfect moment.

Instead of thudding in her chest as it had done anytime the captain was near either physically or in her thoughts, Violet's heart now settled into an easy, familiar rhythm. A rhythm that felt right.

Even as the captain pulled away, Violet could not believe that she had just been kissed. By Captain Jessup no less—the man who had occupied so much of her mind in these past few months. The man who had started as a stranger and had slowly transformed into something of a friend and now this. Whatever this meant.

Violet had not realized how badly she'd yearned for this experience until it was right in front of her. Not just being kissed, but being kissed by this lighthearted, energetic, handsome captain who had slowly crept into her heart despite her best attempts to guard it.

She had not expected that she could produce such feelings in someone else. Especially not someone who was also clearly guarding his own heart.

They stood staring at each other for several long moments. Violet wished she could stand here for the rest of time taking in the captain's usually rugged features now turned soft by the atmosphere between them.

And best of all, his eyes drank her in as if she were just the thing his lonely soul had been looking for. Violet could see in his eyes that he would never tire of drinking her in, of seeing her for who she really was.

In those moments of heartfelt silence with the captain holding her hands in his, Violet could see a different future. His face conveyed possibilities she had long since written away as above her station in life. Right now, nothing else mattered but what they might become.

"May I call you Violet from now on?" the captain asked, leaning his head down again so their foreheads almost touched.

"That would be lovely...Owen," Violet whispered. The name felt blissfully fresh as it slipped out of her mouth.

Owen grinned, his eyes wrinkling at the corners as Violet had seen so often and had come to adore.

"I am so very glad you think so, Violet."

As he tilted his head to the side to kiss her again, the sound of footsteps in the hall jolted Violet harshly back to reality. She pulled her hands away just in time for one of the footmen to appear at the door.

"Ah, Miss Davies. Lady Neil said I might find you here. She requires your assistance in her dressing room. Urgently." The footman gave Violet her orders in a perfectly professional tone. If he thought there was anything odd about Violet standing so very close to one of the guests, he did not indicate it.

"Yes, I'll be right there," Violet responded with as much professionalism as she could muster in this awkward moment. The footman nodded briskly and left the room.

"I'm so sorry, Owen, but I must go," Violet apologized, fearing that she'd ruined their moment.

But Owen simply smiled understandingly. "There is nothing to apologize for. I understand you have your duties.

Come find me again when you have a free moment. I'll be waiting."

Filled with relief, Violet quickly took his hand and pulled him down so she could plant a kiss on his cheek.

She hurried out of the room but turned just in time to see the captain rooted to his spot, eyes wide and a hand on his cheek where her lips had just been.

Violet floated down the hallway on clouds of bliss. For the first time she could remember, she hoped she would be finished with her duties soon.

Owen was waiting for her.

# CHAPTER 12

$O$wen turned his horse back toward the path he had left behind some time ago on his morning ride, favoring the expansive grassy paddock.

He looked around at the landscape with its hills in the distance and well-kept copse of trees that would be green again in a few months' time.

It all looked so familiar, he realized. Owen did not know when he'd begun to feel so comfortable at Gatherford Park.

Despite the sunshine blazing in the sky melting away last night's dusting of snow, Owen's heart sank with each step that brought him closer to the grand house. The world seemed cold—colder than it usually seemed even to Owen.

As he guided the horse toward the stables at the back of the Neil family's home, Owen craned his neck up to look at the many windows that adorned the walls. He wondered if Violet was behind one of them now. He wondered if she ever paused her work to look out the window for him.

Days had passed since their kiss in the drawing room. At first Owen accepted that Violet was busy. Even before that incident, he had hardly seen her. She was always running about for Lady Neil who needed extra assistance after delivering the baby.

But the hours passed and Violet had not come to look for him—and barely acknowledged him when they were in the same room as she brought tea or towels or came to take the baroness away for another change of dress.

He couldn't help wondering if she perhaps avoided him for some reason. But he could not think why. She had seemed so happy when he'd kissed her. And she'd promised to come back to him. He had said that he would wait and still he waited.

Owen sighed as he dismounted and led his horse to the stables, waving away a groom who offered to take the reins from him.

He had no right to complain. In truth, despite their kiss and their reciprocal feelings, Owen knew he still had no claim on Violet's attention.

Her time, of course, belonged to the Neil family first and foremost.

He knew he should not have put Violet in such a situation. They had nearly been caught by another servant which would have caused gossip among the servants, regardless of whether or not the situation had been contrived by her mistress to give them a moment alone.

But Violet devoted herself to her work so wholeheartedly. Just as Owen devoted himself to king and country. His mind understood that but his heart argued.

Perhaps all Owen had done was open them both up to complications.

Yet he could not bring himself to regret it. It had been too perfect. It had been too right.

As Owen brushed down his horse, he thought back to the few times he had managed to glimpse Violet. She had been busy working every time. He saw her rushing up the stairs with a small trinket that jingled as she went. He saw her in the library as he passed by, walking in circles beside Lady Neil and watching her like a hawk for any signs of discomfort. He saw her returning to the servants' area with a large lumpy blanket bundled in her arms and a grimace on her face, no doubt heading to the laundry with another batch of soiled clothes.

He had been privileged to spend some time with her in the drawing room but she remained by Lady Neil's side, sometimes offering to hold the child to give her mistress's arms some relief. She always looked so very happy to hold the tiny fellow.

Though Owen knew Violet must be exhausted from her extra duties, he could not deny that she looked more determined than ever to do an excellent job. And she looked as though she enjoyed it. She had an easy relationship with both her master and mistress and she seemed pleased to be able to help in whatever way she could, awkwardly accepting their ardent thanks.

Just like Owen.

"What shall I do about this, old chap?" Owen asked his horse, maneuvering himself to look into the large, intelligent eye on the side of its head. "It seems our similarities could cause some problems if we don't get ahead of this soon."

Owen patted the great beast on its muscular neck as a goodbye and heading through the stables toward the house. He missed Violet. There could be no doubt on that front. But he certainly admired her dedication to her duties. It had been one of the first things he noticed about her, one of the first things that drew him to her.

If anyone could understand Owen's deep-seated call to serve, it was Violet.

And if anyone could understand Violet's dedication to her work, it was Owen.

He went straight for the stairs after entering the house to change out of his outerwear in his guest chambers. He was halfway up when light footsteps coming down piqued his interest. It could have been anyone in the house but Owen felt that he knew those particular footsteps. He'd strained his ears to hear them down hallways and over plush carpets often enough.

Owen looked up and found his intuition confirmed. Violet rushed down the stairs, her head bent low over some fabric in her hands—something to be washed or mended surely.

She concentrated so deeply on examining the fabric that she seemed not to notice Owen, squeezing herself as close to the railing as possible so as not to get in anyone's way.

Owen hoped that she would see him or sense him nearby but she still kept her gaze on her occupied hands, twisting and pinching at the cloth as her brows furrowed, searching for a solution to fix or improve it. When they finally came to the same step Owen acted quickly.

"Violet!" He called in a loud whisper as he put a hand on her elbow.

Flashbacks to a previous similar scene played in Owen's mind. The day he'd asked her for a carriage ride and she had hurriedly thrown him off. So much had changed since then. Yet he still felt so far from where he truly wanted to be.

Violet's head snapped up, her eyes wide with surprise. She likely had been so focused on her task that she would have been oblivious to the Prince himself coming up the stairs.

But following quickly on the footsteps of her surprise was happiness. Owen's heart melted at the look. She could not have been avoiding him. She wouldn't look at him so sweetly if she had been. Instinctively, Owen softened his grip on Violet's elbow so he held it gently as if he might be about to thread her arm through his and lead her out to a dance floor. Without thinking about it, Owen's thumb brushed over the fabric of her dress slowly.

"Violet, could we have some time together soon? Perhaps we can go out on horseback or in the carriage, just for a short while. I could come down to the servants' hall and have dinner with you," Owen suggested, a hint of desperation in his voice. He could not hide, to himself or to Violet, that he had missed her terribly and craved even just a few moments with her.

Violet fidgeted with the cloth in her hands and pulled her eyes from Owen's. She looked uncomfortable and nervous. Owen disliked causing her any discomfort but with each passing day he feared he might never see her again unless he found an opportunity to snatch a conversation with her.

"Cap—Owen...I'm terribly sorry but I have been so busy. I really can't spare any time right now. Her Ladyship is still in a delicate state and I must do my best to support her as she heals." Violet explained quietly, her eyes finding Owen's again. Now the surprise and happiness were both gone. In their place was regret and melancholy.

Owen pursed his lips together when he heard Violet nearly call him Captain Jessup again. They hadn't had the opportunity to use each other's Christian names again until this moment. When they had been in the same room Violet had been working and the Neil family or the lieutenant were always nearby. She must have grown used to calling him captain again.

"But please know that I do miss you..." She continued softly. She gave Owen another sweet smile that melted his heart yet again but sank it into his stomach at the same time. How silly that they should miss each other when they currently lived under the same roof.

Owen opened his mouth to speak, to tell her he missed

her so dearly, to beg for her time again. But before he could, Violet carefully pulled her arm out of Owen's grip.

"The family and Frank are in the drawing room with the little one. I'm to add this to my mending pile and bring up tea and a blanket for Her Ladyship." Violet gave him one last sad smile and continued down the stairs.

Owen watched her go and his heart sank deeper with every step that took her further away. His mind swirled with unpleasant thoughts.

He had considered the possibility that Violet could be avoiding him. Perhaps her affections for him weren't as strong as his own or perhaps he'd made her too uncomfortable with his forward actions in the drawing room that day.

But Owen did not believe that now. Violet could have a career on the stage if she had fabricated the flicker of happiness overtaken by gloom in her eyes. And she said she missed him. Surely Owen could hold onto that. Soon Lady Neil would be back to her old self and Violet would be allowed a little more free time again.

Owen could wait. He'd told Violet he would be waiting.

He took Violet's information, and what he suspected was her unspoken suggestion, and quickly made his way to his chambers to change and then joined everyone else in the drawing room.

His eyes immediately fell upon Lord and Lady Neil by the fire. The baron read a thick book, his eyes flying over the page as he rapidly absorbed the information as only a scholar like himself could do. Lady Neil sat next to him with her son in her arms. She smiled down at him as his tiny hand curled around her finger. And then there was Davies, napping away in a chair near the happy family, a newspaper folded up on his chest.

Owen paused before making his presence known so he could enjoy the pleasant picture for a moment, the corners of his lips pulling up in a bittersweet smile. Would any home of his ever have such a cozy scene?

With any luck, it would. Owen just had to wait.

He approached the empty chair next to his friend and settled himself down, slapping Davies on his good knee.

The lieutenant snorted awake and shook his head furiously. As soon as Davies's eyes landed on Owen he launched into a half-coherent tirade.

Owen and the Neils laughed at Davies's sleepy fury and he quickly calmed back down as his faculties returned.

"Jessup, you devil. You're lucky only my words went flying and not my fists this time." The lieutenant chuckled and gave Owen a slap on the shoulder.

"I daresay your fists do not concern me any more than your words. I was always the faster of the two of us, if I recall."

True to his statement, Owen quickly leaned back as Davies attempted to land another playful blow to Owen's arm.

Lady Neil laughed again, turning her face down as both her hands were occupied and could not provide her with discretion. "Thank you, friends, for always being so entertaining. I swear, I wouldn't ever need to go to the theater to see a farce as long as you two stay here."

Owen grinned. "As I've said before, my lady, I am always happy to help in any way I can." He gave an exaggerated bow of his head.

A shadow flitted across the corner of Owen's vision and suddenly Violet was at his side. He'd happened to choose the chair closest to the end table where she now set the tea tray down, a blanket draped over her arm.

Owen's chest swelled when he saw the smile she tried to hide and the humor in her eyes that she tried to replace with neutral professionalism. She must have been in the room long enough to enjoy a little of their farce. He wished she could have joined in as she had such a lovely laugh. But no matter. He just needed to wait a while longer and he could spend all his time finding new ways to make her laugh.

"Captain, how was your ride this morning?" Lord Neil asked as their merriment settled back down into a calm, amiable atmosphere.

"It was very peaceful, thank you. Your grounds are beautiful even in the middle of winter. I can only imagine how grand it must be when spring awakens."

Violet handed Owen a cup of tea and their fingers brushed against each other. It took everything Owen had not to toss the cup away and grasp her hand in his. But she slipped away before Owen could act on his mad impulse.

"No thank you, Violet." Lady Neil held up her hand to the cup Violet offered her. "But would you be a dear and hold Joseph while I play the pianoforte? It has been so terribly long since I've been able to practice comfortably."

Violet nodded and Owen could see the excitement ripple through her. She truly adored this little one and had grown quite comfortable caring for him when needed. Lady Neil placed the baby in Violet's outstretched arms and she gently accepted him, smiling as he snuggled himself against her body.

Lord Neil stood from his seat and took the blanket that Violet had laid across the arm of an empty chair. He followed his wife to the nearby instrument and draped it over her lap after she took her seat.

A dull pain shot through Owen's chest as he watched his hosts interact with such deep love and respect and friendship.

The way Lord Neil carefully placed the blanket over Lady Neil's lap, adjusting it until he was satisfied that it adequately warmed his wife. The way Lady Neil smiled up at the baron and took his hand in hers for a moment while whispering something to him. The way Lord Neil watched his wife with amazement and adoration as she stretched her fingers over the keys and went through a warmup exercise.

It all suddenly felt too overwhelming to Owen. It must have been so lovely to openly share their affection and love for each other, to be together every day without fear.

He looked over to Violet who walked up and down before the fire, whispering words of comfort to the little being in her arms, bouncing slightly as she walked to soothe him. Her eyes spoke louder than any words she could have said at that moment. Owen could see her contentment and her devotion.

Another dull pain pulsed through his entire body this time. He wanted that life for Violet. He wanted it badly. Though she may not admit it out loud or use her work or her past as an excuse, Owen knew that she wished for a family of her own—for a love like the one shared between Lord and Lady Neil, a love that could create a new beautiful life. A love that could keep her safe.

Though Owen had begun to hope that he could be the person who could give that life to Violet, he could not shake the apprehension in his stomach when he saw her so lovingly care for her mistress's son.

She was dedicated to this family. And Owen was dedicated to his country. He prayed to God every day that there would be no other wars to call him away from his home again. But he knew that if one did come, he would take up arms again and fight.

Seeing Violet happy and warm and safe with a precious little one in her arms reminded Owen that he would hate to leave a wife and child behind should that call ever come again. He had been extremely blessed to return home this time, mostly unscathed save for a few scars. The same may not be true the next time.

Even if Violet could accept this as a possibility, Owen was not sure that he could accept it and saddle her with that fear and possible heartbreak and a difficult, bleak future as a widow.

Owen's chest tightened as if squeezed by some cruel invisible hand. The huge drawing room suddenly shrank until the walls closed in on him and he could not draw a full breath.

The loving baron and baroness and the sweet, caring Violet and her tiny charge were magnified in his mind and Owen could not escape the longing that accompanied those images as well as their many potential disasters.

"I fear I have taken ill. Please excuse me," Owen announced abruptly, rising from his chair and striding through the room as quickly as possible without waiting for any response.

He rushed through the house in a daze, reeling from the mixture of emotions he had felt today, emotions that made his heart soar and then tore it down the next moment. He knew what he wanted—who he wanted—but his mind would not let go of the pitfalls of such an attachment and the reasons he'd built for years to avoid this very situation.

Owen closed the door on his bedchamber and leaned back against it. Perhaps solitude would do the trick and allow him to figure out these thoughts that whirled through his head, to compartmentalize them and observe them objectively.

But as Owen paced around his room, he realized that his thoughts would not be tamed so easily. Perhaps a nap would do the trick. His hand was on the service bell to ring for the valet to change him into sleeping clothes when a knock sounded at his door.

He sighed and walked back to the door, not sure who to

expect but knowing that he likely did not want to see or speak to whoever it was.

He was right. Davies stood at the door, breathing heavily and leaning against his crutch. Owen gritted his teeth. Company and conversation were the last things he wanted at the moment, the precise reason he'd left the drawing room in such a hurry.

"May I help you?" he asked, unable to hide the tinge of annoyance in his voice.

"Yes, you may. I am in terrible need of a chair. I don't remember you ever walking so fast, or perhaps my leg slows me down that much."

Owen took a closer look at his dearest friend and saw that he indeed looked exhausted. He'd exerted himself to check after Owen and he knew he should be grateful to have a friend who cared so much that he would hobble along on his still healing leg with an uncomfortable crutch as fast as he could manage.

Owen sighed again and pulled the door open further, taking Davies's free arm and guiding him to the nearest chair.

The lieutenant lowered himself down with Owen's help and groaned as soon as he felt the soft upholstery against his back. He took a few deep slow breaths and rubbed his knee above his bulky wooden cast.

Owen planted himself before his friend and crossed his arms defensively. While he appreciated Davies's effort, he still did not wish to have a drawn-out conversation. Especially not when Owen suspected that his friend had seen through his excuse of illness.

"What else can I help you with, Davies, now that I have provided the chair?"

Davies sat up a bit straighter and fixed Owen with a suspicious expression. "Something is off about you. Why did you leave the drawing room in such a rush? What truly ails you?"

Owen glanced about the well-furnished and comfortable room that had been his own these past few months, avoiding the lieutenant's curious eyes. He frowned as he considered lying and claiming some sort of sudden stomach pain or headache.

But Owen knew this would not do. He and Davies had been through hell together and he was his closest friend. They had seen each other in any number of uncomfortable, embarrassing, and emotionally and physically painful situations. And Owen knew that Davies only asked those questions to give Owen the opportunity to come clean himself. There was no use lying to him now.

Owen sat heavily on his bed, the mattress creaking under his weight. He leaned his forearms on the tops of his thighs and folded his hands together, his head sinking between his shoulders as if the weight of his feelings had begun to slowly crush his body in on itself.

"I know it will come as no surprise to you, but I have developed a very strong attachment to Violet." His voice was quiet but it carried through the room and seemed to bounce off every wall back at Owen.

He glanced up to see Davies raise his eyebrows at the mention of his sister's given name but he did not interrupt.

"I believe she has developed an attachment to me as well. I know for most this would be the end of the story. There would be the proposal and then the wedding and then a lifetime of happiness.

"The solution seems so simple when I think of it in those terms. If we both care for each other, what more can there be? But it is not so simple for me. Or for her.

"I know she has worked hard for her position here and she loves the family she serves and the work she does. But it can be difficult for servants who marry to keep their positions. I do not think Lady Neil would turn Violet away by any means, but she would have to divide her time between her duties to two families. I would hate to dull the sense of pride and fulfillment she takes from the work she does and add more stress for her.

"And I also cannot give up my own sense of duty to my country. I cannot risk putting her and any future children in a terrible position should something happen to me if another war comes. I only want her to be happy. She has been through so much already in her young life and she has managed to maintain her kindness and determination through it all. I could not bear to be the cause of more worry and suffering for her."

Owen shook his head after he finished his speech, the weight of his words causing his shoulders to sag. The two men sat in silence for a few moments as they both absorbed Owen's words.

"Well," Davies began, taking a pause to formulate his next words. "Firstly, I would like you to know that I wholeheartedly approve of a relationship between you and my dear sister. I had not considered it in the least when we first arrived but I think the idea came to me much sooner than it came to either of you. But that is not uncommon for people in love. So you need not worry on that count."

Owen glanced up at his friend nervously. He had not mentioned love exactly.

"There is no need to deny, nor state it explicitly. Everything you said speaks of love. And I do agree that Violet feels the same about you though she has not come out and said it to me either. I fear we have not come to that point in our new relationship yet, or perhaps she is just shy.

"As I have said before, my good man, I understand your concerns. But you have already valiantly served your country. There is no way to know if another war will come. But perhaps it is not such a bad idea to sell your commission if you are serious about courting my sister. You are in half retirement now and I know how much it means to you to serve your country. But you have done your part a million times over I would say.

"And should you decide to keep your commission and get called up again, I am sure Violet would be well aware of the risk she would take on in making a match with you. And I daresay she would support you every step of the way. I do not wish to see my sister hurt any more than you do but if I have learned anything about her in these past few months it is that she possesses an incredible strength."

Owen nodded, pondering his friend's words. He knew what Davies said was true. Perhaps selling his commission was not such a terrible idea. He'd very briefly considered it at different points since he realized his affection for Violet but he had banished the thought as the coward's way out. But the lieutenant did have a point that perhaps Owen could be satisfied with the service he'd already provided.

And he certainly knew that Violet was a brave, willful young woman who had survived some of the most awful circumstances life could throw at a person. Perhaps he had not given that quality enough credit.

"Here's an idea, Jessup. Why don't you think of some gift or gesture to present to Violet that will show her you are serious in pursuing her, that will show her what a life with you could be like," Frank suggested.

Owen nodded slowly and ran his mind through various options that did not include an outright proposal. Yet. He wanted to be sure that they both agreed on what kind of life they wanted and if it would be worth the risks before taking the next step.

"Ah!" He sat straight up as the thought hit him like lightning. "Thank you, Davies," Owen cried out as he sprung off the bed and headed for the door. "You are a genius! Sometimes."

He could hear Davies laughing as he sped down the hall to find Lord Neil.

# CHAPTER 13

*T*he delicate glass bottles clinked as Violet wiped them down and rearranged them on Lady Neil's vanity. She always stayed behind in the dressing room after Lady Neil went down to breakfast to tidy up.

Exhaustion made her limbs and eyelids heavy. Violet did not begrudge her mistress for the extra help she required, but she sincerely hoped that she could soon return to her regular schedule. Many of her continuous tasks had fallen behind.

And she missed Owen dreadfully.

"Oh, what could it hurt?" Violet asked herself quietly as she allowed the weight of her tiredness and gloom to sink her aching body into Lady Neil's chair. She had never done such a thing before, knowing how impudent it was to commandeer any of her mistress's belongings as if they were her own unless specifically invited to do so. But surely just this once couldn't hurt. She was so very, very tired. She rested her elbows on the vanity and dropped her face into her hands for a few moments.

But the sudden creak of the door opening caused Violet

to jump up immediately, knocking her knees against the vanity in the process and nearly toppling several of the bottles sitting nearest the edge. She scrambled to right them before they spilled or rolled to the ground.

Her heart thundered and the exhaustion fled her body as a surge of adrenaline rushed through her. She turned to the door, expecting to see Lady Neil's shocked expression upon finding her maid taking a rest that had not been granted. Perhaps she had forgotten something or wished to send Violet on a different errand.

Instead, her eyes beheld an even worse sight. Lord Neil stood in the doorway, eyeing her curiously. Violet would have been embarrassed beyond belief to have been discovered in a state of repose by her mistress though she knew she likely would not have suffered any harsh punishments or scoldings. But it injured Violet's pride to give even the impression of laziness.

Now she was utterly mortified to have the master of the house walk in on her sitting at his wife's vanity as if she had the right to do so.

"L-Lord Neil!" Violet stuttered, her sudden anxiety hiking her normally light voice into an even higher pitch. "Is everything alright? Is Her Ladyship well?"

"Yes, she is perfectly fine." The baron nodded as the surprise left his face, replaced by his usual unintentionally solemn expression. "I have actually come to speak with you for a moment. I know you usually stay behind here after Her Ladyship comes down for breakfast."

Violet's breath caught in her throat, all her senses on high alert. It was exceedingly strange that Lord Neil should seek her out. After all, the last time he had done so resulted in her brother's return to her life.

She took a few anxious steps toward the baron. "How may I be of service, my lord?"

Suddenly Lord Neil's face melted into a reassuring and pleased smile. Violet almost reeled back in shock. She could not fathom why Lord Neil would look at her so. In fact, she was rather surprised that he would look at her with any sort of pleasantness after finding her shirking her duties.

"There is no need to worry. The news is good. I would be happy to speak to my publisher if you are serious about publishing your poetry. Once I have read some samples, of course. I must confess I did not realize you would be interested in taking such a path but the idea of having another writer in the house, and a published one at that, very much excites me. I cannot promise success, however, but I think you may find a very nice readership in time. Her Ladyship and I fully support your endeavor."

Violet's head swirled as Lord Neil rambled on. In fact, this was the most the baron had ever spoken directly to her and possibly the most she had ever heard him speak in one go. Excitement gleamed in his eyes as he delivered this "good news" to Violet but she could not bring herself to see it as such.

Despite her shock, Violet did not forget her manners. "I appreciate that very much, my lord. But may I ask who gave you this information?"

"Captain Jessup. He sought me out yesterday afternoon after he recovered from his illness. He said you had shared your poetry with him and expressed interest in sharing it with a wider audience. He knows I have connections in the publishing industry—though he still does not know I publish myself and I would ask that it remains that way—and he asked if I might mention your work and help your dream along."

"My dream..." Violet mumbled as she turned the baron's words over in her mind. She slipped into shocked silence but her confusion quickly morphed into anger.

"I apologize, my lord, but I fear I may have given Captain Jessup the wrong impression. I have no such desires. I simply like to write a little from time to time. I have no such dream," she said with a strained smile.

Lord Neil's brow furrowed at her statement. "Are you quite sure? If you are shy about sharing your work you need not be. The captain has vouched for your talent. And I know myself how nerve-wracking it can be to show your work to someone else the first few times."

"I am very sure, my lord. The captain is simply mistaken. But I do appreciate his efforts and your willingness to help." Violet nodded with as much grace as she could muster as she fought the annoyance broiling in her stomach.

"Very well. You are always welcome to seek me out should you change your mind." Lord Neil offered a disappointed smile and backed out of the room, closing the door behind him.

Violet took a few steadying breaths and tried to push the conversation out of her mind. She turned her attention back to her work, tidying the room and laying out a walking dress for Lady Neil's first afternoon walk with Master Neil.

Soon she realized that she had pulled out an evening dress rather than a walking dress and shook her head. This would not do. She was too frustrated by this incident to simply ignore it. It refused to be pushed to the back of her mind.

Her next best option was to face it head on. Violet replaced the incorrect dress and stood before the large closet, staring into the expanse of dresses of all different types of fabrics and colors and embellishments. But she did not truly see them.

Instead she saw Owen lying to Lord Neil about her imaginary desire to publish her poetry. Perhaps lying was too strong a word. But he had certainly exaggerated whatever information he'd misinterpreted from their conversations.

Violet could not understand why he would say such a thing to the baron in secret. She had never told him she wanted to publish. To her knowledge she had never even hinted at such an inclination.

She rubbed at her temples as she tried to piece together Owen's logic but all her attempts failed. She could only come upon one explanation.

Owen had always taken risks his whole life—from his decision to join the army and go straight into the heaviest battles to his high speed and high energy hobbies. Perhaps Owen felt that Violet needed to take more risks in her life. Perhaps, if she let him any closer, he would try to push her toward something she knew was not meant for her.

Owen took risks and lived a bold life. But that did not mean that Violet could do the same.

All Violet wished to do was live her quiet life without any disturbances or fanfare. That wish had already been complicated when Frank and Owen had turned up at the door of Gatherford Park. And it only became more complicated the longer they stayed.

She had not anticipated that she might fall in love with her brother's handsome, charming friend. That was the biggest complication of all. Clearly it all hindered Violet from doing her job, the thing that had been most important in her life since she became an orphan and lost her home, the thing that gave her security.

In love. Violet had hesitated to associate those words with her feelings for the captain. She wished that she did not feel so frustrated and despondent when she associated them now for the first time.

Violet may not have had much life experience, staying

mostly inside the homes she served in under the Richards family and now the Neil family.

But Violet was no fool. She knew enough of life to know that being in love did not guarantee compatibility or long-term happiness.

She trusted that Owen's intentions in asking Lord Neil to help her publish had not been malicious in any way. But surely if Owen knew Violet at all, he would have known that the last thing she needed was another distraction stealing her time and focus away from Lady Neil and her many duties in the house.

Violet hadn't had the time or energy to think of what would happen if the captain did ask for her hand. Surely she could not continue as she did now. How could she live separately from Lady Neil and come to the house every day to do her duties and then go to her own home that she would also have to manage? She and Owen would rarely see each other. And she would be too far away if Lady Neil had any emergencies.

In many ways, Violet felt that she owed Lady Neil her life.

It had been the baroness, after all, who had begged her parents to take her in. And the baroness had asked for Violet to be promoted to her personal maid when she began her London seasons and required more attention in dressing and toilette. She had even brought Violet with her when she married though she could have hired a new, more experienced maid who knew how to serve a real lady.

Though her heart longed for Owen, for the life of companionship and love she had never allowed herself to dream of before, Violet did not know if she could bring herself to forsake her mistress.

What she had told the baron was true. She did not have such dreams. She should not have such dreams. Especially when her dream tried to take her to places she had no right to go.

VIOLET BARELY SAW her needlework as thought after thought about Owen's interference in her life raced through her mind. She pulled the thread through the frayed hem listlessly. She would not be surprised if she had to take her seam ripper later to all the work she'd done during lunch. Yet another interference.

A sudden commotion by the entrance of the servants' hall startled Violet and she nearly pricked a finger when she jumped at the sound.

She paused and listened to the banging of doors and shuffling feet and a consistent heavy thud against the ground as someone approached.

"Truly, lieutenant, you need not come down here. The servants' hall is no place for a guest. Please do allow me to fetch her." Mrs. Baird's voice trailed back to Violet from the entryway.

Violet stood from her chair and carefully set the gown she'd been mending on the dining table. Frank burst into the servants' hall a moment later, walking as fast as he could on his crutch, an unsettled look in his eyes and a nearly crushed sheet of paper in his other hand.

"Frank! What has you looking so perplexed?" Violet cried out, surprised not only to see her brother in the servants' hall but to see him in such a shaken state. That was the only way she could describe his expression. Shaken.

He stumbled over his words, unable to string any coherent thought together. Instead he collapsed into a chair and waved the page at Violet, mumbling for her to read it.

Violet took the letter with trembling hands and

hammering heart. She could not guess what the letter might contain but she knew it must be something shocking to put her brother in such a bizarre mood.

She slowly sat in the chair next to Frank and began reading. Her eyes flew over the poorly written lines. The handwriting was difficult to read at times, as if the writer could not hold the pen steady.

The increasingly sick feeling in Violet's stomach told her that the safety she'd cultivated was being threatened once more.

Their oldest brother Samuel had succumbed to disease and passed away several months ago. The letter had been written to both Frank and Violet by their remaining brother, Charles.

A jarring mixture of astonishment, anger, and sadness flooded Violet's senses. She was dizzy with the words she'd just read as they swam through her mind.

Sam was gone. Charlie had tracked Frank down at Gatherford Park to deliver the news. But that was not all.

*Please, brother and sister, I know you have both done well for yourselves. If you could only provide me a modest allowance for a few months...*

Violet turned to Frank, her wide eyes filling with tears that had no definitive source. Even as they spilled down her cheeks she did not know if they were tears of sadness that one of her brothers had died or tears of rage that the other would immediately beg Frank for money after contacting him for the first time in years.

Frank sipped at a glass of water that Mrs. Baird must have brought for him. He breathed rapid and shallow, still processing the letter as well. Of course, Frank had spent much more of his life with Sam and Charlie than Violet had and they had treated each other as brothers.

"Frank...I am sorry to hear about Sam." Violet's voice cracked as she reached a hand out to comfort her brother.

Though he had often denounced all of their actions against Violet, she knew the news of one of their brother's deaths must take a toll on him.

"I must admit I am not sure how to feel right now. You know after I joined the army I lost contact with both of them. I can't say I ever expected to hear from them again for better or worse."

Frank rubbed a hand over his face. He suddenly seemed exhausted and aged.

"And Charlie is only a day's ride away?" Violet asked quietly.

She should not have been so surprised by this. If one brother managed to find her, surely anyone else would be able to. But Frank was a different matter. As far as she could tell from Charlie's letter, he hadn't changed much.

"That is what he says, yes. I'm shocked that he bothered to contact me after all this time..." Frank stared into the depths of his water glass and Violet instantly knew that he was afraid to look at her.

"Frank, you cannot mean that you will go to see him." The words felt disgusting in Violet's mouth as she said them but she could see from the way Frank flinched at the harshness in her voice that she was correct.

He looked at her with desperation in his eyes. "Violet, he sounds like he's in a bad way. He needs help.... And he's lost Sam now. You know those two were always thick as thieves."

Fury threatened to overtake Violet as she stared at her brother. She trembled with it, her heart beat with it, her tears flowed with it.

It took all her strength to hold herself together. She had been abused by her father and her brothers for years. Frank had done what she'd thought was impossible and had grown into a better man. He'd sought her out to apologize and put their future as a family in her hands.

Of course Violet did not wish any of her brothers harm and she had been saddened to read the news of Sam's passing. But Charlie wasted no time in his letter to pester Frank for money. He had confessed that he and Sam had never found steady work and had bounced from village inn to village inn for the past twelve years. And now that Sam—who had always been the craftier of the two—was gone, Charlie had slipped deeper into poverty.

And now he tried to force his way into her life again. And Frank, her long-lost brother whom she'd worked so hard to forgive and accept again, seemed to see no problem with this.

"They were thieves indeed, Frank. They helped steal the joy and love I should have had in my childhood. And I'm sure they have stolen much else since. And yet you will go to him, after everything he put me through?"

The words slipped through Violet's clenched teeth. She feared that if she opened her mouth any further all she would be able to do was scream.

Frank blanched and his eyes darted about uncomfortably. He seemed torn as he took a moment to decide what he would say.

"Yes. I think I will go to him."

Violet took a deep shuddering breath. "Frank, I implore you to burn this letter and leave that man to wither away wherever he has landed himself. He has only reestablished contact with us now because he needs financial help. If he'd had any money to sustain himself I doubt he would have written at all, even to tell us about Sam."

Frank gave an exasperated sigh and dragged a hand down his face again. "I simply cannot say I am opposed to reconnecting with him. That has been my mission these past few months since I've been here, in the past year that I searched for you. Family and forgiveness has been my mission. Surely you can understand that better than anyone."

Violet's anger could no longer be controlled. She stood so quickly from her seat that the chair toppled backwards. Frank jumped at the sudden movement, staring at Violet in shock.

"How dare you suggest there is anything even remotely similar to these situations? I did nothing wrong. I was just a child and yet you all put the blame on me for causing Mother's death and sinking our family into ruin. You've come here to ask my forgiveness for the part you played and I granted it. But you were never the instigator or the worst offender. I know that now. You were barely more than a child yourself.

"But Sam and Charlie were relentless. They knew well enough that what they and Father did was horrid. And now he seeks to take advantage of us to avoid taking responsibility for the poor choices he and Sam made.

"Can you so easily forgive that? Forgive the years of my misery he participated in? I thought you came here because you realized what happened in our family and what you all did was wrong. Are you truly going to forgive someone who did not even write a single word of remorse?

"Perhaps you have forgotten in your time here, but I am under no obligation to forgive anyone after what I've been through. And I cannot fathom that you would say you care for me and regret our past in one breath yet run back to Charlie the moment he comes calling looking for money as if it can all be swept under the rug so easily."

Violet's voice echoed against the stone walls as she unleashed her pain and fury upon her brother. Her tears streamed down her cheeks in hot angry rivers but she did not care who heard or who saw this appalling scene. Frank's eyes were wide as he simply sat and watched her tirade.

Violet's energy was nearly spent. She needed to escape.

"If you think we will ever be a happy little family again you are sorely mistaken." Her voice dropped to a near whisper, cold and resolved. She turned on her heel and rushed out of the servants' hall.

"Violet!" She heard Frank try to call after her but she was too fast, propelled by the final burst of her outraged strength.

She thundered up the stairs, oblivious to the other servants and anyone else who passed her by. She could hardly think about manners at a time like this and she had not a care in the world if anyone thought her disgraceful or discourteous.

Once back to her room, Violet slammed the door shut and leaned her back against the hard wood. Her lungs gasped for breath from her wild dash through the house and from the shock of all this terrible news.

As her senses slowly came back to her, Violet realized that she still held the letter in her hand. She brought it closer to her face and her eyes wandered over the various offensive phrases written in Charlie's shaky, most likely drunken, handwriting.

Violet's stomach churned as she read over his one line about Sam's death and all the following lines about his pathetic position.

She felt utterly confident that the man would never have attempted to find her or Frank unless he thought he could get money from them. He had discovered somehow that Frank was a lieutenant now, and even lieutenants in half-retirement received a comfortable enough payment—and that Violet had secured a position in a large, wealthy house though even a lady's maid did not often have any income to spare.

But perhaps this development would have been easier to bear had it not been for her brother's reaction.

Violet still could not believe that Frank would be so

willing to meet with someone who had caused her so much pain for so many years. He even wished to help him despite every indication that he was being used.

The sickening realization nearly knocked Violet to the floor. She had been betrayed by her family once again—by someone who had claimed to regret his actions and the suffering she'd gone through. Violet could see it no other way. If Frank went back to Charlie and gave him what he wanted it must mean that he still sided with that horrid man.

Violet had been cast aside yet again. She thought she'd escaped the cycle long ago, when she started life as a maid. Frank reappearing in her life had shaken her deeply and she realized that perhaps her past could not be escaped so easily. But she slowly learned to trust Frank again and she thought she'd escaped the cycle again, that she could learn to forgive and offer her brother a place in her life.

But she had not escaped the cycle. It would be impossible to escape, she realized. This was Violet's fate—forever being chased by the nightmare that haunted her.

If Violet could not escape this cycle from her past, how could Violet be sure that she would escape it through her future? How could Violet be sure that any man she married would not mistreat and abandon her and their children? Or perhaps her children would turn into tyrants as well.

No matter how hard Violet tried to build her life, her past would find her and crumble it again. She could not let this cycle repeat. She could not suffer it again or allow another generation to suffer it.

A warm tear landed on Violet's hand and brought her attention back to the cursed letter she still gripped in her hand. The words were blotchy in several places from where her tears had made the ink run.

Another wave of anger swept through her and she tore the letter into shreds.

# CHAPTER 14

Owen closed the heavy double doors behind him, shutting out the wind that had picked up toward the end of his afternoon ride. He shivered and brushed a few flakes of snow off his coat.

A rapid clacking of shoes against the polished wood floor caught Owen's attention. He walked a few steps further into the back foyer and a smile spread across his face when he saw Violet coming toward him. She had been busy with work again so they hadn't had a real word between them since he'd caught her on the staircase. And he was pleased to see that she seemed eager to approach him.

But his smile quickly disappeared when she came closer and he saw the ice in her eyes. She looked more tired than Owen had ever seen her.

Owen made a note to himself to speak with Lady Neil soon about returning her duties to their usual load or asking one of the other maids to pick up extra tasks.

Of course, Owen knew that the news of her other brothers must weigh heavily upon her as well. He'd heard it from Frank and if the news affected Frank this deeply, he could only imagine how it affected Violet. But she had continued her work and Owen hadn't had a chance to speak with her about it yet and offer his comfort.

"Violet, I'm so very happy to see you," Owen said cheerfully when Violet stood before him. He hoped to bring a smile to her face or at the very least let her know that he still thought of her constantly and missed her dearly.

A chill swept over Owen and for a moment he thought that someone had snuck behind him and opened the doors again. But this chill was even colder than the wind outside. It came from Violet.

His attempt at cheer quickly fell away. "I'm terribly sorry to hear about your—"

"Enough. I do not wish to speak of that." Violet interrupted him with a sharpness Owen had never heard in her voice before. It took him aback and sank his heart. He had hoped that Violet would see him as someone she could confide in.

"I understand the situation may be too raw to speak of right now but I am here to listen whenever you are ready. Always."

Anger twitched over Violet's face. It seemed that her anger was not directed toward the news about her two eldest brothers but rather toward Owen himself.

"I am sorry, Owen, but I do not feel it is prudent to speak to you about anything, including my family, because I cannot trust what you will do with that information," she spat, her voice quiet and cold but conveying her displeasure loudly enough.

Owen was so surprised that he took a step back. Confusion rippled through him. "I'm sorry, Violet, but I do not understand. What have I done wrong?"

"You told His Lordship that I wished to publish my poetry."

A small frown tugged at Owen's mouth. "I thought you would have been happy with my gesture of encouragement. I thought I was doing something good for you."

Violet scoffed and shook her head. "Maybe you don't know me as well as you thought. If you had, you would have known that publishing is the last thing I want and that I would not appreciate you discussing such matters with His Lordship behind my back."

Owen's head spun from the venom in her voice, but he could not let this go by without defending himself. His pride bristled and he stood straighter as he spoke.

"I am sorry you feel that way, Violet, but I assure you my intentions were good. I think you need a bit of a push sometimes. You have so much talent and you should pursue that which makes you happy. I mean truly happy. I fear that if I don't encourage you, you may not take action to seek a better life."

He tried to keep his voice as calm and rational as possible, but he could feel the hurt bubbling up and threatening to spill over.

Violet simply stared at him, her expression nearly blank as she processed his words. Owen immediately knew that he had said something even worse and almost wished her anger would return. Anything would be better than the barely interested way she looked at him now.

"You have no right to assume what is best for my life or what will make me happy. Serving this family is my true purpose in life. It may not seem very noble to you but I am honored to have this position and do this work that you seem to think is so beneath my dignity. I do not need to be pushed in any direction by anyone. I've made my choices in life and I am proud of them. What I need is to be left alone."

Her quiet, calm words ripped through Owen's chest but

she turned on her heel and walked away before he could fathom a response.

His head still spun as he watched her leave, unable to do anything but stand in his spot as he replayed the scene in his mind.

OWEN WAS NOT much in the mood for company after his confrontation with Violet so he had kept to himself in his guest room once he'd snapped out of his confused daze long enough to drag himself upstairs.

He'd sat on his bed, in the chair, stood by the window, and paced all around the room. His nervous energy cried out to be released with a walk, a run, a gallop, a boxing match, a hunt, anything but being trapped indoors. But he did not wish to risk running into anyone else lest his thoughts betray him. And he certainly did not wish to run into Violet until he was ready.

The more he'd thought about her words, the more Owen understood his error. While he still felt correct in his assessment that Violet held herself back, Owen could see that he had gone about encouraging her the wrong way and he certainly hadn't helped matters with his word choice.

Finally, Owen's anxiety built up so fiercely that he felt he might burst if he stayed in his room a moment longer. He knew Violet likely did not wish to see him or speak to him right now, but he could not stand to leave them in this state.

He stormed out of his room and through the house straight to the servants' hall. Mrs. Baird, the kind housekeeper, was just on her way back to the servants' hall as well and she looked surprised to see Owen walking her way with such determination.

"Captain Jessup, there is hardly any need for you to come

down here. Surely I can have a footman or maid bring you whatever it is you require," she explained, eyeing him curiously.

"Thank you, Mrs. Baird, but I need to speak with Violet right away. I thought I might look for her here."

The housekeeper sighed, her eyebrows drawn up in exasperated surprise. "That's twice in one day our honored guests have come to the servants' hall looking for Violet. Come this way, Captain."

Owen followed her into the servants' hall and immediately spied Violet sitting by the fire on the far wall. She had her small notebook in her lap and she frowned down at the page, her eyes narrowed as she methodically placed each word.

He paused for a moment to enjoy the scene, the turmoil in his heart easing just a bit. He almost did not want to disturb her but he knew he must say his part. After that he would leave her alone as she wished. Owen stepped closer and coughed.

Violet looked up in surprise and quickly hid her book when she saw Owen.

"Why have you come down here? You could summon me just like anyone else."

"But I am not just anyone else, am I? I needed to see you right away. I've been thinking all afternoon about our...discussion earlier today. It does not sit well with me and I seek to resolve it."

Violet bit her lip but nodded and stood before Owen. He could see that she guarded herself when she looked at him and his heart sank. He had never meant to make her feel as though she needed to protect herself around him. In fact, he'd tried to do the exact opposite over the past few months. And all it took was a few poorly chosen sentences to build those barriers back up.

But even worse, Owen could see the hurt in her eyes that she tried but failed to hide. He may not fully understand her reservations, but he knew he'd caused her pain and that could never be acceptable.

Owen sighed and this time chose the words he'd carefully planned in his head while he'd paced about his room all afternoon.

"Firstly, I want you to know that I am terribly sorry for the position you and the lieutenant have been put in with this news of your other brothers. I can't imagine how shocking and distressing it must be. You have all my support and prayers."

Violet's jaw clenched when he mentioned her brothers and her eyes turned dark. Owen did not wish to push her to speak of it if it would distress her too much.

And in any case, Owen had come to the conclusion that perhaps he should not be the one she should confide in after all.

"Now I would like to sincerely apologize for speaking to Lord Neil about your poetry without your permission or knowledge. I truly did not think it would upset you in this way but after taking some time to consider it, I now see your point. However..."

Owen paused as he pondered the best way to phrase this next part. He could see Violet bristle in anticipation of what he would say.

"I see that I went about the situation the wrong way, but I do believe you may not be allowing yourself to live to your full potential. You see...I've seen so many dreams taken away long before their time. I simply don't want you to have any regrets."

Owen watched Violet's reaction as he spoke and gladly noticed her soften as she contemplated his words.

"I appreciate your concern, Owen. But I urge you to

understand that I have accepted my lot in life. I am content here, truly." She gave a small but unconvincing smile.

Owen stared into her eyes for a long moment, reading deeply into the hesitation, regret, and melancholy he saw there.

Violet blushed under his gaze and looked away. "Why do you stare at me so intently?"

"For as many times as I've heard you say that you are grateful for your position, that you are proud to serve the family, that Lady Neil is a wonderful mistress, all things I know to be true...I have never heard you once describe yourself as happy."

Violet's green eyes widened in shock. Perhaps she had not realized it for herself or perhaps she had simply never allowed herself to realize it. But before she could try to explain it away, Owen had one last thing he needed to say.

"Remember, Violet. Happiness is worth fighting for."

Owen bowed his head and turned his back to Violet. As he walked out of the servants' hall, leaving her with those thoughts, Owen's heart did not feel any better as he'd hoped it would.

Owen had said more than he'd intended and his words carried a realization for himself as well.

Happiness was worth fighting for. He knew this in his bones. He served his country so that every English man, woman, and child could have their chance at happiness.

And he would fight for Violet's happiness with all his power. Even if it meant he would have to remove himself from her side to secure her long-term happiness.

He'd already hurt her once even with his best intentions. He couldn't risk the possibility of causing her worse pain in the future.

## CHAPTER 15

*T*he curl fell out as Violet's pin failed to hold it up yet again. She sighed and took the same soft strand of hair, winding it around her finger before trying again.

A million pieces from yesterday's events raced through Violet's mind, one chasing after another without giving her any reprieve. The same had happened all through the night. She had no idea how she still stood with any energy in her body.

"Violet, please stop."

Violet started at the sound of Lady Neil's voice and she dropped the curl once more. She glanced into the mirror and saw the baroness's eyes examining her reflection, blue eyes meeting green eyes through the glass.

"I'm terribly sorry, my lady. I don't know what is wrong with these dreadful fingers today." Violet picked up the same strand of hair she'd been working and fumbled to put it right.

"It's quite alright, Violet. But please stop for a moment. I have heard the news so I know there is something weighing on your mind."

Violet let Lady Neil's hair dangle over her shoulder. She gave a small nod. Surely everyone in the house must know by now that her eldest brother was dead and the other had been reduced to an impenitent beggar. But Lady Neil could not know of the other situation that troubled Violet.

The baroness's head tilted to the side and she looked at Violet curiously through the mirror. "Perhaps there is more than one something—or someone—weighing on your mind."

Violet flushed and lowered her head. She may have enough energy to stand and attempt to do her work but she did not have enough energy to fight.

"I hoped that you could run into town today and pick up a few items for me. There is a special package waiting in the bookshop that I had special ordered for Lord Neil's birthday. I trust you will retrieve it and deliver it to me with the utmost discretion. And I think a little fresh air will do you some good."

Lady Neil smiled kindly at Violet and Violet found herself happily agreeing. Some time outside of the house and away from the walls that enclosed her troubles would be welcome indeed. And the weather had been uncommonly nice for this time of year.

It was still cold with dustings of snow but many days were pleasant enough to be outside as long as one properly bundled themselves. The thought of the outing enabled Violet's tired body to resume her task and finally complete it.

"Thank you, Violet. You may go get yourself ready now. I can manage the rest myself." Lady Neil's elegant fingers sifted through one of the small plates on her vanity that held brooches and rings and decorative hairpins, searching for a complimentary piece to her dress and hair.

Violet curtseyed and made her way to the door of the

dressing room. But just as she opened it to exit through Lady Neil's bedchamber, her mistress's voice called out to her again.

"Oh and Violet, a footman and Captain Jessup will be waiting for you with the carriage."

Violet paused in the doorway and look over her shoulder at Lady Neil. The baroness sat at her vanity, her eyes locked on Violet through the mirror, but her expression remained unreadable.

For a shocking moment Violet almost protested. But when Lady Neil tilted her head as if waiting for Violet's argument, she knew she must accept this order just like any other.

With a tight smile, Violet nodded and left the room.

VIOLET HAD ALWAYS ENJOYED the small town just outside of Gatherford Park's grand estate. She made her way here a few times a month depending on Lady Neil's needs. The friendly townspeople had welcomed the new mistress of Gatherford Park—and Violet—with joy.

She was nearly thrilled to see it today as the carriage finally came to the town entrance and Violet's eyes drifted over the old stone buildings where she purchased fabrics, trimmings, cosmetics, stationary, and the occasional candy for Lady Neil.

As soon as the horses came to a standstill Violet lowered herself out of the carriage. She could not stand to sit next to Owen a moment longer with nothing but silence and an uncomfortable air between them.

She wanted everything between them to return to how they had been just the day before yesterday. Before Lord Neil suggested she publish her poetry, before Frank had received that letter from Charlie, before Owen had told her that she lived a small, safe life.

But Violet did not know if anything could ever return to its former state, no matter how badly she wished it.

For now, she had to get through this outing with everything on her list and without crumbling under the pressure of everything going sour in her life all at once.

"The walkways are icy, Miss Davies. You should have waited for me to help you down." Owen came around to her side of the carriage after securing the horses to a post. She could hear the concern under his voice beneath the veneer of distant civility.

"Thank you, Captain Jessup, but I am quite alright. I know how to stand on my own two legs."

Violet turned to head down the street to their first destination, but not before she saw Owen's small frown and Andrew's wide-eyed surprise. It must have seemed exceedingly unusual to the footman that Violet should speak so callously to one of their guests.

Andrew had no way of knowing—and Violet had no way of explaining—their actual relationship. She had all she could do to manage her feelings about Owen tampering in her life and Frank's ill-advised plans to help Charlie.

"Miss Davies, Lady Neil mentioned she has a favorite ice shop in town. Are we near it?" he asked politely, his eyes taking in the town and the nearby buildings—taking in everything but her.

Violet slowed her brisk walk and pointed to the storefront in question across the street. "It's just there. Lady Neil treated me to an ice from there just before we left Gatherford Park for the London house. It is not quite like Gunter's but it will do." She tried to keep her voice steady and equally polite.

Owen drew up to her side and despite the conflict within

her, Violet's heart fluttered at his approach. If there was one thing she loved more than having him by her side at all times, it was the feeling she got when he entered a room or came near.

It took all her willpower not to thread her arm through his as they walked down the street just like any other couple.

But Violet knew they were not like those people. Perhaps they never would be.

As she, Owen, and Andrew made their way through the town, picking up the odds and ends on the household shopping list, Violet continued her efforts to remain cordial to the captain.

But it was difficult to convey any subtle sentiment with an oblivious footman around. Violet did not miss the way the poor young man's eyes darted between them, confusion and curiosity momentarily revealing themselves, though he did not pry. Violet vowed to put in a good word for him with Mr. Taylor when they returned.

All through their errands, Owen remained perfectly polite, nodding at Violet's observations and occasionally answering her in a pleasant tone. But Violet could see through it all. He sought to keep things professional between them.

He smiled, but it never warmed his eyes. In fact, if Violet could put a word to the atmosphere surrounding him, it would be melancholy.

Some fabric caught Violet's eye as she paused at a shop window displaying pretty new bonnets.

"How lovely. Perhaps I can try recreating them back at home..." Violet muttered to herself, momentarily forgetting her troubles as her eyes scanned the bonnets, soaking in as much information about the fabric, fit, pattern, and color as she could so she might pull them out of her memory later.

"Lovely indeed," Owen agreed in his pleasant but forced

manner. "I should very much like to see this one on...Lady Neil." He coughed as he finished his statement and quickly looked away from the shop window, away from Violet's eyes reflected in the glass.

Violet looked closer at the bonnet and frowned. She knew Owen had meant to name her and not Lady Neil, but he continued to hold himself back from such statements that would have been natural to both of them just a few days ago. Instead, Violet could only agree that the bonnet would indeed suit Lady Neil very well.

Their next stop was the bookshop, where Lady Neil had had a special gift created for Lord Neil for his upcoming birthday.

"Ah, Miss Davies! I haven't seen you around here in some time." The old shopkeeper, Mr. Grant, greeted Violet warmly, his smile broad with surprise.

"I'm terribly sorry I've stayed away. Her Ladyship has been in special need of me since the little one was born." Violet returned his smile and made her way down the aisles of books to the counter.

"Always so dedicated to the baroness and her family. It may be bold of me to say so, but I do believe Lady Neil hit the jackpot when she chose you for her lady's maid." Mr. Grant winked at Violet as he rustled around behind his counter and produced a thick package wrapped in brown paper.

Violet smiled at the compliment but she could never resist the urge to correct it. "Thank you, Mr. Grant, but it is quite the opposite. I am the one who hit the jackpot."

The shopkeeper scoffed and his eyes connected with Owen's, who had followed Violet through the store. Mr. Grant shot an exasperated expression to the captain and Violet felt rather than heard him chuckle in response. She sighed as Mr. Grant placed the heavy package on top of the other boxes Andrew carried. She must be boring everyone with her insistence on this matter.

Violet thanked Mr. Grant on Lady Neil's behalf but did not leave the store right away. Instead she browsed around one of the far shelves that held trinkets and baubles as she usually did when she paid the bookshop a visit. Mr. Grant always had some new figurine or snuffbox or brooch on his shelf of non-book goods.

Though they were usually small bits and pieces the shopkeeper had picked up here and there, they were often above her personal budget. But still, Violet enjoyed looking and brushing her fingers over the items.

A small hand mirror caught Violet's attention and she picked it up, turning it this way and that and watching the way the sunlight from the street glimmered off its silver back. When she turned the mirror toward her to examine her reflection, she noticed a large figure quickly walk out of view.

Owen ducked behind the nearest bookcase when he realized that Violet had seen him watching her. But despite his usual agility and self-proclaimed love of speed, he was not fast enough to keep Violet from noticing the sadness in his eyes.

He quietly made his way to the door of the shop and Violet quickly followed, calling out her thanks to Mr. Grant once more as she emerged back onto the street.

As she caught up, she observed Andrew say something to Owen as he adjusted his grip on the several boxes and packages he now carried. Owen glanced back to Violet and reached his arms out to the footman, likely offering to take some of the load. But Andrew smiled gratefully and turned away, walking in the direction of their carriage.

Violet hurried, her footsteps clicking against the pavement. She planted herself by Owen's side before he could find himself another excuse to avoid her. She could no longer tolerate this forced distance that they had both been maintaining.

"Owen, please tell me what bothers you. If this is about yester—" Violet whispered urgently, reaching out a hand to touch his arm when she was sure no one was nearby. But he pulled his arm away and stepped back, surprising Violet into silence.

She stared up into his eyes and watched as his sadness and regret submerged beneath neutrality. She watched as he closed himself off from her.

Violet pursed her lips together. She knew she had been pushing him away right from the start. Even after they had become closer than she could have possibly hoped for with their kiss in the drawing room, Violet had not gone out of her way to find time for Owen in her schedule. Though she missed him desperately, her fear had held her back. And though she had thought her reaction yesterday to his talk with the baron and his well-intentioned encouragement had been caused by pride, Violet saw it for what it really was now.

Fear. It all came back to fear.

And now her fear had pushed Owen even further, possibly for good. And she so hated to see the pain in his eyes. He tried to mask it, but Violet saw through the façade. He mumbled something about being perfectly fine and began to walk back to the carriage.

"Owen, wait. Tell me, please. Are you well?" Violet hurried behind him, keeping as close as she dared without irritating Owen and arousing curiosity amongst the other townspeople who were out and about.

He stopped so suddenly that she nearly bumped into this arm. He turned to look at her, his face grave.

"I did tell you. I am perfectly fine. I've just been thinking that our time here is coming to an end—myself and the lieu-tenant, I mean. The last time Dr. Slaterly visited he gave Davies permission for long distance travel."

Violet's heart plummeted and her ears felt as though they were stuffed with cotton. She could no longer hear the sounds of the small but active town. She could only hear Owen's words echoing again and again as she stared at him in silence for a moment.

How could she have allowed herself to forget that Owen and Frank were not permanent residents at Gatherford Park? Surely they would want to leave someday. Violet just hadn't thought that day would be anytime soon. She had grown so used to both of them in the house that she could hardly imagine it without them now—without Owen's inviting smile and warm eyes and contagious laugh.

"Do you really want to go?" She whispered, her throat tight and dry, the question scraping against her as she forced it out.

Owen nodded solemnly. "Yes, we should. Davies wishes to meet with your other brother and I think I should accompany him to ensure the meeting goes well. We cannot know what kind of state, mental or otherwise, that man is in. And Davies is still far from his usual abilities."

Violet's heart dropped even further. She imagined it must be somewhere far beneath the earth's crust by now. Charlie could steal not just Frank from her but Owen as well. But Violet knew immediately that that was not the case. Owen would not distance himself from her like this if that was the only reason he wished to leave. This was one heartache she could not blame on anyone else.

Her eyes dropped to her feet, all her power and energy to rectify the situation suddenly drained. Even when Owen's hands came into her view, grasping her own, Violet could feel nothing but dread. Once, this touch would have sent a thrill of happiness through her. It no longer carried possibility, visions of a new life they could share together. Now it carried finality and the crumbling of what little time they'd managed to steal.

"Violet.... This is for the best. I think my presence will only cause you harm and suffering, if not now then at some point in the future. But I do hope that your brother and I will visit again soon. Perhaps then we will have clearer minds and hearts."

"Will you change your mind even if I argue?" Violet fought to keep her voice steady, a monumental feat given the way Owen's thumbs brushed over the backs of her hands and the way his gaze pierced her.

"I already know what you will say. For now let us return to the carriage and make our way home—to Gatherford Park, I mean."

Owen let go of Violet's hands and they fell limply against her dress. He turned away from her, his shoulders slumped slightly and his footsteps falling heavily on the pavement.

Violet could only follow behind, her head low as she realized that she had run out of time and done nothing to extend it. She'd known for weeks that their time was running out. She just didn't realize how quickly until it was too late.

# CHAPTER 16

*V*iolet eventually caught up to his side as they made their way back through the town. Owen fought to keep his gaze straight ahead despite every muscle in his body telling him to look at her, take her hand, hug her, kiss her.

He could do none of those things now. Not after making his position clear. The only question that remained would be if they could pick up where they left off when he and Davies quit Gatherford Park.

Owen had intentionally left his words open ended. He did not like to speak in absolutes. But the heaviness in his heart told him that time apart would likely only solidify his hesitations into convictions—and the same could very well happen for her.

He could sense Violet's dejection as they walked side by side for what would likely be the last time for the foreseeable future. His heart felt as though it shattered in slow motion, the cracks growing wider and deeper until eventually they would burst apart all at once—and he could only hope that he was nowhere near Violet when it did.

Owen thought back to the look on Violet's face when he'd told her that he and the lieutenant would be leaving soon. He felt like the lowliest monster for bringing that flash of pain across her face.

But as they pressed themselves closer to the buildings along the street to allow a young couple, arm in arm, to hurry by them to some happy destination, Owen knew that he could become an even worse monster.

If he began a life with Violet and something happened to him or if he put her in harm's way somehow.... The possibility of being hurt or killed in war or some accident and abandoning her to fend for herself again, or of bringing her to the dangerous battlefield or turning over their carriage during a ride or any number of other scenarios in which he could accidentally harm her.... Owen shook his head to keep himself from finishing those thoughts.

Owen needed to be a monster now to spare Violet from an even worse monster in the future.

They soon came upon Andrew at the carriage, securing the many items they'd bought on their shopping trip and Owen offered his help. The sooner they could get home and he could retire to his guest chambers for a reprieve from this despondent atmosphere the better.

Two approaching figures caught Owen's eye and he used his peripheral vision to observe two men coming straight for the carriage.

They looked rough, their clothes faded and patched and days old stubble cast shadows on their faces, but that did not put Owen off. He knew many rough looking men who were kinder and more gentlemanly than many of Society's self-proclaimed best.

Even still, Owen kept his guard up. Something about the way they eyed him and the Neil family crest on the side of the carriage did not sit well with him.

"Don't think I've seen you around here before, sir. What about you, Tommy?" The shorter of the two men, and certainly shorter than Owen, strolled up to the carriage and looked Owen up and down.

"Can't say I have, Eddie. What's a sharp-looking lad like you doing in our humble little town?" The taller man came forward now, just a step too close for Owen's comfort. But he would not back down from these obvious troublemakers.

"Good afternoon, gentlemen." He gave a slight bow of his head. If they seemed to think him a sharp-looking lad then he would certainly play the part. "You are correct that you have not seen me here before. I am staying at Gatherford Park with the Neil family. I am out today helping to run errands for the lady of the house."

He continued securing their goods and shot Andrew and Violet a cautionary glance when he saw the men smirk at something in his response.

"Must be nice, living the good life up in the big house," one of them sneered, perhaps Tommy.

Owen felt Violet stiffen next to him at the rude tone in the man's voice. Knowing how much pride she took in the family, it did not surprise Owen that she would not take kindly to someone making a mockery of her employers.

"I don't think this will fit here. Would you take it round to the other side? I'm sure you and Andrew can figure it out."

Owen took the box in his hands and passed it to Violet. He wanted to get both of them away from these unpleasant men. Violet furrowed her brow and bit her lip, hesitating for a moment. But she nodded to Andrew and they went around to the back of the carriage with the parcel.

He breathed a quiet sigh of relief and returned his attention to the two men.

"In fact, I am only here visiting briefly. I was a captain in the army, you see, and now that the war is over I have been making my way around the country visiting family and friends."

Owen smiled with as much friendliness and charm as he could muster, hoping that his simple explanation would be enough to satisfying whatever they hoped to get out of him.

To his great dismay, this only seemed to irritate them more. They glanced at each other with distaste, their lips curling up in matching snarls.

"How nice," Eddie growled. "A fancy captain whiling away his days in fancy homes."

"You're right, Eddie. I bet he sat around his tent all day long ordering other soldiers like our old buddies to die." Tommy spat the words out like venom, his fist opening and closing several times.

Owen could hardly believe the words he'd just heard. He had certainly met others who'd had mixed feelings about the war or even disapproved of it entirely and he could certainly understand why they might feel that way. The war had left almost no one in England untouched.

But never had he been met with such open contempt aimed specifically at him. Never had his service been derided so rudely. In truth, there were dishonorable men who claimed to serve their country only for the rewards and acclaim or those who rose through the ranks only to order others around.

Owen was not that man. He would much rather face a thousand bullets alone than send anyone in his place while he hid in safety. Everything he had done had been for his countrymen, both at home and on the field.

It took all of Owen's strength not to unleash his anger upon these two imbeciles. Instead, he harnessed all the excellent breeding and restraint that had been instilled in him throughout his life. He would not stoop to their level and allow them to goad him into confronting them—though he desperately wished to do just that.

"I am sorry to have given you such an unfavorable impression of my character when you have only known me for less than five minutes. But in truth, I am not terribly concerned about any of that. I simply wish to be finished with my errands and leave in peace. Now, if you don't mind."

Owen stood to his full impressive height before bowing his head to the two men again. He turned to head around to the other side of the carriage where he hoped Violet and Andrew had stayed out of sight. But Tommy and Eddie seemed to think that their fun with Owen was far from over.

"Oy! You can't just come to our village and act like you're better than everyone!" Eddie shouted, slamming his palm against the side of the carriage.

Owen wheeled around and watched in shock as the two men began to stir up a ruckus.

"Don't you take a swing at me!" Tommy cried out, turning toward the street to ensure his voice carried out to the other townspeople.

"Gentlemen, stop this nonsense!" Owen shouted, taking a step toward them.

The throw happened so quickly that Owen nearly missed his chance to dodge it. He felt knuckles graze against his jaw as he leaned back to dodge the punch. But he was not so lucky with the second blow, which landed on his stomach as he tried to avoid the first.

He doubled over, his stomach throbbing from the impact. But he managed to bury the pain beneath his anger and he righted himself in time to sidestep another punch. He caught his present attacker in the shoulders and pushed him away.

"Owen!" Violet's cry from behind him distracted Owen. He looked over his shoulder to see her and Andrew emerged from their hiding spot.

"Help! Someone help!" The footman called out.

Violet was frozen in her spot, her eyes staring in terror at Owen.

Before he could yell for them to get away and run for help, one of the men seized the opportunity to land a hard blow on Owen's cheek.

He toppled faster than he thought possible.

"Owen!" Violet cried again and she ran faster than he thought possible, throwing herself at the man who'd just punched him.

She grabbed the man's coat, trying to pull him away from Owen. With the wind knocked out of him, all he could do was gasp out pleas for her to stop and get away. But his pleas went unheard or ignored.

He tried to stumble to his feet again but the soreness in his cheek from the punch radiated throughout his face and around his skull resulting in a dizzying headache. His eyes could barely focus as he watched the man try to shake Violet off him.

But they snapped to attention the moment he heard bone connect with bone as the man's elbow caught Violet's jaw.

She too toppled faster than he thought possible.

Her limp form on the ground was enough to banish any pain and dizziness from Owen. None of that mattered now. He surged forward, his rage powering his arm as he threw himself at the man who'd harmed Violet and drove his fist into his already crooked nose.

The man fell backwards onto the ground and Owen was on top of him in an instant. He pulled his fist back to strike another punishing blow, his chest heaving with fury and adrenaline, sweat dripping down his temples and neck.

But before he could strike again, two strong arms wrapped around his, still poised in the air for the next blow, and he found himself being yanked to his feet.

Owen heard Andrew's voice in his ear but did not hear what he said. The blood rushing through his brain drowned out anything else and now that he'd been removed from the attacker, the dizzying headache returned in full force.

"Violet..." was all he could mumble as he tripped over his own feet, Andrew working hard to steady Owen's larger and more muscular frame.

Andrew said something again but Owen still could not hear. His bleary eyes glanced around at the scene until he finally spotted her. She sat up on the ground, surrounding by townspeople while others wrangled the two men who'd attacked them.

Owen immediately pulled himself out of the footman's grip and dropped to the ground next to Violet. He gripped her shoulders and allowed his eyes to unabashedly examine her face. He barely noticed the people surrounding them and their mutterings.

"Violet, are you well?" His words were breathy and his voice cracked, the combination of overwhelming emotions from the event making his throat raw.

"Yes, Captain, I'm just fine. A little sore but fine. But what of you? They hit you so hard..."

Violet sounded as overwhelmed and distressed as Owen had. He took her hands in his and gently pulled her to her feet. Now that the scene appeared to be under control, the two instigators dragged away amidst jeers and swears at Owen, Owen took a good look at Violet's condition.

Her black work dress was covered in dirt and bits of gravel clung to the soft skin of her palms where she'd tried to break her fall. A red mark bloomed along her jawline, the area already beginning to swell.

Monster.

That word that had rung in Owen's head just a few minutes before came roaring back. Hatred surged through him as he realized he'd put her in this position. However unintentional it had been, she'd still been hurt because of him. Because he attracted trouble and risk into his life. Because his profession made him a monster to others for a different reason. Because she'd tried to protect him.

All Owen wanted to do in that moment was take Violet in his arms and kiss her despite the dust on her lips and the footman and other townspeople nearby who would surely see. He did not care about any of that. But he did care about Violet.

And because he cared so deeply for her, he instead dropped her hands to her sides and took a step back. He straightened his shoulders and clenched his jaw.

"I told you to stay away. You were foolish to step in. You could have been hurt even worse." He tried to keep the sorrow and pain out of his voice, masked beneath coldness and distance.

Violet's eyes widened and her mouth fell open slightly in surprise. Owen's words had hurt her. He hated himself all over again for causing her still more harm, but he needed to end this now.

"I just wanted to help.... I couldn't just stand by and watch you be attacked," she whispered, still staring at him in shock.

Owen's façade crumbled slightly and he softened at the fear and worry in her voice. But he needed to hold as firm as he could to his stance, even if he could not force himself to be completely cold.

"I know, and I do thank you for that. But it was unnecessary and you needlessly put yourself in danger. I am a trained fighter after all. I could have handled the situation on my own."

Violet frowned. "Not when your opponents fight dirty, forcing you take on two at once and striking you when you aren't looking."

Before Owen could rebut, a few villagers returned to the small group from Gatherford Park.

"Is everyone alright aside from being a bit shaken? Does anyone need the doctor?" A kind young man asked.

Owen opened his mouth to insist that Violet be taken to the doctor immediately but she quickly insisted that she was perfectly well, or would be soon enough. Owen forced himself to bite his tongue.

He knew her injury likely only needed a bit of ice to bring down the swelling and mitigate the bruising but he could not stop himself from wanting to insist that Violet receive the best care, the best attention, the best of everything—a habit he would need to quickly learn to suppress. Owen did not fool himself into thinking he could ever break it entirely. Still, when they returned to the estate he would ensure that Mrs. Baird was made aware of the situation and tended to Violet.

"I'm terribly sorry you had a run in with those two scoundrels. They only came to town just before winter but they've already caused more than their fair share of trouble. Quite a nuisance, if you ask me. I hope we can be rid of them soon," said an older woman, her nose scrunched in distaste.

Owen nodded at the information, unsurprised. He suspected that if he asked around he would easily discover that those two men had also been run out of the other nearby towns.

"Thank you all for your help. You've been very kind and generous to us. I will make your good deeds known to Lord and Lady Neil. And the same goes for you two," Owen announced as he turned his attention to Violet and Andrew. He nodded for them to climb into the carriage so they could leave this drama behind and he spurred the horses away as soon as the reins were in his hands.

The ride home—no, not home, Owen had to remind

himself once again—was a grim and silent affair. After Owen privately offered his thanks to both Violet and Andrew once more, everyone slipped into their own thoughts.

The ride felt far longer than Owen remembered. His heart broke with each moment that passed in pained silence and stillness.

$\sim$

OWEN KNEW that he should go upstairs at once, that he should call for a footman to ready his bath so he could wash away the grime and sweat that made him feel disgusting. But he knew there was something else that would not be so easily washed away.

Instead, Owen followed Violet to the servants' hall. Despite his best intentions, he could not keep himself away. At least not until he could be sure that she was truly fine.

"Violet, are you sure you are quite alright? I saw what happened. I saw how hard he hit you, how hard you fell."

Violet stopped, straightening her shoulders and lifting her head before turning to face him. "Yes, I am fine. As I keep saying."

Owen's heart sank at the coldness in her voice but he knew he deserved it.

He'd thought it would be the best way to do this, to go about separating them until they both had a chance to consider what they wanted, what they could accept in their futures. He could make himself unappealing to her so that she would not miss him when he left. So that she would not want him back if he returned.

But Owen could not do it any longer. If he must hurt her, let it be with the truth.

"I'm so sorry for being harsh after the confrontation, Violet. I do appreciate your willingness to help me. But I see all too clearly now what I had feared before. You will be hurt because of me. Perhaps not physically like today. Emotionally is more likely. For that reason I feel it is necessary for me to go. As I said before, I do not wish to stay away forever. But I think you should have the opportunity to return to your normal life, life without me, and see that you do not need me."

Violet lowered her eyes and took a shaky breath. "Is this really what you want to do?"

Everything in Owen screamed to say no, to take it all back and take her in his arms. But he allowed the final thread holding his heart together to snap.

"Yes. It is."

Violet nodded and turned away, walking toward the servants' dining table and sinking into a chair. Owen saw the tears in the corner of her eye before she buried her face in her hands.

He rushed away, calling for Mrs. Baird. Like a coward, he could not bear to witness the damage he'd caused.

"Captain, is everything alright? I've just heard from Mr. Taylor that Andrew came back from town in quite a state. He said something about a fight breaking out."

Mrs. Baird hurried out of the storeroom when she heard Owen calling. She gasped when she saw the state of his clothes and the bruise on his cheek and his disheveled hair and the distress in his eyes.

"Good Heaven..."

"Mrs. Baird, Violet was hurt in the scuffle and she needs your help. She'll have some bruising to her jaw tomorrow and it's quite swollen and red right now."

Without another word, the housekeeper rushed past Owen toward the servants' dining area.

Once he knew that Violet would be cared for, Owen nearly ran upstairs as fast as his sore body would allow. But instead of going straight for his room once he reached the guest wing, Owen checked the guest sitting room first. He threw the door open and found the lieutenant reading the newspaper by the fire.

"Jessup, what's—" He started, shock etched on his face as he took in his friend's state.

"Davies, we must go. As soon as possible. We should find your brother right away. Let us not delay any longer." Owen quickly interrupted Davies, his voice hard and determined.

The lieutenant reeled back in his chair for a moment, surprised by the intensity of the request. But he nodded and mumbled his agreement. For once Owen was extremely serious and Davies knew better than to argue.

Owen did not say anything more. He returned to his room and began packing.

He needed to get away from Violet as quickly as possible.

He could not stand to see the heartbreak in her eyes, the heartbreak he had caused.

$\mathcal{V}$iolet stood at the large front facing window in the drawing room. It was the best vantage point to watch the proceedings downstairs without risk of being discovered.

Her heart barely beat as she watched Frank and Owen bow to Lord Neil and kiss Lady Neil's hand before climbing onto their carriage.

As Owen spurred the horses onto the pathway leading away from Gatherford Park, Violet's heart sank to depths she had not thought possible, even deeper than it had fallen yesterday.

Tears slipped down her cheeks but she did not brush them away. She needed to feel this. She needed to feel the pain and guilt.

She hadn't said goodbye to either of them. She knew her heart would shatter if she stood before Owen and saw the pain in his eyes, knowing that he did not truly wish to go.

But she had failed over and over again to encourage him to stay, to truly open herself up to him. But her fear had gotten the better of her one final time and it was too late now. The least Violet could do was admit that she had been a fool to hold herself back and that she had brought this heartache upon herself.

She even felt guilty for not saying goodbye to Frank though she still had not forgiven him for insisting on meeting with and helping their brother. He had come all this way to reconnect with her, after all, and she still appreciated that effort. Violet had grown very fond of him in his time here despite her initial reluctance. She'd often felt that they really were a family again, or at least getting very near it.

But again, it was all too late. Violet's fear had also kept her from truly accepting her brother again. And in her fear she had declined to see them off, knowing full well that she had no way of knowing when she might see either of them again.

She had begged Lady Neil to tell Frank and Owen that she was extremely busy with something else and could not spare a moment to say goodbye. Violet hated to see the disappointment in her mistress's eyes when she repeatedly denied the lady's attempts to talk her out of this decision. And she knew that no matter what excuse Lady Neil gave on her behalf, the men would see through it.

But Violet knew she would hate seeing the despair in Owen's eyes and the hurt in Frank's eyes.

Even just watching him leave from the window broke her heart.

As the carriage grew smaller, nearly to the bare tunnel of trees that separated the main estate from the rest of the lands, a tiny movement from the carriage sent Violet's heart tumbling all over again.

She could have sworn that she saw Owen turn to look back at the house for a moment. But not just at the house. At the upstairs windows.

Something in the profound misery that weighed on her body told Violet that he had indeed been looking for her.

Suddenly unable to hold herself up any longer, Violet allowed her knees to give out and she slid into a chair next to the window. She just needed a few minutes to let her tears flow before she went back to her duties. Still, Violet hoped that no one would come into the room looking for her.

She covered her face with her hands as the full weight of another abandonment settled into her bones. Frank had chosen Charlie over her once more. Owen had chosen to remove himself from her life to protect her and protect himself from the responsibility of hurting her.

Bitterness mingled with heartbreak as Violet came to the cold realization that this was always bound to happen. She was no one important and she never had been. Violet was an afterthought to everyone in her life. She was just a maid, a position she was lucky to have at all. She didn't deserve a grander, more exciting life like Owen had encouraged. Violet had proved that herself many times over in these past few days and weeks.

As the tears continued to flow and the emotions continued to rip through Violet like a whirlwind, she next wondered if she should have fought harder to keep Owen near her. She should have become even closer to him after their kiss. She should have spoken up yesterday when he'd said he wanted to leave. She should have told him then in no uncertain terms that she wanted him to stay. That she wanted him.

But Violet had always had trouble trusting the strength of her voice. She'd convinced herself that if his mind had been made up, she was powerless to change his opinion. She'd been powerless her whole life, yet when she'd had the chance to use the power she knew she had, she'd let it go to waste. She'd let Owen walk away.

Instead she continued to live her life in hiding.

Yesterday's events flashed through her memory. He had

been cold to her after the fight. He'd said he didn't need her, that he never had and never would. He may have rescinded the harshness of his statements later, but Violet felt that she was inconsequential to him.

This was the life she had made for herself, the life she had chosen. She was proud of her hard work. But, sitting alone in the drawing room with the image of the carriage carrying Owen and her brother away, Violet knew that she had lost something hugely important in her efforts to maintain the safety she'd fought so hard to cultivate in her life.

Footsteps echoing up and down the hallway outside the drawing room pulled Violet out of her morose thoughts. For a servant like her, emotion needed to be tucked away during working hours. She had already indulged herself to much.

The next best thing for her short of getting Owen and Frank back would be to throw herself into her work with a vigor and determination the likes of which this house had never seen before.

Violet sat up straight, pulled her shoulders back, lifted her chin, and wiped her tears away. She pushed her broken pieces back down into darkness. She had tasks to tend to and duties to fulfill.

She had mustered up her resolve at just the right time. Violet stood from the chair as she heard quick footsteps approach the drawing room.

"Ah, Miss Davies. Lady Neil requests your presence in the library," the footman stated.

"Does she want me to bring tea? A blanket?" Violet asked, her professional voice sounding foreign to her.

"No, Miss Davies. She just asked for you."

Violet nodded and smiled her thanks. She dragged herself out of the drawing room, away from the window where she'd last seen Owen. Her body felt as though it were shackled around the ankles with weights.

Once inside the library, Violet spied Lady Neil at the small pianoforte in the far corner of the room. Lord Neil had purchased several new instruments and scattered them throughout the house so she would always be able to practice wherever she was.

Sweet, gentle notes floated into the air as the baroness's agile fingers pressed into the keys with just the right timing and feeling. Violet had always envied her skill. She had learned a bit of music and practiced on the pianoforte and harp when she was younger, before everything had fallen apart. Whenever she heard her mistress play, she wondered if she might have been proficient if she'd had the opportunity to continue learning.

Violet approached the instrument and Lady Neil stopped playing when she heard Violet's footsteps drawing near. She curtseyed and smiled when she stood by her mistress's side. The smile felt painful, like it was wrong to use these muscles that had once felt so right when Owen had still been in her life. It felt like a lie.

"How may I assist you, my lady?"

"Come this way," Lady Neil instructed, leaving the pianoforte behind in favor of a seat by the fire. As the baroness sat, Violet planted herself by the armrest, awaiting further orders.

"Please sit." Lady Neil waved to the open chair next to her. Violet stared in surprise for a moment. Though Lady Neil always treated Violet with respect, she hadn't expected her mistress to ask her to have a seat as if they were equals. There was something unusual in the air between them. But Violet lowered herself slowly into the chair. It was still a command, after all.

"It is my turn to ask what I can do for you, Violet," the baroness said kindly, her blue eyes brimming with concern.

Violet blinked rapidly at Lady Neil's words, another wave

of surprise sweeping over her. She did not feel comfortable with these open displays of worry and sympathy. Especially not when they came from her mistress. She had always known that Lady Neil was exceedingly generous and kind, and she knew by now that such behavior should not shock her. This was the person Lady Neil had always been.

But Violet knew the baroness was under no obligation to care about her and she lived her days expecting the lady's care and concern to vanish or be ripped away somehow at any moment. It would be easier to deal with should Lady Neil ever find fault with her and bring the comfortable nature of their working relationship to an end or even dismiss her entirely.

In fact, Violet lived all her days expecting to be thrown over and cast aside. It would be easier to deal with should it happen again. At least, she'd thought it would be easier. Now she was not so sure.

Violet put on her fake smile again. "There is nothing I need help with, my lady, though you are very kind to offer."

Lady Neil sighed, her gaze sad but knowing. "Violet, you know I see you as more than just my lady's maid. You are a companion, a friend. I know there are certain boundaries between us that others may think we must observe, but I do not care overmuch for such boundaries. I speak to you now as a friend and I wish to know what troubles you as a friend.

"You see, I know you hide your pain because you feel it is not right to share it with me. But I can see it in your eyes. Just as you have become attuned to my needs and wants and emotions over the years, so too have I become attuned to yours. I wish you would stop thinking that I do not care for you or notice you, or that I only care and notice because it is my nature to care for and notice everyone. Or that I will toss you aside if you make the smallest mistake or behave as any human would in these circumstances.

"So please, Violet, share with me your thoughts and concerns and aches, no matter how burdensome you think they may be. Helping a friend is never a burden."

Fresh tears bubbled up at the corners of Violet's eyes again. This kindness shocked her though Lady Neil was right —it shouldn't shock her. But it only shocked Violet because she had trained herself for so long to expect the worst, to expect that she meant nothing to anyone who meant anything to her.

Looking at Lady Neil now and seeing the sincerity in her expression, Violet felt that she could come to accept her mistress as a friend as well. She did not wish to deviate too much from her role, but it comforted her to know that she need not distance herself so much or brace herself for rejection.

In fact, Violet had often felt that she and Lady Neil could have been friends in another life. But she had always kept those feelings at bay, knowing they would be impossible to act upon. But tonight in the library, the two women were friends, regardless of their birth or ranks or pasts.

Violet could keep her emotions contained no longer in the midst of this kindness that she had craved for so many years but had been too afraid to let near. But she let it near now and she allowed herself to fall to pieces before Lady Neil.

Her mistress leaned forward and took one of Violet's hands in hers, rubbing gentle circles with her thumb. She did not rush Violet, she simply sat with her and whispered words of comfort until Violet's tears subsided enough to allow her to speak.

"I am in love with the captain, my lady. But no matter how close we got I would not let my final wall down. And I pushed him away after he tried to encourage me to publish. I insisted that my place was here as your maid, that I had no business wasting time trying to write verses worthy of being published.

"And after the debacle in town yesterday he'd said he didn't need my help. In truth, I don't think I helped much at all as this bruise on my jaw can tell you. He apologized for it later but I can't help feeling it must be true. I got in his way. I will only hold him back if he chooses to shackle himself to me. He lives a bold, exciting life and I do not.

"And now Frank has abandoned me again for our worthless brother. I thought that I was important to him, important enough for him to track me down and follow me here and give me time to learn to accept him again. But I am not more important than that wretched man who helped ruin my life. I am not important to anyone, save for Your Ladyship and the rest of the Neil family but even then it is only because of the service I provide. At least that is how I always used to think of it."

The words spilled out of Violet amidst her shallow breaths and cracked voice. She had thought the words many times over but had never expected to say them aloud, especially not to Lady Neil. But now they hung in the air, heavy and pitiful.

"Violet Davies," said Lady Neil after a moment of silence.

Violet looked up in shock at the sternness in the baroness's voice. She rarely heard Lady Neil use such a tone, even when the situation would have allowed for it. Violet's heart stopped as she realized that perhaps she really had spoken too out line.

But Lady Neil's eyes still showed only concern. She took Violet's other hand as well and took a deep breath.

"I know your family history is awful. I can't tell you how shocked I was the first time I heard it from my mother, some years after you'd started working in my family as a scullery maid. You'd just been promoted to housemaid and I thought you seemed like such a pleasant, diligent girl. I told Mama that I might like to have you for my maid once I came out in Society and she told me your tragic story.

"I was so shocked by it because I never would have suspected it when I saw you about the house working or when I requested something of you. You always had a smile on your face and accepted every task with grace. I knew then that you were not just a dedicated worker but a strong, uncommonly kind young woman. I had no idea how you managed to remain so positive and professional given everything you'd gone through but I respected you immensely for it."

The breath left Violet's body as she took in Lady Neil's words. She had never dared to hope to hear such words from her mistress. But hearing them now, Violet's damaged soul felt a little soothed. In fact, it felt wonderful to know that she was so appreciated and even respected by such an exemplary lady as her mistress.

"As awful as your past is," Lady Neil continued, "and as much as I wish it had never happened to you, it made you stronger and kinder. I know you fear that your chance to have a happy family has long passed. But not all families are horrible. They do not need to follow the same pattern.

"You know better than almost anyone that my family is far from perfect. But I plan to learn from their mistakes with the family I've created and you can do the same. Not every man will become like your father and brothers.

"And I suspected that Captain Jessup cares for you very, very deeply and that is why he has left in such a hurry. I could not convince him to stay at Gatherford Park no matter how hard I tried, because he felt that he had put you in too much danger.

"Sometimes...the people who care about us most do things that they think will make us happier and keep us safer in the long run, not realizing that it will do the exact opposite. You may remember a similar situation I was in with Lord Neil before we married. And I am living proof that such fears can be overcome.

"The captain worries that his career in the army will cause you to suffer or that you will end up hurt in some way if he remains near you like you did yesterday. Such occurrences are so rare but to the mind of someone riddled with fear, all they can see are the million ways something can go wrong instead of the million more ways it could go right."

Lady Neil paused and allowed Violet time to digest her words. Of course she remembered the courtship between her mistress and her new master. She had seen the pain it caused Lady Neil for weeks. But just when everyone had thought hope was lost for the two of them, they managed to overcome their obstacles and now they were very happily married with a precious infant son.

Perhaps Lady Neil had felt just the same as Violet now felt. Perhaps that meant Violet could correct their course somehow.

But she could not be completely satisfied with Lady Neil's words. Not yet.

"But my lady, if I should marry—" Violet started, but the baroness held up a hand to silence her and she immediately snapped her mouth shut. Lady Neil smiled understandingly. She seemed to already know what Violet would say.

"If you should marry, and I certainly hope you do, I want you to remember that my greatest wish is for you to be happy. Henry and I both adore you and we agree that you should pursue the path that makes you happiest—and the same goes for the rest of our staff. Of course we want you all to enjoy your time here, but we understand that circumstances and desires change.

"Should you leave the family at some point, for one

reason or another, we will find a way to get along without you. It certainly won't be the same and we would miss you dearly, but you shall not use us as an excuse to avoid your true happiness, wherever it takes you. And that is an order," Lady Neil chuckled as she saw Violet open her mouth to protest.

Violet sighed and sank back into her chair. She contemplated her mistress's words with a strange, dizzying mixture of anxiety and hope. But her heart swelled when she realized that the pain and regret she saw in Owen's eyes confirmed what Lady Neil had said. He did care for her deeply, so deeply that he was willing to sacrifice his own happiness to do what he thought would be best for her.

Lady Neil was right. Owen had been right. It could rest on no one's shoulders but her own to create a better future for herself. No matter how scared she might be of rejection and abandonment and heartache. She would never know how bright and loving and safe the future could be if she did not give it a chance. And the first step toward taking that chance was getting to Owen.

But just as this newfound resolve lifted Violet's spirits, they were tempered once more by doubt. It was one thing to find Owen and another to convince him that she needed him in her life despite all the time she'd spent holding him at arm's length and eventually allowing him to walk away—that she was willing to spend her life with him come hell or high water and anything in between.

"My lady, I fear I have been such an irreversible fool. I pushed him away when he only wanted to help. I was afraid of losing my security when all this time I have never felt safer than when I was with Owen."

Lady Neil surprised Violet with a laugh. "I am not the one who needs to be told this. But I think you know what you must do. Now go find this Owen fellow you speak of and do it."

Violet blushed when she realized she had used Owen's Christian name so casually in front of someone else. But she had little time to wallow in her embarrassment.

She must act fast if she had any hope of catching up.

A FEW COLD snowflakes landed on Violet's face as her curricle rumbled along the road. She muttered a prayer under her breath that the weather would hold out until she could overtake her brother and Owen. Hopefully one woman on a curricle would be faster than two men in a carriage laden with suitcases.

Violet had no idea how long she'd been driving, pushing the horses as hard as she dared. The creatures surged forward, pulling against their harnesses in perfect time with each other as Violet tapped them with the reins. Their hooves clattered against the gravel and her heart thumped in time with the motion.

Just as the snow began to fall in earnest, Violet finally spotted their carriage. She urged the horses into one final sprint, shouting promises that they would be rewarded handsomely with warm rub downs and several sugar cubes each.

The horses jerked forward so hard that Violet nearly toppled over the side but they flew faster than ever toward Violet's goal.

She finally drew parallel to the carriage and shouted for them to stop. Owen and Frank both whipped their heads around to stare at her in amazement. Owen yanked on their horses' reins and brought them to a stop.

Violet climbed down from her curricle as Owen and

Frank both did the same. Owen simply stood and gazed at Violet in shock for a moment while Frank came around from the other side of the carriage, slow and careful on his crutch.

Violet took a moment to catch her breath while both men watched her in silent confusion.

"I am so, so sorry I did not say goodbye earlier," she gasped out, thoroughly winded from the adrenaline of her high-speed chase.

Her eyes glanced back and forth between the captain and the lieutenant as she meant the apology for both of them, but she could not help her eyes lingering on Owen.

Frank stepped forward and grasped Violet's hand. "I am glad you have come now. There is no need to apologize. I think all will be right from here on out." He smiled warmly and then coughed. "Oh my, there's a...quite a wind coming up. My old leg, you know...can't tolerate a chill for very long. If you don't mind I think I shall return to the carriage and my pile of blankets."

He gave her a knowing smile before he walked back around the carriage to resume his seat.

Now only Owen stood before Violet. Snow gathered on his shoulders and the brim of his hat and his lips and eyelashes just as Violet had seen before—it had been one of the first moments she'd allowed herself to feel her affection for the captain.

"Violet, what on earth are you doing out here?" he asked quietly, curiosity and a hint of pain in his voice. Violet knew that he did not like to see her out in the cold especially now that it had started to snow, racing over the road to catch him.

But if Owen had taught her anything, it was that sometimes a little risk was necessary, especially when the reward was a lifetime of love and happiness.

Violet's mind had been so occupied with her eagerness to

catch up that she had not given any thought as to what she would say if she did achieve this opportunity.

Her heart hammered against her ribs as she felt Owen's eyes watching her, waiting for her answer.

She reached below her coat into the apron she still wore and pulled out a folded sheet of paper. Thank God she'd had the foresight to bring it along just in case her words failed her as they currently did. With trembling fingers, she held it out to Owen.

"I think this should explain everything." Violet swallowed the lump in her throat as he carefully took the page, his heavy gloves brushing against hers.

She watched him closely as his eyes drifted slowly over the page. He read intently, mindful to absorb every word and phrase of the poem she'd written a week ago, inspired by her feelings for Owen.

He softened as he reached the end, his eyes glowing with what Violet hoped was happiness.

"Violet, I cannot tell you how much this means to me," he whispered, taking a step closer. "But you know I fear what may happen to you or myself if—"

"Please, Owen, accept my words as they are written there and as I say them now." She quickly interjected, taking another step forward, finally closing the distance between them.

"You are worth any risk. I tried to hide from it for so long, but I am ready now to live the life I never thought possible because you make it possible. I know I am safe with you. I trust you with my heart, my life, my future."

Owen stared at her for a long silent moment. There was that look in his eyes again. Longing. But this time it was not just longing. It was longing that had finally been satisfied.

His lips did not respond with any words but rather with something far better—the next kiss, the kiss that Violet had dreamed of since their first in the drawing room. The kiss that would be the start of all others.

The snow continued to fall around them as Owen's lips pressed against hers with such a tender desire she had not known was possible. And she returned it with all the love and admiration her heart contained.

They could stand under snow, rain, wind, sunshine, and anything else life may throw at them. Violet knew without a doubt in her soul that as long as they stood together, hand in hand and heart to heart, they could overcome anything.

# CHAPTER 18

Owen climbed into the curricle after helping Violet into the seat next to him. The snow still fell around them but he didn't feel the cold at all. With Violet pressed up next to him for warmth, Owen found he didn't mind winter very much at all. In fact, it seemed to have some distinct benefits. He smiled down at her bundled up form, her head huddled down on his shoulder.

The curricle lurched forward, following behind the carriage he had just been in, the carriage that had been taking him away from Gatherford Park and Violet. Frank now drove it back toward the Neils's estate.

Just a few months ago Owen would have complained of the cold and snow and begged to go back inside as quickly as possible or cursed spring for being so far away.

But now Owen felt that there could be no moment more perfect than this. His mind replayed his shock at seeing Violet all the way out here so suddenly and his even greater shock at the poem she'd given him which told the tale of a sad, troubled young woman who loved a brave, kind soldier.

He'd given up hope that he would ever read or hear such

words from Violet, or that he deserved to read or hear them, no matter how desperately he'd wanted to. But he knew now that she accepted him and all his risks. Right now there was nothing more important than having Violet by his side and making her happy every day for the rest of his life.

Owen and Violet rode in happy silence for a few moments, allowing themselves and each other to soak in the events of the last few minutes and revel in the feeling of their hearts finally coming together. Owen breathed in deeply, his lungs soaking up the sharp winter air, tempered by the warmth swirling through his chest.

But there was one thing that made Owen curious. He finally ventured to break the silence.

"I must confess I did not know you knew how to drive a carriage."

Violet looked up at Owen and smiled shyly. "I've only had the opportunity a few times and I prayed during the entire race that I wouldn't get overturned and end up like poor Frank. That wouldn't be a very romantic ending."

Owen laughed, the sound echoing over the barren landscape. "You are a woman of many talents, my dear."

A lovely rosy red bloomed over Violet's cheeks at the pet name and her eyes went wide in surprise.

"I hope my best talent will be making you happy," she whispered breathlessly.

Owen smiled, his eyes softening with love as he looked down at his sweetheart. "I don't think you will have any issues there. In fact, you are already off to a great start."

Violet returned his smile, her gaze speaking louder than any words ever could. Owen's heart continued to swell to unimaginable sizes. He had not thought his heart capable of containing such immense happiness and love.

Warmth radiated through his body, starting from his chest and travelling to every last inch—but most of all where

Violet's body pressed against his. He wished to hold her forever, to draw from her warmth and share his with her. He wished to share everything with her.

As they lapsed into another comfortable silence, Owen knew that whatever life they chose from here on out would be the exact life he wanted.

Any life with Violet in it was the life he wanted. The life he needed.

THE SUN HAD JUST SLIPPED below the horizon when Owen, Violet, and Frank returned to the Neil estate. The poor butler Mr. Taylor received quite a shock when he found the group in the foyer, dusting off their coats and hats and bonnets. Owen thought he must be sick of them saying they would leave only to show up again a few hours later. But Owen hoped this would be the last time for a long while.

Violet asked Mr. Taylor to allow the three of them to warm up in the servants' hall which the old man agreed to though Owen could see he felt odd bringing guests downstairs instead of upstairs. But Owen would follow Violet wherever she walked, whether it be to the servants' hall or the drawing room or around the grounds or the other side of the world. The possibilities felt endless to Owen but best of all each one felt just as wonderful as the last.

As the butler left them to their own devices in the main servants' area, Owen held himself back when he saw the way Davies observed his sister with anticipation. Surely he must have many things he wished to say to Violet as well. He hovered nearby but just far away enough that he could not make out the quiet murmurings of their private conversation.

Owen smiled when he saw the Davies siblings wrap their

arms around each other from the corner of his eye. Violet burrowed her face in her brother's shoulder, her eyes closed and a small smile on her face. Owen had never seen them share such a loving moment and happiness surged through him for both of his dearest friends—perhaps even his soon-to-be family, he realized with a jolt.

Davies rested his chin atop his sister's head and his eyes searched the room until they met Owen's. Owen smiled to the lieutenant and he returned the smile, a tear of happiness twinkling in the corner of his eye.

This had been a long, often difficult journey for all of them and Owen was beyond thrilled that his friend finally had the ending he'd wished for from the start. And of course he was thrilled that Violet had the resolution she had sought for years though she'd never allowed herself to admit it.

He considered himself very lucky indeed that Davies had begged him to join this mission and that he'd agreed despite his reluctance. Though he'd began this voyage with no stake in it, Owen couldn't help feeling that he'd somehow gotten the ending he hadn't realized he'd been wishing for all along.

Violet and Davies separated from each other but Owen could see the love connecting them now. They both looked at peace. The lieutenant beckoned Owen over and as he approached, Violet announced that she would get a pot of tea ready for them, excusing herself from the two men.

Owen felt suddenly nervous, his limbs buzzing with uncertainty. Davies had long known that his best friend had an attachment to his sister. But Owen couldn't help worrying that now that both his and Violet's feelings had been made known, the lieutenant would rescind his positive feelings about their relationship. He stood next to Davies and awaited his sentence, or at the very least a lecture.

But the lieutenant simply put a hand on Owen's shoulder and smiled.

"Thank you, my friend," he said quietly but earnestly.

Owen furrowed his brows. "What do you have to thank me for, Davies?"

"For making my sister so very happy. For joining me here when you did not need to. For being the most excellent friend a man could hope for. And I think you should get used to calling me Frank now."

Heat prickled under Owen's skin at the compliments. Though he normally would have brushed them away with a joke or some insistence that it was simply the right thing to do, Owen allowed himself to feel the pleasant sensations course through his chest at receiving such kind words from his best friend.

"I'm happy I could help, Frank. And rest assured that I plan on doing my very best to continue making Violet happy. That is, if you'll give me permission..." Owen's eyebrows lifted in anticipation of his own unfinished question.

Frank chuckled and gave Owen a gentle slap on the arm. "Of course you have my permission. Though knowing Violet as I do now, I doubt she would have listened to me if I'd said otherwise. She can be terribly stubborn when she wants to, that girl."

"I wonder where she gets that from," Owen scoffed. But a bolt of happiness shot down his spine at Frank's approval of his intentions. All he need do now was secure Violet's approval, though he imagined he would receive no opposition there.

"I told her that I would still see Charlie, but only to determine for myself if he has improved his character at all. If he hasn't I will cut ties with him right away, once and for all."

"Good, I'm glad to hear it. That will be a large weight off of Violet's shoulders. I know she hasn't been easy for you to get close to, Frank, but she does care about you immensely. That is why she was so upset when you agreed to meet with him. She was afraid she would lose you again."

Both men glanced to the fireplace where Violet removed the teapot and brought it to rest on a nearby end table with a hot pad. She worked with a smile on her face and seemed completely unbothered by anything in the world. Mrs. Baird had joined her, busily setting out a tray of biscuits and cookies.

"I was a fool for that, I know that now. I cannot tell you how glad I am that we can move forward now and be a family again. Even if it's just the two of us. And you I imagine soon enough, Owen. She called me brother, you know." Frank smiled proudly at Owen, his hazel eyes shimmering in the firelight. "But I think I shall go upstairs and change out of these cold clothes. I will return shortly."

Frank left Owen behind in the servants' hall and when he turned back to Violet, he now saw that she sat in a chair next to the fireplace. Mrs. Baird wrapped a blanket around her shoulders as Violet's hands clutched a warm cup of tea.

Owen approached, bringing another chair closer. Mrs. Baird gave him a warm smile that lit up her entire face with happiness as she settled a blanket around him and pressed a cup of tea into his hands. It warmed Owen to see how beloved Violet was in this household and that everyone seemed just as accepting of him.

And it warmed Owen even more to see Violet smile with such contentment when he sat across from her. He vowed to put that look on her face every single day no matter what it took.

Mrs. Baird hurried off, mumbling something about fetching another blanket for the lieutenant when he returned. Owen selfishly hoped that none of them would return for a while though he guessed that was their design.

Once the housekeeper's footsteps receded to the linen

closet, Owen put his cup of tea on the end table and Violet did the same. She reached her hands out to him just as he reached forward to take them.

"What did Frank talk to you about?" she asked, tilting her head curiously.

"Just that he was glad I make you happy and how he plans to sort things out with your brother. Possibly something about you being stubborn."

Violet chuckled and shook her head. "Brothers. What can be done about them? But I must confess that I am so very glad to have both you and Frank back in my life. Having a family is so much more important than I realized. I had trained myself for over a decade to give up any hopes of having a happy, loving family. Yet my family, old and new, turned up right on my doorstep when I least expected it."

Her green eyes stared softly into Owen's as she spoke. The way the firelight made the green dance stole Owen's breath away. It took him a moment to recover from their sublime beauty before he could respond.

"I wholeheartedly agree. Given my career, I never expected that I would have a family of my own or that I would even want to. But you showed me that having someone to fight for, someone to love is a worthwhile cause. Indeed it is the most important cause. And I am so grateful to you for showing me that."

He lifted her hands to his face and kissed her knuckles, relishing in the feeling of her warmth against his lips.

When Owen sat up again, Violet removed one of her hands from his grip and placed it gently on his cheek.

"I also want to thank you for encouraging me to take a risk every now and again. I've decided that I will talk to His Lordship about publishing some of my works. I don't know that I will ever join the ranks of our great poets, but I think it could be nice to share my thoughts with others even if they are few."

Owen's eyes widened in surprise and when Violet's face split into a smile, he threw his arms around her and held her tight. Her arms slid around his back and he could feel her hands clinging to the back of his coat. He marveled at how perfectly she fit against him, how warm she was, how sweet she smelled, how much love he could feel emanating from her as they grasped each other.

"Wait a moment, Violet." Despite everything in Owen's body yearning for him to never let go, he pulled back from the hug and held Violet at arm's length, peering into her face. "Are you sure this what you wish to do? I do not want to pressure you."

Violet smiled. "Yes, I am sure. You were right. I have been content here but I have never been truly happy. I let fear hold me back for too long. And now that you've shown me that I can and should have more than just contentment, I want to pursue things that will make me happy. Including you. No matter what happens in our future, no matter where life calls us, any time I have with you will be worth it."

A tear slipped down Violet's cheek and Owen quickly brushed it away. He jumped in surprise when Violet's finger swiped at the corner of his eye. He hadn't realized that he too had been so overwhelmed with happiness that his own loving tears had made an appearance.

He cupped her small round face in his hands, hands he had once thought were too rough and stained to ever be so gentle. But it all felt so natural now, as if this were the real purpose of his hands all along.

"I promise, Violet, that I will do everything in my power to protect you, your happiness, your dreams...and the life we will create together."

Violet rested her hands over Owen's. "I know. I trust you completely."

Owen grinned and simply stared at her for a moment, amazed that he was about to say the words he'd longed to say for months.

"I love you, Violet."

"I love you, too, Owen."

The fire bathed them in a warm, sweet glow as he leaned forward and felt her lips against his own, soft and slow and gentle but full of love and hope and excitement.

Owen could look forward to the future now in a way he had never thought possible. Because Violet was his future.

# EPILOGUE

*V*iolet's hands shook in her pretty lace gloves, the blooms in the small bouquet trembling with her nerves. She stared down at the flowers and marveled at the brightness of the colors and the sweetness of their scent, allowing her anxious mind to get lost in their simple beauty for a moment.

A sniffle at her side brought Violet back to the present. Lady Neil stood next to her with a handkerchief in hand, dabbing at her eyes.

"You look absolutely beautiful, my dear. I am so very happy that this day has come."

Violet smiled and wrapped her arms around her mistress in a warm hug. Lady Neil returned the gesture earnestly, still sniffling.

"Thank you for being such a wonderful mistress and friend to me. And thank you for being here with me on this day and allowing us to use the Gatherford Park chapel."

"Oh hush now. It is an honor to help you prepare on your wedding day and I would see you wed in no other place but right here at your home."

PENNY FAIRBANKS

Violet felt her own tears threatened to spill at the word "home." Gatherford Park had been her home as long as it had been Lady Neil's. She just hadn't allowed herself to think of it in that way. But she happily did so now. Gatherford Park wasn't just the place she worked. It had become her home. And now she would have her own home on the grounds with Owen in the little cottage gifted to them by Lord and Lady Neil.

A knock interrupted their many sniffles as Lord Neil and Frank entered the small side room where they awaited the start of the ceremony.

But Violet's tears returned in full force when she saw the warmth and happiness in her brother's eyes. He walked forward confidently, his crutch long since abandoned and his leg fully healed. He took Violet's hands in his.

"You look lovely, sister."

"Thank you, brother. I can't believe we're sharing this moment together." Violet's voice trembled and Frank brought out his handkerchief to catch her falling tears.

"It would have been unimaginable to either of us several months ago, wouldn't it? How strange life can be. Strange but amazing."

Violet could only nod her agreement as her emotion continued to swell and threaten to make her a blubbering mess just minutes before walking down the aisle.

Lord Neil appeared at Frank's side with a warm smile. "You do look very lovely, Violet. And I am happy to announce that I have good news to share on this already wonderful day."

Violet's heart stopped and she gripped Lady Neil's hand for support as she waited to hear Lord Neil say the words she'd looked forward to for weeks.

"The publisher has gone over the samples you sent him and he would like to publish a volume of your poetry."

The baron grinned, his excitement nearly eclipsing Violet's. He had been serious when he'd told Violet the first time that he would be thrilled to help her through the process and he'd nearly fallen over in shock when Violet approached him after Owen's return to inform him that she would accept his assistance.

Lady Neil gasped while Violet simply stared into the distance in silence, Lord Neil's words still ringing in her head. But Lady Neil did not allow her much time to ponder the amazement of it all. She squeezed Violet in a tight hug while a round of congratulations sounded through the room.

Violet laughed in excitement as much as disbelief. She wondered for a moment if this day could get any better and laughed at her own silly thought. Of course it would get much, much better. Soon she would be Mrs. Jessup.

"I cannot wait to get to the altar and tell Owen the good news!"

"Of course you are excited, dear Violet, but do not forget that you have other things to say to the captain at the altar first," Lady Neil chuckled. "Are you ready?"

Violet took a deep breath before answering. "Yes, I am. But first I would like a moment alone with my brother."

The baron and baroness nodded and quietly left the room. Violet took a hesitant step towards Frank.

"Charlie?"

Frank did not answer right away but took one of Violet's hands and smiled ruefully.

"He has recently taken up a job at a shop in a nearby village. He seems more serious about getting himself into a better position after the little...discussion I had with him."

Violet let out the breath she'd been holding. She recalled all too well Frank's first meeting with their brother. He did not share all the particulars with her, but she knew that after much yelling and threatening to leave Charlie destitute for good, Frank managed to finally start turning him around.

The work would be long and hard and neither Violet nor Frank trusted that Charlie would change his ways. But they'd agreed to give him one chance to put himself right if he wished to be in their lives again as he claimed he did.

"I am glad to hear it. I think I should like to see him after Owen and I are settled in our cottage."

"Do not worry about that right now."

Frank held his arm out to Violet and she took it, nerves shooting through her again. She did not know why she should be so nervous. She had no fears whatsoever of being jilted. In fact, she would not have been surprised if Owen had slept at the altar in his excitement. But still, it was a momentous occasion and all eyes would be on Violet.

Her brother gave her an encouraging smile as they left the side room behind and stepped into the chapel.

All worries of whether she might trip over her dress or drop her bouquet or say the wrong words left Violet in an instant.

Warm spring sunlight filtered through the tall windows and bathed the aisle in an angelic glow, each pew adorned with a beautiful arrangement of flowers.

At the altar stood Owen, a perfectly placed beam of light shimmering over him.

Violet swore she could see the tears in his eyes all the way from her end of the aisle. Her nerves melted away when she saw his smile.

All the guests stood as she and Frank began their walk. The Neils were at the front on one side while Owen's family whom she'd gotten to know over the past few weeks stood on the other side. The entire Gatherford Park staff was also in attendance. Mrs. Baird's eyes watered as Mr. Taylor patted her on the shoulder, both looking for all the world like proud parents.

But Violet did not worry about all these eyes on her anymore.

All she wanted to do was walk towards those comforting brown eyes she loved so dearly, to stand beside the man who had opened her heart and her life to so many exciting possibilities.

Her body felt as though it might float away as Frank removed his arm from hers but Owen quickly took her hands, keeping her grounded before him.

Violet could see the absolute joy and adoration in Owen's eyes as he smiled at her. He mouthed a silent "I love you" to her and she did the same.

"Welcome, everyone. We are gathered here today to join Captain Owen Jessup and Miss Violet Davies in holy matrimony," the pastor began.

THE DAY WAS TOO beautiful not to spend outside. A feast had been spread out over the great lawn behind the house, in perfect view of the blooming gardens.

Violet watched happily as her family and friends gathered, conversing and enjoying their time together under a beautiful spring sky.

But most of all, she loved the feeling of Owen's hand in hers.

As if on cue, Owen's hand squeezed hers. Violet looked up at her husband curiously, surprised by the way his eyes shifted about nervously.

"What troubles you, love?"

"Let us remove ourselves from the festivities just for a moment. Will you join me for a walk around the lawn?"

Confused, Violet allowed Owen to lead her from her chair at the dining table. Everyone had finished their meals for the most part and simply sat or stood around the table talking.

She rested her hand on his forearm as they began a slow circuit around the rest of the party.

"Owen, what's the matter?" She asked again, unable to contain her curiosity, a twinge of worry shooting through her chest.

"I have a surprise for you, my darling wife."

Owen smiled as the new word left his lips and Violet felt her worry drift away on the cool spring breeze.

"You have already given me the greatest gift of all today, my dear husband."

Owen stopped and turned to face Violet. His large hands gripped hers. "I think you will like this gift anyway. You see, I've decided to sell my commission so we can remain here for as long as we wish now that you've found a new position as Lady Neil's companion."

Violet blinked rapidly in shock, her mind processing the words as quickly as she could. Shortly after she and Owen announced their engagement, Lady Neil had offered to change Violet's position from lady's maid to companion, allowing Violet a bit more freedom in her duties and removing the necessity for Violet to live within the main house. Of course Violet had gladly accepted.

"Owen, that is really not necessary. I know how much your service means to you and I would hate for you to give it up on my behalf. You know that I will fully support you if or when duty may call for you again."

They had had this conversation numerous times leading up to the wedding, in regards to both of their careers. Neither wanted the other to give up their sense of duty. Thus they both agreed that Violet would maintain her position for as long as it suited her to do so and that should Owen be called away again, they would constantly be in each other's hearts and prayers.

Owen chuckled and trailed a finger down Violet's cheek. "I know you would and I greatly appreciate that. But I have given it much thought and I have come to terms with the fact that I have done my duty to my country and I can be proud of that. Now it is time to fulfill my duty in another way."

Violet tilted her head, her eyes narrowed suspiciously. Her husband did not lack for wild ideas.

"I can fulfill my duty by becoming a great husband to the nation's treasure and most beloved poet. And by bringing more brave, smart, caring little Englishmen and Englishwomen into the world," Owen said with a grin.

Violet couldn't help laughing. Yes, her husband was truly full of wild ideas.

"I don't need to be the nation's treasure, you know. I only want to be your treasure. But I agree with the rest of your plan. In fact, I can't wait for our new adventure."

Owen leaned down and gave Violet a quick kiss on the lips.

She threaded her arm through his once more and they continued their walk over the bright green grass, the warm sun shining down upon them, a soft breeze brushing against their cheeks.

Spring was Violet's favorite season indeed, made all the sweeter by her husband at her side.

\*\*\*

THANK you for reading Violet's and Owen's story! You can read Rosamund's story here, or any of the other books in my complete Regency Romance series, Resolved In Love.

If you want to stay updated on my new releases, you can sign up to my newsletter and receive my stand-alone novella, *A Lifetime Of Love*. Happy reading!

# ABOUT THE AUTHOR

Penny Fairbanks has been a voracious reader since she could hold a book and immediately fell in love with Jane Austen and her world. Now Penny has branched out into writing her own romantic tales.

Penny lives in sunny Florida with her charming husband and their aptly named cat Prince. When she's not writing or reading she enjoys drinking a lot of coffee and rewatching The Office.

Want to read more of Penny's works? Sign up for her newsletter and receive A *Lifetime of Love*, a stand-alone novella, only available to newsletter subscribers! You'll also be the first to know about upcoming releases!